S0-EQC-103
Main   Aug 2021

This item no longer belongs to Davenport Public Library

FRIENDS
of the
Davenport Public Library

"Celebrate The Printed Word"
Endowment Fund
provided funds for the
purchase of this item

Morgan's Medicine

Center Point
Large Print

Also by Julia David and available from Center Point Large Print:

Love Covers
Love Flies
Love Protects
Truitt's Truth

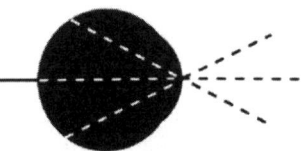

This Large Print Book carries the Seal of Approval of N.A.V.H.

Love's Pure Gold

Book 2

Morgan's Medicine

Julia David

CENTER POINT LARGE PRINT
THORNDIKE, MAINE

This Center Point Large Print edition is published in the year 2021 by arrangement with the author.

Copyright © 2020 by Julia David.
All rights reserved.

Scriptures taken from the Holy Bible, New International Version®, NIV®. Copyright © 1973, 1978, 1984, 2011 by Biblica, Inc.™ Used by permission of Zondervan. All rights reserved worldwide. www.zondervan.com The "NIV" and "New International Version" are trademarks registered in the United States Patent and Trademark Office by Biblica, Inc.™
Scripture quotations from The Authorized (King James) Version. Rights in the Authorized Version in the United Kingdom are vested in the Crown. Reproduced by permission of the Crown's patentee, Cambridge University Press. Read more at http://www.cambridge.org/bibles/about/rights-and-permissions#XJ2I7IqlEcFocUHv.99
Scripture quotations marked MSG are taken from ***THE MESSAGE***, copyright © 1993, 1994, 1995, 1996, 2000, 2001, 2002 by Eugene H. Peterson. Used by permission of NavPress. All rights reserved. Represented by Tyndale House Publishers, Inc.

The text of this Large Print edition is unabridged.
In other aspects, this book may vary
from the original edition.
Printed in the United States of America
on permanent paper.
Set in 16-point Times New Roman type.

ISBN: 978-1-64358-974-9

The Library of Congress has cataloged this record under Library of Congress Control Number: 2021935059

"A cheerful heart is good medicine, but a crushed spirit dries up the bones."
Proverbs 17:22 NIV

"Gold is good in its place; but loving, brave, patriotic men are better than gold."
Abraham Lincoln

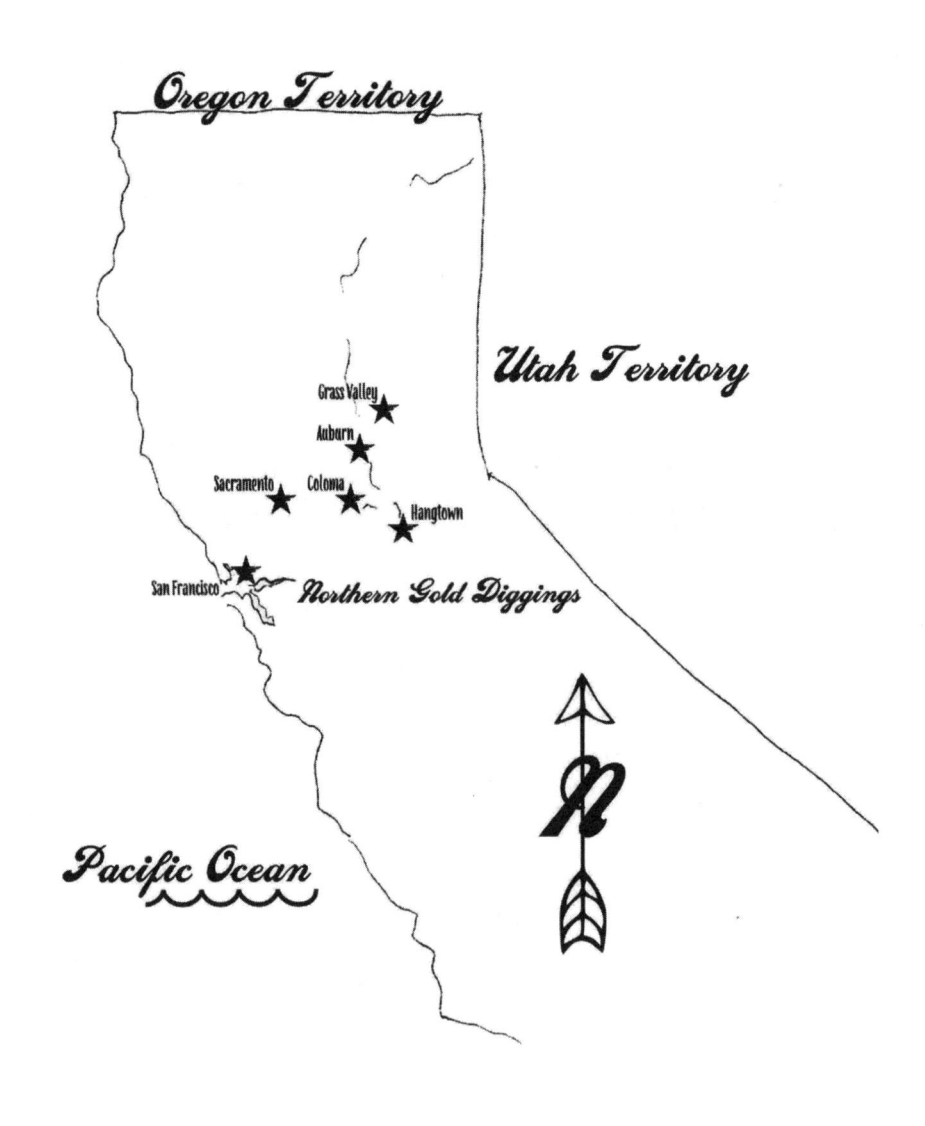

One

*San Francisco Bay
Late spring, 1851*

A heavy clunk sounded in the night. *When had she dozed off? Had something hit the side of the ship?* Emery leaned up on her elbow and listened. Sensing the large, selfish pig, Arnold Snider, still asleep in her bed, she closed her arms around her head and squeezed her shaking body into a ball. Winding her arms and legs tight was her only comfort for the damp, cold night. How dare the man drift into a peaceful sleep in her bed?

Another sound caught her attention. Her head rose higher. So many sounds on this evil, horrid ship from hell. But nothing was as wrong as the body of Arnold Snider sleeping next to her, wrapped in her blankets. She'd rather slumber with the hundred vermin in the bowels of this ship than be near him. His own wife lay only three doors down. Surely Mrs. Snider must wonder where he is. Another creak sounded. Was it her younger sister trying to return to their room? Dare she light the lantern and make the monster take his leave? Would he just awaken and press her to meet his filthy needs again? Another creaking sounded as Emery pushed her feet to the floor. Her narrow cabin door swung open, and Emery jumped off the bed. Shadows of unrecognizable men with a dim lantern and expressions of anger and confusion filled the doorway.

"Is that Arnold Snider?" a whiskered man with a crooked nose asked. His eyes narrowed beneath the brim of his torn hat.

Emery gripped the collar of her white nightgown and pinned herself against the corner wall. Arnold rose up, dazed, and pulled the slipping blanket around his belly. Shaking from head to toe, Emery wondered if they were here to give Arnold what he deserved. A drop in the bay of San Francisco would be fitting. As soon as the intruder met her eyes, she carefully nodded her head, yes.

In one fluid motion, Emery watched wide-eyed as the three men squeezed through the door, gagged Arnold's mouth, and bound his legs and hands.

"You've taken everything from us, you yeller coward," the man with dark hair growled as he roughly tied the last knot around Arnold's ankles. "Hiding away, thinking no one would find you out in the bay."

In a confusing instant, Emery realized they were not sent by her father for her and her sister Gianna's rescue, but their hatred apparently ran as deep as hers. A sob of gratitude rose in her throat as one of the men reached out for her. She gladly moved around the bed toward him. Finally, she and Gianna would be free from this rocking rat hole. But before Emery could utter a word, the man with the crooked nose jerked his bandana from his neck and pulled it across her mouth. Her hands rose up like fire to pull it loose. *No, no!* Emery tried to yell past the thick fabric against her useless tongue as he easily pulled her hands back while another man wrapped her waist with a metal band of some kind. A padlock clicked through the band as Emery tried to plead with her eyes. *My sister, my sister!* Her words would not come out. She twisted from the man, now tying her wrists to the metal band. *Why, why? Are they going to throw me overboard?* The man with the crooked nose jerked her by the elbow and stopped her where Arnold lay like a strapped pig for roasting.

"Take one last look at your wife, Snider." He growled low and flung a piece of paper on the bed. "When you meet us here with the gold you stole, you can have your pretty little wife back."

Every fiber came alive in Emery as she squealed from the back of her throat and shook her head no. *"I'm not his wife!"* Her cries sounded like muffled noise inside her head. *"No, no!"* She tried to shake loose from her bands as they dragged her from the tiny, cold cabin and up the stairs to the top deck. *"Gianna!"* Tears streaked down into the rag in her mouth. Emery jerked and tried to kick a barrel to wake someone up. Now spiking pain radiated into her stockingless toe. *"Gianna!"* Her pleas were cut short as someone wrapped a thick arm around her waist and lifted her off her feet.

Like she was nothing but a sack of potatoes under his arm, the man with the crooked nose flipped his leg over the railing and lowered them down until someone touched her bare legs and bore her weight. Pushed onto the bench of a small rowboat, Emery reared back. The face of the man tending the boat was the same face as the man with the crooked nose, only this other man, with a straight nose, stood glaring into the dark shadows.

Clawing her fingernails into her own hands, she needed to determine if this absurd moment was *not* a dream. Before she could gain her sanity, the men crowded in, smashing her between them. Taking the oars, they began to row like sailors fighting high waves. Emery searched the darkness in every direction, looking for some explanation. The bay's slight swells were calm, and the water lapped unevenly as their boat began to leave the Snider ship.

"Abner, do you see anything?" the dark-haired man asked as he rocked back and forth rowing.

"Nothing but their dinghy floating out to sea."

Emery raised her shoulder and cocked her chin to it, rubbing and struggling to knock the tight bandana from its grip around her mouth. If she could only scream for her sister. The man with the straight nose shook his head at her and pulled his jacket off.

"Shoulda brought her a dress or blanket or somethin'," Abner croaked. She froze with wide eyes as he pressed his coat over her shoulders. "Sorry for touchin' yer legs," he murmured, looking away quickly. The coat smelled like dirt and sweat. Emery shook, from her throbbing toe to the top of her head. They were rowing away, leaving the ship and her younger sister abandoned in Hades.

"Thanks for the suggestions, Abner." The man with the matching face sneered. "Since you just sat in the boat while we did all the dangerous work, you can do the kidnapping next time."

A jolt radiated down her core. *Kidnapping?* Emery understood those American words. Were they using her as bait to get their money back? Likely from Arnold taking out his cash and gold, causing the bank to go under in Hangtown. What would they say when they realized she was not Arnold's wife? Just a lowly servant girl who . . . Emery closed her eyes; the ache in the back of her throat tried to squeeze it shut. She tried to breathe through her nose and think of anything other than what had taken place on that foul ship.

What would they say when they realized Arnold wouldn't pay a red cent for her?

They'd kidnapped the wrong woman. Finny, his very pregnant wife, slept soundly three doors down from her cabin. Would it benefit Gianna and her to play the part until she could escape? Stunned by the befuddled escapade, Emery rocked forward and tried to cover her eyes. Her dark, thick curls hung around her face. The metal band cut into her skin. She looked at it closer. It looked like a barrel ring. The two bolt holes lined up where a heavy lock was hung. Her wrists were bound with thick rope and doubly secured by the lock. If she did use her legs and jumped over, she would go right to the bottom. Suddenly, her spine arched. Then who would save Gianna?

"More to the left." The dark-haired man pulled his oar deep into the bay water.

Bumped around by the men's rowing, Emery tried to focus on the small flickering lights from the shore as they grew closer. They were moving to the side of the bank, away from the pier. The cold water on the floor of the small boat froze her bare feet. Her toe throbbed, and she fought to keep her breathing steady. A wave of dizziness and nausea swept over her, making her gasp for air. *How could this be happening?* Shock and emotion constricted her throat and the gag clogged her mouth; it was going to suffocate her. She would choke on her vomit and die. *Gia, forgive me.* Her head felt thick, and her limbs went to ice. *Forgive me, Mommi and Poppi; death, come . . . quickly.*

"Whoa now!" Clayton shot his arm out as the dark-haired young woman pitched forward. "Abner, grab her."

Abner steadied her shoulders, and her body drooped forward. "She ain't breathin'."

"Then take the gag out, idiot!" Clayton quickly lowered his voice.

"Just probably passed out." Farly leaned into his rowing. "Let's get back to the horses. Silas, put your back into it, man."

Silas and Farly rowed harder as Abner pulled the gag down around her neck.

"That's better. I think she's breathin' now." Abner pulled her limp body inside his arm and tried to tuck his coat around her. "Who told us she had red hair? I know it's dark tonight, but this ain't red hair."

Except for the exertion of rowing, a strange silence fell upon the boat. No one wanted to admit anything. "Quit playing nursemaid, Abner. You're a miner, and you don't know nothin'. When we get to the shore and that cold water hits, she'll come to fast. Be ready to gag her mouth."

Emery felt her body shift, and she opened her eyes. The men were pulling the rowboat through the waves as she lay on the cold, wet planks. Disoriented, she reached for her face. *Her mouth was freed; oh, thank God, she could breathe!* The sand scraped the bottom of the boat, and Emery pushed up with her bound hands. Bewildered, she looked back and forth, hearing only the gentle crashing of waves. Now what? In the darkness of the land, could she run? With another full gulp of air, she gripped the wooden side and rose to step out. Rough arms came from somewhere as a man grabbed her and she struggled against him. The coat around her shoulders fell into the boat, and her half-wet nightgown clung to her body. She couldn't even raise her arms to try and cover herself. She sucked in a mortified gasp, as he lifted her and carried her to shore.

"If you scream, that gag is going back on," he said, just a breath away from her ear.

Abner set her on her feet, but her legs gave way, and her knees dropped onto the sand. *Where were they?* Bending forward, Emery raised her bound hands and tried to brush her hair from her face. Had they made it? Back to where? San Francisco? The shivers started again, coursing through her body.

One of the men ran and brought a group of horses from the brush, while someone gripped her elbow and led her upward until the sand turned to rocks. She winced as rocks cut into her sore feet and throbbing toe. The four men searched left to right while gripping their horses' reins. They moved quickly with few words. The dark-haired man talked about keeping the plan the same. Before she could get her bearings, the man with the crooked nose pulled a stirrup out. "Put your foot in," he barked.

Emery tried to obey, but her legs wobbled so hard she could barely raise them. He grabbed her ankle and slid her bare foot in and gripped her waist. As soon as she could center her own weight and swing her leg over, he did the same right behind her. The horse jerked unexpectedly, and she had to grab the saddle horn not to tip off. His boots replaced her feet in the stirrups, and they galloped away from the brush.

A hazy string of clouds covered the moon, but she could see her bunched up white gown and bare legs hanging over the saddle for all the world to see. These men had no conscience, no scruples—just like Arnold Snider. How long till they would want to violate her?

Her stomach cramped with nausea again. Arnold had promised her trinkets and tiny pouches of gold if she met his manly needs. Her rebuttals and avoidances had only kept him at length a few short weeks.

Emery gasped as the horse pulled to the right and galloped down a trail.

When she and Gianna asked to be taken home, Arnold had threatened to take them from the bay out to sea. She and Gianna cried into the night, thinking they would never see their family again. But when the boat didn't move, she could only pray and hold onto the hope that his were useless intimidations and he would leave her be.

The day he'd pinned her in the hatch where they kept the dry goods was when the nightmare started. Her refusal had only made him madder. She'd swung to slap him, but he'd caught her wrist and pinned it behind her. When the Lucifer had finished with her, he said if she spoke a word of this, he would drop Gianna overboard. *Accidents happen all the time,* the vile man had threatened.

Emery dipped to the side to avoid a low branch coming at her. Nothing mattered. Not what happened on that ship or what happened with these men. Poisoned by disgust, she was already dead inside. Her mommi would say: "Keep God close and keep your hope closer, *mi niña.*" Long gone were these sweet sayings and pinches to her chin. No more loving smiles for the woman she was becoming. Every sensibility that felt good and pure in her had been taken.

The jarring of the galloping horse knocked her regrets back and forth. Those girlish daydreams she'd had—for her family to prosper in America—were gone. How stupid to think that as her family sailed away two years ago from Pamplona, leaving their pain and loss behind them, they would start a happy new life working in the gold-laden rivers of California. How could she have had such vain schoolgirl imaginings? The disgrace she had endured as a maid for the Sniders had drowned every budding hope, every childish dream.

The man drew the reins to a sharp right, knocking himself into her clasped arms. The horse strained up a steep hill, and her bare legs chafed from the damp seawater and saddle leather. With her hands bound, just like being out at sea, there was nothing she could do.

Helpless and hopeless, so familiar. Emery gripped the saddle horn.

There was nothing she could do.

Two

Auburn, California

The cold creek water swished over the edge of the flat mining tin and doused Morgan's scarred hand. He ignored the cold sensation and kept the swirl going in his pan of water and pebbles. This daily mining at his creek often found him with wet boots or wet cuffs, something his time as a military war surgeon never did. Allowing the water to slosh over the side, he saw the specks of gold he'd been hunting for all day. Morgan shifted his weight on his left leg and dropped his knee into the rocky, muddy bank. Picking the feathery soil apart, he mused how this simple, mindless work certainly had benefited his body and soul. Clear creek water ran more forgiving than the blood that soaked his clothes during the war. The specks of gold shimmered their approval for his day of work.

Securing the lid to his tin of gold, Morgan sat on a fallen log and crossed his ankles. The vines of berry bushes along the creek had found new life after a long winter.

Morgan stretched out the pinch in his back and took a long, deep breath. This land in the California territory had been fruitful and abundant. The trees rustled with a light wind, and little birds flitted from branch to branch. He wished no one the hardships he'd endured to get here. Nevertheless, the west was a new land, open for many, like him, who needed the reprieve and solitude. From his past to this, he felt almost favored. As soon as he'd seen this cabin, this land, he knew he'd found his own Eden. Last night's sleep had been as agreeable as this day. A restful, full night's sleep replaced the nightmares that often woke him in a cold sweat.

Morgan lifted his gaze to the blue sky, painted with a few white, downy clouds. Lately, he didn't claim to be Adam in the garden, talking to God. Today felt like the many times he'd wondered if, once removed from the bloody war, his faith would someday find light from the darkness of disbelief.

Peace felt possible at this moment. In the stillness, he waited. Filled with sincerity, he whispered, *"Thank you"* to the heavens. Some random sermons from many hours in the chapel at Rush College came back to him. "Thank you is often the most earnest form of prayer," one of the chaplains had encouraged. Simple enough to remember, and the prayer felt true to his tiny mustard seed of faith.

Morgan stood and brushed off his pants. No amount of anger or questions would bring back his brother and the other seven doctors who had set out to heal the men serving in the war for Texas. They had been just like him—eager and a bit too naive. His honor-bound heritage required him to dismiss his scars, his nightmares. He walked upright on two legs. For all the unfathomable reasons, he was still alive.

Morgan gathered his mining tools and opened his canvas bag. A piece of corn tortilla lay at the bottom, and he grabbed it before dropping his things in. Carlotta, his housekeeper, was getting more feeble, but she took enough care to see him fed. Popping it in his mouth, he chewed, reminding himself he was indeed hungry. Tossing the bag over his shoulder, he hiked around the edges of the creek and stopped. Was someone calling his name?

Morgan stomped through the brush and past a thick grove of oaks. Wasn't he just thanking God for the peace and solitude? He knew so few people in this gold rush town of Auburn. Who would . . . ?

"Doc!" rang out through the scrub trees. Morgan smiled and picked up the pace. The Derry brothers called him Doc from their time in the war. It had been months since they'd last stopped by his humble cabin.

Catching sight of them standing in his yard, he dropped his mining bag and had to laugh. These two matching faces had been his constant source of amusement throughout the horrid days of the war. Wide-eyed and smiling, he opened his arms and jogged to them. Hugging and patting their backs, he rocked them side to side. "What, what are you doing here?" Being taller and older, he grabbed each of them by the nape of the neck and gave them a shake.

"We come to get some more medicine." Abner's eyes twinkled, mocking the past when Morgan tested his inoculations on them.

"There isn't any known medicine or solution for the two of you." Morgan still had hold of them, now gripping their shoulders. A warmth stirred in Morgan, seeing their faces, hearing their voices; they had such a dire history. He felt a kinship born of the worst days of his life that had been shared with these two backwoods twin brothers. Maybe his small thankful prayer to God had blessed him with this good fortune.

"Did you see Carlotta? How long can you stay?" They turned to walk across the dry grass to his cabin. The usually talkative brothers stopped suddenly. Morgan followed their stares right up to his cabin, and his long strides abruptly froze in place.

"What—what is that?" He glared at the brothers. It looked like a wild woman in a dirty nightgown with long, unkempt hair flowing around her shoulders. The unpresentable woman's head hung toward the ground as she sat on his simple wooden bench under his porch eaves.

"Good God, Abner!" He dipped his head to Clayton. "What have you boys done now?"

"She needs a doctor," Clayton said, nodding to his brother. "She done kicked something and broke her toe. It's all purple and big-like. It pains her when she walks."

Morgan hadn't moved an inch. "And what is she doing with that rope binding her wrists next to her waist? What is that metal band around her?"

"Ah, well now." Abner pulled off his old torn hat and scratched his dirty hair. "That was kinda a mistake. It was, was Farly—"

"Farly McGregor? He's part of this, too?" Morgan looked around and noticed only two horses tied to a tree.

"See, when we got on the ship in the bay . . ." Clayton started.

"Ship? What ship? This woman is from a ship?" Morgan huffed, shaking his head. These brothers had robust intentions but peanuts for brains. He rolled his lips tight, suppressing a growl.

"You know how we lost what gold we had when Arnold Snider took it from the Hangtown bank?" Abner asked.

Morgan looked at the bent-over woman. Why was Abner talking about Hangtown? "What happened on the ship?"

"Just let me say it," Clayton cut in. "I'll do it quick-like."

Morgan raised his hands, imploring them with impatient eyes. "Please do."

"This here's Arnold Snider's wife. We took her off the ship where he's been hiding out. We need her to stay here for one week, and then we are going to return her in exchange for the gold he stole. All fair and even. No one needs to get hurt." He cleared his throat. " 'Cept that bad toe. But we didn't do it, she did. Ahh . . . and Doc, you'll like this. She don't talk or carry on at all. So it will be like she's not even here." Clayton nodded with a slight smile and walked toward the cabin.

"Wait. Just wait." Morgan's voice grated as Abner went to get their horses. "She's not staying here."

"Just one week, Doc." Abner turned to take his horse. "You got Carlotta to help and . . . and . . . she needs some doctorin'."

"No!" Morgan bellowed. "I will not be part of this. It's against the law what you've done. You know that?" Morgan stared them both down. "This isn't your Kentucky mountain-folk ways, 'eye for an eye' nonsense. Snider's probably got the city and the county law out looking for you all."

"That's why we need to leave her here. We already split with Farly and Silas. We gonna cover our tracks." Clayton moved to mount his horse.

"Boys, I mean it. Do not leave her here. I will take her to the law in Auburn, I will." Morgan felt his chest squeeze as Abner mounted his horse. Morgan tried to grab the reins, but the horse swung to the side. "No amount of gold is worth sitting in prison for the rest of your life." He could feel the blood pulsing in his neck.

"We's saved your life, Doc." The brothers pulled their horses away from Morgan's yard. Abner drilled him with a stubborn expression. "With this favor, we'll call it even."

Before Morgan could find his next rebuttal, they kicked their horses and were gone, down around the tree-lined road from his home.

Morgan slumped his face and shoulders toward the ground, warring against their stupidity and his anger. They had pulled him from the burning surgical tent, yes. Yes, that was the day he should have died, but this . . . this *plan* of theirs screamed insanity.

Unlocking his jaw, he straightened up, pulling his unkempt, wavy hair behind his ears. Squinting with a frown, he looked her up and down. Poor woman, not even a robe or cape for covering. Feeling disheveled from mining alone, he tucked the loose tail from his shirt back into his pants. Should he get Carlotta? She often napped this time of day, which explained why she hadn't heard the ruckus. Maybe he could approach this distressed woman first and hopefully soften the shock that his housemaid was going to soon experience.

Morgan looked down the trail where the Derry brothers had left, and then back to the woman bound and sitting on his bench.

He should've ridden away with them.

Three

Emery kept her head down but heard every word. These kidnappers were dropping her off with their friend from the war. How quickly his delight in seeing them had changed. His voice sounded smart, like Miss Cassidy, who had helped her and Gianna learn to read and pronounce words correctly. The man tried unreservedly to convince the brothers to change their minds. Would he take her to the law in this town, as he said?

Emery shivered at the ridicule she would receive because of how she looked. Then what would she do? Helpless nagging pain tried to close her airway. Thank God the gag had remained loosely around her neck on the ride to get here. Breathing slowly through her mouth, Emery tried to calm the rising and falling of her chest. Maybe this Carlotta would be someone she could confide in? A sound like feet moving came near her, likely sizing her pitiful state up and down.

"Ma'am. Mrs. Snider." His words were calm but strained. "I . . . I can only apologize for what you've been through. I assure you—"

She peeked up through her mass of hair, only seeing his clothes and shoes. He wrung his hands together. Spots on his cuffs and shirt were wet.

He paused and exhaled. "I . . . I don't know why I'm standing here like a fool. Let me get you a blanket." He stepped up on the porch and turned before he opened the door. "Or, please, why don't you come in and sit by the fire? I will get the housemaid, Carlotta, to assist you."

Emery bit the corner of her bottom lip. This man called her Mrs. Snider, yet she was only a servant. Her brain hurt from reviewing every option inside and out on the rough ride here. Should she continue the ruse or tell him the truth? Which one would get Gianna off the ship? Little did she know she was going to be dropped off with another man, changing everything.

"What the devil?" he snorted as he bent to untie her from the porch post.

"Stop!" Emery curled her legs up and pulled on the rope. "Leave me be."

"Ma'am . . . I . . . I think you should come inside. I promise I will not hurt you." Morgan waited, not gaining any compliance. Slowly, he sat on the porch step. His knees came up to his chest, and she could see him drumming his fingers across his ankle. "How is your toe? Would you like me to take a look?"

"No." Pulling her nightgown over her feet, Emery twisted on the bench away from him.

Morgan stood and walked away a few feet before turning around. "I will get Carlotta to assist you." He crossed over the porch again and stopped at the door. "I must know this. Forgive my impudence, but did any of the men who took you . . . do anything cruel or untoward?"

Emery had no idea what the last word meant. "Cruel" described every moment she lived intimidated and terrorized by Arnold Snider. She understood what he meant and, peering up through her hair, slowly shook her head no.

A few minutes later, a squatty, dark-skinned woman in a plain brown dress stood in front of Emery with her fists on her hips. Emery glanced up through her thick tresses. From the look of her wrinkled scowl surrounded by thin, white hair pulled into a low bun, Emery wondered if the man called Morgan was safer.

"Dose boys done *loco*." Carlotta frowned. "Leaving you here with the doctor. Aye ya, *tsk, tsk*. What do you want first? Bath or some food? You look to need both."

Emery couldn't think. How far was Hangtown? Could she make it on her own to find her family? Her toe throbbed every time she stood.

"I say the bath," the old Mexican woman broke in. "I have hot water on the stove." The short, elderly housemaid had the nerve to pull on her arm, lifting her from the bench. Emery refused to disrobe in any strange place for a bath.

She pulled free. "No." Sitting back, she curled into a ball.

Carlotta's fists were back on the square hips.

"I'm sure you can take care of yourself, *señorita*, but this rope is tied to this porch, and that band, not good. I say we work to get it off now."

Emery pushed her arms against the metal band. It had become like a belt she'd grown used to. She dropped her head low and rubbed her forehead. "*No necesita asistencia.*"

"*Que?*" The woman reached in and pulled Emery's hair up from her face. "*Tu hablas español?*"

Emery's head lifted slightly. She shrugged a shoulder. "I am from Spain—north-central Spain and south of France. My people are Basque. So, *sí*, yes, some Spanish."

Carlotta seemed to feel she'd suddenly found a confidante and began to rattle off about her days in Mexico before the Americans made it Texas. She told Emery details about the war that ravished her land. Dr. Morgan was a good doctor, Carlotta recounted, who had offered her a job after she had buried her second husband. Emery listened, noting the difference in how they pronounced words. After she'd nodded along and tried to follow Carlotta's story, Emery felt her eyes drooping with fatigue.

"Just a blanket, *señora*," Emery asked.

Carlotta frowned. "You come *en la casa*." She pointed to the door. Emery shook her head no.

A wrinkly hand of dismissal waved at Emery, and the old woman turned on her heel to leave.

Listening closely, she made out a few sentences of what Carlotta told the man in the cabin. Undoubtedly, they were both frustrated for the inconvenience she caused them. Just a blanket and the corner logs to her right would do. Emery stood carefully. Coiling her rope, she hobbled to where the cabin logs crossed. Sitting in the space, she could rest her head in the crook. Eyes drooping, a wave of numbness covered her. *Nothing mattered but Gianna.*

"Mrs. Snider."

Emery jerked awake. Morgan knelt on one knee, holding out a thick woolen blanket. For the first time, she could see the man's face. Her torso nudged back until her head bumped the rough log. He seemed younger than his strident voice. He had wavy brown hair that touched his collar, a strong nose and jaw, and encompassing dark eyes. He looked nothing like the Hangtown doctor that had come to care for Miss Cassidy's fingers. This doctor hadn't shaved in days and yet his dark stubble mixed in with red- and white-patched skin on his cheek. Had he been burned recently? He looked at her with his own curiosity and wiped his hand across the area she stared at. It was too late. She looked away, stricken. She shouldn't have been studying him.

He raised the blanket. "I would rather you come inside. I have a room ready."

Still tethered to the metal band, Emery inched her hands upward to receive the blanket.

"I can have a cot for Carlotta put in your room. I sleep in a room on the other side of the cabin." Their eyes met again, and Emery needed him to go. His kind voice and actions pulled her thoughts apart. *Who could she trust?*

"No, no, this is all." She unfolded the blanket. Morgan followed her rope to where it coiled and knotted to the porch post.

"I suppose the twins thought this would be an acceptable place to keep you for a week." He lifted the rope, and she saw the jagged red scars on his hand.

A new thought distracted her, and Emery raised a sad smile. *Twins,* of course. In all the bedlam and rush, she'd no time to see that for herself.

"We both know this is completely unacceptable." Morgan rubbed his forehead, pinching his temples. "How can I help you?" He waited, and her brain froze at a loss to form any sensible words. Seemingly impatient, he took in a deep breath and spoke abruptly. "I would like to take you into Auburn. I can find you a room there and, if you want to go to the sheriff, I will handle the Derry boys."

Her mind whirled. What would be her story to the lawman? She was a ragged nobody, not worth his time or attention. Her life was a tale of shame and humiliation. No, thank you, she would keep that to herself. It would be of no help anyway.

He brushed his fingers under his chin. "I could go for your husband myself. Bring him here?"

Her eyes flared wide with panic. "No, no, please. Promise you will not!" She clenched the blanket. "You don't know him." Emery grasped for some believable words. "He would likely kill your friends, and maybe you."

Morgan rolled his head side to side and stood. "I don't know the best way to return you to where you belong. I need *some* guidance." He sat on the bench and looked at the post. Before she could stop him, he pulled his knife from its leather case over his back pocket. In one swift move, his long arm reached her rope and cut it from the porch post.

"Sir, please." Emery panted. "What are you doing?" Her voice cracked with strain, feeling as if someone had set her adrift on the ocean, but she had no ability to swim.

"Mrs. Snider, I, myself, do not know what to think of my friends' barbaric behavior." Dr. Morgan's brow furrowed with concern. "But I am not destitute of honor or principle."

Emery's throat constricted as she gaped at the frayed rope. He was trying to do the right thing. How could he know that his attempts were making it worse?

"Now, raise your hands and be very still." His

intentions clearly focused on the rope around her wrists.

Her head violently shook no, and she tucked her hands between her knees.

"Mrs. Snider. Please help me . . . help you." He held his mouth open to say more. "I . . . I would never do anything to hurt you."

The irony hit Emery. She almost believed the deep warmth in his gaze. This one seemed so valiant, so close to trustworthy. Her toe throbbed, and her stomach rattled for something to eat but, mostly, she wanted to scream from the treetops: her name was *not* Mrs. Snider.

"I'm keenly aware that I look . . ." Morgan stopped as she watched intently. He carefully pushed the knife back in its case. ". . . Frightening. The war left many of us disfigured." Standing a bit taller, he shoved his hands in his pockets and looked out to the fading light of the evening. "The actions of the Derry brothers have me visibly distressed. I apologize. I know your name, but I don't recall if I introduced myself. I am Morgan Hastings."

She watched him turn to her. With her chin down, she glanced at him from the top of her eyes.

"I was a surgeon in the Mexican-American war."

"What is a surgeon?" slipped from Emery's mouth before she could stop herself.

"A doctor, a physician, but I specialize in cutting into the human *bod*—"

He swallowed and leaned on his other leg. "I, uh . . . help repair and uh, yes, repair . . ." He raked his fingers through his soft waves. "The point is, you can trust me. I've sworn an oath to help people."

What had Mr. Snider sworn to her? The list of his green-bellied lies ran endlessly in her mind. She wrapped the blanket closer; this log corner was all she had to trust in. For tonight, its solid sides braced her body from Lucifer's touch, rocking ships, and pounding horses.

Tonight, that was enough.

Four

I cut into the human body? Morgan put another log on the low coals inside the fireplace. That sounded like the *perfect* thing for a frightened, abducted woman to know. Why not just tell her he was a butcher instead of a surgeon? That would have been more apropos. She likely knew what a butcher did. He blew out a puff and brushed his hands against his pant legs. As if there wasn't already enough fear in her eyes. He should have told her he was no longer a surgeon, just a lowly but happy miner. Morgan shook his head and squeezed his temples. Could he think of anything worse to say to get a woman to come into his cabin?

Circling around his kitchen table, he noticed the sun had dipped behind the trees. How could he blame her for hovering in the corner of his porch? Even Carlotta had taken her some water and food and tried again to coax her to her senses. But this strange young woman would not budge. What if she was gone in the morning? How far could she get shackled in such a fashion? The image of her hobbling through the woods in her locked bands and dirty nightgown rattled him.

Could he do anything right?

He knew so few women and, even less, how to

interact with them. His poor communication was evident. He'd never read one page in his medical journals about such a stupefying situation. His brother, Ronald, had been the confident, witty one. Ronald often found himself the life of the weekly supper party, teasing and entertaining the young women of Chicago.

Morgan ran his palm over his scarred right hand. How many countless hours had he spent reading and writing with the vow of fidelity to his sacred learning? None of those hours gained him chivalry or deportment with the fairer sex. Morgan bent his stiff, damaged fingers and closed his eyes.

He could still see Ronald's large smile. Ronald's constant bravado had left Morgan, the younger brother, aware of his own predisposition to social dullness. Finally, Ronald had settled on a dear family friend, a lovely young woman, Miss Olivia Bradstreet, to marry. Their fathers were both doctors and already close friends. The families meshed perfectly. Their courtship didn't look too difficult—in fact, they both seemed to enjoy each other's company immensely. Of course, she'd said yes. They were to marry as soon as he returned from the war in Texas.

But that was not to be.

Faint shadows on the floor drew Morgan's eyes upward until he stood and glanced out his front window. Mrs. Snider looked to be asleep. His shoulders dropped as he chewed on the corner of his bottom lip. What could he do differently? It felt cowardly and irresponsible to retire and leave the poor woman out in the cold.

Morgan walked to the desk where he kept his medical books and opened the drawer. Pushing past some letters he'd not yet mailed to his father, he reached for the small tintype photo of Olivia, remembering that horrid day a year ago when Ronald's hand had shaken so violently as he'd pulled the photo from his blood-soaked vest and pushed it into Morgan's hand. "Tell her how I loved her," were his brother's rasping last words.

Morgan ran his thumb over the genteel face in the picture. Her soft eyes appeared forlorn. How could she have known her fiancé would never return? Morgan felt the familiar twist in his gut and set the photo down. It almost felt irreverent to have something so personal in his scarred hand. Taking a deep breath, he looked back to the window and slowly exhaled.

Something about this kidnapping seemed amiss.

The earlier offer to return her to her husband provoked an unusual fear. What had she said? Snider would only kill the Derry twins? Any rational man who had had his wife kidnapped would do so. Why did she protect the ones who took her against her will? Morgan stepped closer to the window and peered out. Could she be a bit daft? Some of the men he worked on in surgery had been so, saying the most peculiar things at times.

Was the story from the Derry boys even true? It would explain why she would not let him help her. Carlotta said this young woman was Basque, that her people came from the area around Spain and France. That explained the Spanish he'd overheard and the soft accent in her few words. Gossip said her husband, Arnold Snider, was *not* a saint. Morgan had had no interactions with the man, but the papers had made various speculations. The Derry boys believed it to be true that Arnold Snider was the cause of Hangtown's bank going into bankruptcy. Their hard-earned gold had unjustly found a way into Snider's pockets. The bank reported that Snider's withdrawal had matched his deposits, yet something had gone terribly wrong. Everyone else who came to withdraw their deposits had been turned away from the bolted door. Left with only lame excuses and empty pockets, the town had been furious!

Rubbing his fingers through his hair, Morgan stepped to his front door and opened it. It had started to rain. He ran his tongue inside his cheek as he thought about his predicament. This arrangement would not do. Despite his current choice and location as a backwoods miner, his overriding good breeding and privileged education were ramming through his conscience. The porch creaked as he stepped out.

"Ma'am." Morgan stepped closer, and she didn't move. "Mrs. Snider." Was she alive tucked inside that blanket? There was one way to find out. Bending down, he scooped her frail body into his arms and lifted her from the corner. Her head fell forward on his chest, and he thought he heard her whisper. "Poppi, *por favor*, please get me away." Pushing the door wider with his foot, he took the four steps to the bedroom on the right. Her long lashes flickered open as they entered the dark room.

"No, no, no." Fear radiated from her eyes. She tried to raise her hands, but they caught on the rope and padlock restraints.

"Just sleep here." Morgan lowered her onto the straw and feather mattress. He straightened the blanket back over her legs as she tried to rise. "You will be safe here, and it is starting to rain." His body blocked her ability to stand. Her round eyes widened in fear. Flipping to the other side of the bed, she dropped onto the floor in the corner of the room. Frantically, she quickly tucked the blanket around her limbs and huddled beneath the woolen fabric. He'd seen those same vacant eyes of terror and shock on the battlefield. Even in the shadows, it was akin to what he saw in her at this moment. He hadn't meant to frighten her again.

"Mrs. Snider, I will leave you." Morgan took a step back, retreating. "Is there anything you need? I can awaken Carlotta to—" he stopped as she adamantly shook her head no. "Would you like the door open? It aids in the heating of the room." He held the knob, waiting. Her shoulders seemed to relax, and she blinked a tired, sorrowful expression.

"No, Dr. Hastings."

Morgan stilled after pulling the door closed. Staring at the crackling fire across from him, he paused at the use of his name on her lips. It was strange, but it seemed almost lucid. His mind swirled as he released the knob. *What now? Could he sleep? Likely not.* Was she just frightened, or truly unstable in mind and soul? Her long hair had fallen back when he laid her on the bed. White and blotchy-faced, she seemed younger than he would have imagined. Her skin was so ashen, nothing like the Mexicans of Texas and California. He'd heard of the Basque people, but knew little of their origin.

Grabbing some reading materials off his desk, he settled into his soft chair by the fire. His boots rested on a stump of wood he used for chopping kindling, and Morgan felt his body relax for the first time since he'd seen those impetuous brothers. His fuming anger at the twins had lessened somewhat. Their plan was still unimaginable and beyond ridiculous.

Surely in the morning light, he'd be able to reason with Mrs. Snider and see to her safe return. Morgan positioned his paper to find a stream of firelight and wondered about her actual age. Holding her in his arms, her tired, soft round eyes were hard to ignore, and her young face was far from common. Truthfully speaking, she was lovely, even in her stricken state. The observations constrained his rambling thoughts. What if her husband and the law tracked this escapade to his cabin door?

Exhaling, he shook his head and realized his eyes had been reading his favorite publication—*The New England Quarterly Journal of Medicine and Surgery*. Still, his mind hadn't registered one word. Dr. Oliver Wendell Holmes was defining a widespread belief in medicine and the proposed germ theory of disease. Usually interesting and thought-provoking, he'd read it over many times. Morgan tried to start again before he dropped his damaged hand and the journal into his lap.

Shaking his head, he tossed it onto his desk. There was no purpose in rereading it anyway. He was a miner now. A simple, profitable trade that didn't require steady hands or personal engagement with people. Likely, seeing the Derry brothers or having a distressed woman dropped into his peaceful day caused the revolving recollections about the war and his brother's death. Morgan rubbed his palm over his weekly stubble. Would the affliction of those memories ever find any healing? Fatigued, he closed his eyes. Tomorrow, he would reason with the young woman and return her into her husband's waiting arms.

Emery's untethered head bobbed forward. Jerking awake, she listened. Fighting exhaustion, she still heard no movement from outside the door. Carefully she gathered the cut rope and stood. Her bones ached from top to bottom and from every side. The bed looked like a fluffy cloud and had felt heavenly the few seconds she'd laid there. Taking a careful step forward, Emery winced at the stabbing pain coming from her big toe. Her feet were as cold as river ice, and yet the pain was real.

After setting the chair under the doorknob, she slowly lowered herself back to the bed. Like the first bite of sweet bread from her mother's stove in Pamplona, her body melted into the comfort. Pulling and tucking the blanket around her the best she could, Emery held the barrel band taut at her waist and laid on her side. The soft, cold pillow next to her cheek seemed like something from a wonderful dream. It even smelled crisp and clean. Maybe all this was a dream? Yet, unmistakably, she'd watched Arnold Snider put that pouch of gold in her father's hand.

"Two months," her father had said, patting her

back goodbye and guiding her and Gianna onto the San Francisco Bay wooden pier. Emery had wondered if she would ever see her family again. Every instinct in her being had known they were being sent into the devil's den. Her father could only see the family's survival in that pouch of gold.

How could she blame him? He had fathered two females first. They were little help with a pick and back-breaking work in the rock. His own gold claim could barely feed a cage of mice, let alone a family of seven.

A groan escaped the back of her throat, and she huddled deeper into the bedding. The log cabin remained silent except the light patter of rain tapping the roof. Rising an inch to get the band from cutting into her ribs, Emery remembered this exact silver barrel band sitting on the deck days ago. The crew usually threw everything of no use over into the bay, but somehow this useless circle of metal had become a trap around her waist. No matter how she sucked in and maneuvered, she could not get it past her hips. Darkness settled into shivers on her skin.

What of Gianna? Her younger sister, not yet seventeen, must have been shocked to find her gone. Was she terrified and crying tonight? Was Gianna begging to go home? Emery's fists tightened. What lies had Arnold told Gianna? And his wife? Heavy with child and needy at every turn, Missus Finny would certainly notice her maid missing. Emery ground her teeth. How desperately she wanted to pray that ship would sink to the bottom of the bay, but first, she needed to get her sister off.

That was her only hope.

Five

Emery awoke to the gray light coming through the window and voices outside her door. "I will get my husband's Mexican spurs. Those will wake her up."

Quickly, she raised on one elbow. Spurs? The old woman would use them on her? Hunching over, Emery pulled the blanket around her back and arms the best she could. Standing quickly, she approached the window. Her body wavered like she was back on the ship; she groaned, likely from rising so fast. Peering at the cloud-covered sky, Emery felt annoyed. She'd overslept but didn't need to be prodded by these people to rise. Looking closer, something out the window drew her attention.

Maybe a dozen little birds pecked at the ground, looking for their morning seed or worm. Some would chase the others off, and then more would fly in to replace them. They were mesmerizing, so miniature, brightly colorful, and determined. The rain-saturated ground should bring elation to her being. Dirt, dry grass, earth—anything would be better than a bay of green-blue water entrapping her and Gianna like a floating prison. She turned towards the door, removed the chair and inhaled. How would she get this wavering to stop so she could compose herself and—

A loud knock blasted her silence. The door opened. Carlotta stood in the opening. "*Señorita*, you are up. I have eggs and tortillas getting cold. You must come and eat." Carlotta signaled her forward.

Emery's eyes darted around the room. What choice did she have? Gripping the blanket tighter with her bound hands, she followed the woman into the center of the cabin. The warmth and smells hit her suddenly. Just looking at the plate of food on the table made her mouth water. Before she could sit and scoop up the waiting food, an abrupt panic arose. Dr. Hastings was missing. Was he going to town for the law?

"*El hombre.*" Emery tried steadying the panic in her voice. "Where is the man?" she said, trying to breathe slowly. "Dr. Hastings?"

Carlotta pointed to the table. "Sit." She handed Emery a fork. "He in the barn. Thinks you don't like him."

Carlotta nodded to the food, and Emery felt the need to obey. She could reach the plate and scoop the eggs into the tortilla but had to lean her face into the plate to take a bite.

Carlotta pushed a cup of milk in front of her plate. Emery hadn't had milk in months. Glancing up at Carlotta, she wondered if it was a calculated tease. She could not reach the cup. Carlotta raised her eyebrows with a smirk. "What is *loco* with you? You won't let him cut your rope there? You afraid he cut your skin?" She let out a cackle and wiped her hands on her dingy white apron. "He has a box of those doctor tools he use in the war." Carlotta snickered. "If he cut anything wrong, he could fix the damage, *sí*?"

Emery didn't know if she was serious or mocking her. Her belly growled for more food, and she leaned forward for another bite.

"He doesn't think his hand will work," Carlotta smirked. "But I've seen him do many things. His fingers are stiff, but they still work." The short, weathered woman inched the cup halfway to the edge of the table. Emery looked up, slowly chewing. This *señora* was as shrewd as a hawk watching her nest.

Emery's blanket picked the wrong time to slip from her arms and land on the floor. Exposed and embarrassed, Emery knew she couldn't reach it and Carlotta made no motion to help. Thick, worn, brown hands rested on the table next to her plate. "You will, *señorita*," her voice void of kindness as Emery tried to lean away from her, "let me help you dress and get free of those bands, *sí*?"

Emery nodded slowly, though she would prefer to hide in a corner. She had nothing clean to wear, so any clothing, even a shift from an old woman, would be more proper than what she was currently wearing. This Carlotta was much like her own *abuela*—when grandmother spoke, the household obeyed.

"*Sí, señora.*" Emery glanced, then averted her eyes. The cup of milk inched to the corner of the table.

Bending to drink the last drop of milk, Emery looked up to spot a horse and rider galloping across the yard. Before panic set in, recognition of the hair and size of the man made her straighten up. It looked like Morgan Hastings. Now what was he doing? Waiting with bated breath, there didn't seem to be anyone else with him.

Carlotta wrapped her apron around the last heavy pan of hot water. "Come now. The bath is ready." Carlotta walked around the kitchen wall into the next room.

Emery stood up from the chair and felt waves rocking her body again. Reaching out to steady herself with the table, she bent down to retrieve her blanket. Breathing deeply to calm her stomach, she noticed the room had dark wood floors covered in the center with a blue and brown rug. Two large chairs near the rock fireplace, a desk, and the table was all there was. Humble. Far from Arnold Snider's fine, shiny house in Hangtown.

Her first real job had been cleaning his wood floors and expensive furniture. To think, back then, she'd felt pleased with her fortunate opportunity. What an innocent child she had been. Clutching her blanket, Emery felt a nervous shiver run up her back as she walked around the corner. Behind the wall, a simple bed sat covered with a colorful *serape*; a thin wooden wardrobe stood next to it. The high-sided tin tub sat a few inches from the rag rug on the floor.

Carlotta pursed a wrinkled frown and motioned to Emery. "Come close to the tub and rest your hands on both sides of the rim."

Emery stepped closer, eyeing the large kitchen knife in Carlotta's hand. Allowing the blanket to drop around her feet, she slowly separated her wrists as much as possible then pointed the fingers of her right hand down toward the warm water. The fingers of her left hand touched the tin, and Emery held her breath. Straining to pull her wrists apart, Carlotta touched her tongue to her top lip and slowly sawed the rope back and forth. As soon as her hands were freed, Emery staggered back.

Carlotta flashed a crooked smile. "*Muy bueno.*" The old woman's worn *huaraches* kicked the rope to the corner.

Emery pulled her elbows back and stretched her shoulder blades, neck, and arms. Waiting, staring down into the warm water, shouldn't she feel some joy? Some freedom? Rubbing her tender wrists, she unknotted the bandana that hung around her neck and tossed it into the corner where her rope bindings lay. Staring at the rope and bandana, a strange tingling started in her nose, and her eyes began to fill. What did any of this freedom matter? She would always be a captive to carry the shame alone, never forgetting the things done to her against her will. The milk in her stomach turned sour, just like everything else in her. Emery tried to stiffen her jaw. She would not cry in front of Carlotta. She could soak in that tub until her skin dissolved, but it would never remove the real stains she bore.

"*Niña*, come now. This water, *es muy bueno*." Carlotta touched the padlock. "What to do with this? Aye, aye." She shook her head.

"I've tried. I can't get it off." Emery's hand came up quickly to wipe her dripping nose; as she rubbed both hands over her cheeks, her arms felt like feathers.

Carlotta stepped back and dropped the soap and a rag in the water. "Here is your towel." She pointed to the cloth on the bed. "Now, you have your hands. You can get clean." Carlotta picked up the corner of a quilt and hooked it on the opposite wall. "You won't be disturbed, *niña*."

Emery thought she saw a glint of sadness in the old woman's face before she turned and allowed her privacy. Alone, the windowless room felt heated with the kitchen's black stove, a thin wall away. With this kind of warmth, no wonder the old woman preferred the cozy corner to the other front room. Emery took a deep breath and pulled the soiled nightgown up and under the metal band. With one last look around the area, she pulled it over her head and stepped into the tub. Sitting down quickly, the warm water rose and covered her limbs as she pulled herself into a ball. Her skin tingled with warm goose bumps and, just for a moment, she dipped her shoulders to allow the water to soak her hair. Sinking a little lower, she could rest her head on the back rim.

Emery slowly closed her eyes. All her days in California, she'd never had a bath so wonderful. Her last real bath was in their two-story stone home in Navarre. One privilege of being the oldest was she would always bathe first, then Gianna, and, finally, they'd try to scrub the little boys clean. It would end in a battle of trying to keep most of the water in the tub. Scrubbing the family wash came next and, finally, the diapers. Pulling in a deep sigh and letting it out slowly, she thought, *Oh, to be a queen of luxury today, with the warm water all to myself.* The lavish minutes ticked by until Emery's elbow knocked into the edge of the metal band at her waist. She opened her eyes and reached for the rag. *Stupid goat, I'm the queen of nothing. Nothing but pain and indignity.*

Minutes later, before Emery could finish towel drying her hair, she heard a noise in the front and wrapped the towel around her body. Carlotta's arm extended through the quilt wall. "Here, this for you." Carlotta wiggled a package in the air.

Emery took the two steps quickly and took the brown paper bundle from her grip. "*Gracias*." Emery held the package. "What is it for?"

"Look and see. If you need help, call for me," Carlotta said, turning into the kitchen.

Emery dropped it on Carlotta's bed and pulled the string apart with one hand while gripping her damp towel at her chin. Shrinking back, she gaped at the lovely white fabric of bloomers and a chemise. Soft, cream-colored long stockings seized her attention. Carefully setting the beautiful underthings aside, her eyes widened. A cream-colored blouse with full sleeves and a blue skirt the color of late evening completed the impressive ensemble. Emery held her hand over her open mouth. Everything shined so feminine, so new and crisp. Was Dr. Hastings waiting outside to take her to town? To the law? For a brief careless moment, she'd forgotten that she remained trapped between two worlds with no way to be free. Her shoulders dropped while something wilted inside. These things would be like wearing a costume of sorts. Running her hand down her face, Emery clutched her cheek and then squeezed her bottom lip. Whatever misfortune came next, at least she would be clothed.

• • •

Carlotta mumbled something about coming in her room as she shuffled around the corner. Emery had hoped if she took long enough to dress, maybe Dr. Hastings would leave her be. "I'm sorry. I can't seem to get this braid right." Emery separated the clean strands.

"*Aye ya ya.*" Carlotta looked her up and down. "Someone knows how to pick women's clothes right. These fit you well, *señorita*. You," Carlotta blinked, shaking her head, "you no look like the same person." She turned Emery's shoulders away and began to braid her long tresses. "I have a strip of leather here." Carlotta reached for something off her bureau and secured the long braid with a small bow. "And take this." Before Emery could refuse, she pinned a broach onto the neck of her cream blouse. "I never wear it." Carlotta shrugged. "Some *gringo* gave it to me when he was dying."

Emery nodded a wary thanks. "Please, have your room back." Emery scooped up her filthy nightgown. "I will do the wash, empty the water, and then I will scrub the floor." The disbelief in Carlotta's eyes pinned her still, and she tried again. "I will be very quiet. I will. You won't even hear me."

Carlotta's gray and black brows furrowed, and she lifted the corner of Emery's blouse, revealing the metal ring. "This must come off next. Go."

Carlotta pulled Emery's elbow around the quilt door. "The doctor need to help you."

Emery's feet stumbled forward with the unfamiliar layers of her new blue skirt. Once out in the kitchen, she held the table for support. Morgan stood by the fire and turned to see her. His chin lowered notch by notch, but his eyes got wider the longer he stared at her. Cheeks flushing, she looked to the floor. Of course, it was him who rode to get her the lovely new things. Her hands were free now, so Emery covered her cheeks. "It's very warm in here," she mumbled.

He looked around the room, scratching the back of his head. "You . . . you look well." His face flushed, and he pulled on his ear. The silence lingered on with uncomfortable space between them. Emery pulled her braid over her shoulder and then flipped it back. The tall, lithe man had shaven, revealing a kind mouth. A strong jaw gave way to muscled neck and shoulders.

"Would you sit for a moment?" Morgan gestured to the soft gray chair.

Emery held his eyes one last second before moving. Something about his face—even blotched by red and white scars, his countenance brought no fear to her. Maybe it was the warmth of his deep brown eyes or the calm in his voice that pulled her? *Or being fully dressed.* Possibly after being threatened and mistreated on the ship, there wasn't much else that could be done to her.

"Ah!" Morgan hit the heal of his palm against his forehead. "Shoes." Rolling his eyes, he growled. "I forgot shoes."

Emery looked down at her toes peeking out covered with the new stockings. She would never tell him they were the best pair she'd ever owned. "No matter." Emery sat, feeling like a spoiled woman in such a soft chair. "My toe pains me and . . . and . . ." *I have nowhere to go.*

That truth didn't leave her mouth.

Six

Morgan sat stiffly and cleared his throat. He already branded himself a clumsy oaf when it came to women. The experience of asking for women's *things* at the mercantile was enough to rattle him for days. Thankfully, the clerk yammered on about the change of the town's name as she fetched all the items, leaving him to answer only a few minor questions. But shoes, good Lord, how could he forget shoes? Morgan glanced down at her feet, wondering her size. Cracking a small smile, he tried not to react to the total transformation sitting a few feet in front of him. The simple, sweet beauty of Mrs. Snider was fetching . . . *beyond fetching.*

"Auburn was formally called Dry Diggings." The words came suddenly from his tied tongue. Cracking his jaw to the side, he looked to the fire. *Why did he say that?* The woman had far greater concerns than the goings-on of this mining town. "So." He leaned forward, grasping his hands over his knees. Again, he couldn't help notice she nervously pulled her braid over her shoulder and fidgeted with the end.

"You know I feel dreadful for the actions of my friends and . . . and I would like to assist you in any way." Morgan rocked back and tapped his fingertips together over his lap.

Emery chewed on her bottom lip. "I thank you for taking me in." She looked everywhere but at him. "What I was hoping . . . since you mentioned the town here, Auburn?" She finally looked at him with a brief sweet smile.

"Yes." He nodded, smiling back. "I could send word for your husband to gather you there."

"Oh, no." Her round eyes widened further, and she leaned forward. "Not that. I was hoping to send word to my family. They live outside of Hangtown."

"Hangtown?" His face lit up. "That is not far. I could take you myself."

"No." Emery squirmed in her chair and, obviously uncomfortable, she stood. "The fine breakfast is . . . is . . . rolling over in my stomach." She pressed her lips together and crossed her arms over her chest, rubbing her elbows. Walking the few steps to the kitchen, she ran her hand over the wood table as she circled it. "That is not necessary." Appearing tongue-tied, she looked down, shaking her head. "I just have something important to relay about my sister. It's very important." Her face flushed from pale to pink.

Morgan stood. This confusing, nonsensical reasoning was happening again. Past the pretty round face and deep molasses brown eyes, the woman sounded addled. *She's been kidnapped and taken from her husband, but she needs to relay something important about a sister?*

"Mrs. Snider." He took a quick step closer.

Suddenly, an alarmed expression covered her face, and he stopped, feeling the indignation from her eyes sinking into him. Her confusing stance hit him anew. Talk was common about women who'd traveled by land or sea to arrive in gold country, only to find it a desperate place. Their mental capacities had collapsed under the strain. Yet Arnold Snider was said to be the richest baron in the area.

"Please, sir. I . . . I . . . insist, I mean . . . that you would call me by my given name. Please," she said, her tone coarse. "Just call me Emery."

Morgan blinked, wondering . . . *Did the Derry brothers threaten her?* Another thought occurred to him. "Have you incurred your husband's wrath in some way? Do you suppose he will blame you for this misfortune?"

Clutching her hands under her chin, she took in a deep breath. "I can't expect anyone to understand. I have overstayed my welcome, and this is none of your concern." She stepped around the table and faced him. "Could you give me directions to this Auburn? I will make arrangements for myself and soon pay you back for these fine clothes."

Morgan felt his ire rise at her insistent dismissal

of help. "No, that will not do." He shifted his weight and paused. "You have money? For a room? To send word or to travel to your family?" He studied her. *How did their cordial smiles turn into a rash standoff?* "And I hate to remind you, you have no shoes."

Her petite nose flared, and she reached for her blanket that had been left on a kitchen chair. Flinging it over her arm, face like a flint, she headed for his front door.

"Mrs. Snid . . ." He stopped his plea as she opened the door, walked through, and let it slam behind her.

He lowered his head and pulled his hand across his face. Did she have a rational bone in her body? Watching her through his front window, she paced the front porch. A growl caught in the back of his throat. What was he missing? Had he been removed from society so long that he could be that confusing?

Emery realized she had come back to the porch where she'd started. The front porch was dry, but the yard was wet and muddy from the rain. Scanning left to right, the quiet area reassured her it wasn't as despairing as the ocean, and at least she had the use of her arms. Groaning, Emery pulled the blanket tight around her and went to lean in her old corner where the logs crossed. Dr. Morgan Hastings would not control her and tell her what she could and could not do. She'd rather ruin these beautiful stockings and explain the metal ring to her parents than put up with his notions. The man claimed to be here to help her. Yet he had balked at her request to get word to her father about Gianna.

No, she could not find her way herself. He knew she had no money. Even if she did, what questions would her parents ask? Why is Gianna in danger? How could this kidnapping occur, and how could she have been mistaken for Arnold Snider's wife? And even more troubling, what was Snider doing in her and Gianna's bed? Emery could hear their questions as she shook her head, pulling the blanket across her face. All she had figured out so far was to perhaps write a note. Just one simple thing to explain that Gianna is in danger and get her off that boat.

Numb and exasperated, she lowered her chin. "I don't know what to do. *Dear God, what am I to do?*" Existing between bitter woman and hurting child, she didn't expect an answer for one like her. Crying and hiccupping softly, she crumpled to the porch floor and curled against the rough log cabin. Letting the tears flow, she dropped her head to her knees and sobbed. It was upsetting to cry on her new things. The crisp store scent smelled so good. After a few minutes, her groans and sniffles calmed down a bit. Something slowly pulled on the corner of her blanket, until she had to look up. The sunlight replaced her darkness when she saw a white handkerchief.

"In the military, a white cloth is a sign of surrender," Morgan's voice calmly explained. How long had he been sitting on the bench outside of her blanket cave, rudely eavesdropping on her? Slowly taking the handkerchief from his hand, she used it to blow her nose.

"Or it comes in handy as a handkerchief," he said, with a half-grin and wide-eyes.

Oh, this man with his calming tone was wasting his time. Arnold Snider had tried kindness and gifts. Emery wiped her eyes and wet nose on the cloth. Today, because she was abandoned and without any recourse to save her sister, she would decide to hate this man too.

"Your friends will get no gold from Arnold Snider." Her voice cracked with bitterness. "And I will never see my sister again. They are gone, halfway to the edge of the ocean." She waited for a reaction, but the tall man just stared out at his land.

"The rush for gold." Morgan sighed. "How many found out the hard way—money can't buy you a penny of peace." He ran his fingers through his long waves, securing them behind his ears. "It can't cure dysentery or yellow fever." Glancing over his shoulder, their eyes met briefly before he stared out again. "It can't stop a bullet from lodging into your chest or heal burning flesh."

His voice trailed off, and it seemed he was done making his point.

He turned to face her. "How do you think the Mexican government feels about selling this land we live on, now that the streams and rock have revealed gold? A tin of nuggets can turn allies into enemies." He frowned. "Some will spend a lifetime seeking tiny flecks, pulled and gathered from these diggings. Water so cold, frostbite turns the toes black. All for fortune." His voice was hushed. "But it won't bring my brother back." His eyes narrowed at her. "Or your sister."

Emery thought those were the clearest words he'd spoken so far. Her family, her existence, and her future had been controlled by glistening gold flecks. His forlorn musings sounded better to her ears than any of his sad attempts to help her.

"The Bible says heaven has streets of gold." Morgan shrugged one shoulder. "Maybe that was the gold's sole purpose, all it was really created for." He looked back out to the trees.

Emery stood and stretched her back from the discomfort of the hard logs. "You were a surgeon? In the war?"

He nodded lightly, turning to lean against the porch post.

"And your burns?" she asked. "If you don't wish to tell me . . . are they from the war?"

His brows rose quickly, and he stretched his scarred fingers on his right hand. "I wouldn't be here if it wasn't for the Derry twins. They were just wet-eared teens. Assigned as stretcher-bearers." He smirked lazily. "The surgical tent was supposed to be protected from battle, but on this day, I was elbow deep into cutting . . ." Sitting up straighter, Morgan cleared his throat. "Trying to repair a . . . a wound. I don't even know which direction the ammunition came from. I just remember it was loud, and before I could look up, the log poles and tent came down on top of me. I think I was knocked out for a few minutes. I don't remember the smoke or the flames. Just those matching faces covered in soot, hovering above me."

"Abner and Clayton," Emery whispered. They were sort of comical the way they talked and badgered back and forth. Now she was able to make sense of their words; Morgan's caring for her would make them even. They had saved his life.

"Everyone else in the tent perished." He huffed.

"How dreadful." She couldn't help the genuine pity expressed in her heart and voice.

Rising, he stretched his torso. "I can't hold the instruments properly anymore, and my hands begin to shake. Doing the simplest medical tasks . . . I can't explain it—something akin to a panic riddles my being." Emery suppressed a shudder, wishing she hadn't pried. His skin seemed to pale.

"I think I'll take a walk." Morgan stepped out onto the soggy grass. "I'll make it short, and then I'll ride back into Auburn and fetch you some shoes." He gave her a firm nod before he walked away.

"Wait!" Emery clung to the post as he turned to look at her. "Enjoy your walk. If you want me to go, I will, but if I could stay longer then I don't need the shoes." That sounded jumbled to her own ears.

"You are welcome to stay," he said matter of factly before turning away.

The doctor walked out to the tree line with a confident gait. He shoved his hands into his pockets, his shoulders slumped slightly, pulling his tan shirt taut against his back. Why did she assess him and stare after him now? Hadn't she said earlier she would hate him also?

Without malice toward his friends or her, he said she could stay. Though paralyzed at first, now there seemed little need for fright inside the walls of his cabin. Her arms were free, and the strange man truly seemed to care, even to be eager to aid her safe return. Emery blew out a long breath as he stepped out of sight. It didn't matter that he was close to her age and favorably handsome.

Closing her eyes, she squeezed her hand over her face—*stupid girl*. Nothing mattered. Even in light of forgiveness of sin, she would never have what other young women her age had—purity and honor to bring to a marriage. The most important things would never be hers to pledge.

Seven

Morgan's walk led him to circle back to the barn for his mining bag. Mining would serve to distract him until the late afternoon clouds brought on more rain. He needed a day of quiet to think.

Something in her story didn't make sense. Or was he just thinking of the unstable woman he'd agreed to share his cabin with? The rain sprinkled lightly on his hair and shirt. The Derry brothers had asked for one week. How could he allow her to stay and then turn his back as she was taken away by those brash numskulls? The ridiculous scenario gripped his belly until it hurt. What about her husband? What kind of offense was harbored between them that his own wife didn't seek him out? She talked and moved with a certain youth and innocence. Was Snider cruel to her?

The same questions rolled over and over, and none of them made any sense. He spent the next hours finding little gold, and soon grew weary of mining and searching for any rational solution for the kidnapping of Mrs. Snider.

Morgan entered his barn and put his equipment away. After forking hay to the horse and cow, he filled the water trough. Bewildered, he leaned against his workbench. The greatest difficulty with this unannounced guest would be in keeping his mouth closed. Could he possibly share a space with her and not ask questions? His head tipped back. *Impossible.* He'd always had to know answers.

Finding reliable results, diagnoses, or solutions had thrilled him in medical college. From a young age listening to his father, he needed to understand how bones healed and the body pumped blood. Those mysteries he could learn with confidence, but to try to make sense of the ways of a young lady sobbing on his front porch—he was a perplexed man at a severe disadvantage.

Shaking the rainwater from his hair, Morgan fingered it back and jogged to his cabin. Carlotta was sitting at the table, while Mrs. Snider had donned an apron and was stirring something on the stove.

"She say to let her cook," Carlotta said, shrugging a shoulder. Mrs. Snider had a rich husband and possibly her own cook. Would it be edible? Carlotta didn't look too worried. As soon as his unexpected house guest flashed her deep brown eyes at him, he remembered her words, "Call me Emery."

"I hope you don't mind." She waited.

"No, whatever you two want." He felt like an intruder in his own home. "I will change my shirt and . . ." *This was awkward.* ". . . Then be back." Opening his bedroom door, he rolled his eyes. Yes, his belly growled, and whatever simmered in that pot smelled wonderful, but this would not do. He was a bachelor and she a married woman. Mrs. Sni—Emery, couldn't cook for him and be . . . be . . . around. People would talk. He bit his bottom lip and unbuttoned his shirt. *What people?* This cabin couldn't get any farther from his family's fine home on Green River Avenue. He opened his wardrobe. *What shirt?* The brown one had started to fray at the collar and cuffs. Carlotta had made him a light green one, but the arms were a bit short. Morgan roughly pulled it out and hurried it over his arms. Rolling up the sleeves, he shook his head. Now he wondered if he was an addled hermit. Without clear answers about her situation, he would go mad. Possibly, with effort, he could keep silent for a day, maybe two, but then she would have to explain and quickly move on from here.

Carlotta pointed to her spices, and they spoke back and forth in Spanish. Emery prepared the supper with confidence, only substituting a few things here and there. As soon as Morgan came from his room, the Spanish quit flowing and silence replaced the chatter in the small kitchen. Had she made the right choice after thinking of staying in her room all day? Helping Carlotta with the floors and wash was good for her hands and heart. Somehow the conversation flowed into preparing the meal and Emery had asked to do the cooking. But now, the way he cautiously approached the table and took a chair, it seemed like an intrusive, brash decision.

"It's called Tolosa soup." Emery ladled a large thick scoop into a bowl. "At my home outside of Pamplona, we had sheep and goats." She carefully set it in front of him. "But cow milk for the cream is fine, and no goat cheese, but—" She waited as he blew on a spoonful of the steaming soup.

He nodded after taking a bite. "It's good."

Emery felt her insides relax. "And the skillet bread is thick and good for dipping also." Sliding a plate of round bread in front of him, Carlotta eyed her with wide eyes. "And me, please." Emery realized she'd been watching him. She filled another bowl and set it before the waiting elderly woman.

Morgan looked up from eating. "Please sit, join us."

Emery turned to the stove and back to the table. "I was taught to wait until the man had his fill." She lifted a simple smile, but Dr. Hastings stopped eating, drumming his fingers on the table. Something about that did not sit well with him. The way his tongue rolled around the corner of his mouth, he seemed to be holding his words back. Pulling in a shaky breath, Emery took another bowl. Placing a small scoop inside, she pulled out the chair and sat. Stirring the hot liquid, Emery decided to keep her head down. What had she said wrong? He'd seemed cordial to her earlier, even sympathetic. Where had his forbearance gone?

"Where did you learn to cook like this?" He broke into her thoughts. His voice was low and steady with little scrutiny.

"At my mother's and grandmother's hand." Nodding, Emery took a small bite.

"Your family had sheep and goats, you said?"

She finally looked up, and his face appeared interested, not angry. "Yes, before the floods of '46. A month of rain and standing water as far as you could see. We had to live in the second story of our stone home. Many animals drowned." She shook her head. "Then disease took the goats, and the sheep all died." Morgan shook his head and chewed. "My father believed there was no way to start over. We sold what we could, said goodbye to all we'd ever known and . . . and," her tone weary, "found ourselves on a ship to America."

Carlotta huffed and shook her head. "Aye, aye, America." She broke off a piece of bread and sopped up the last drippings from her bowl.

"Where did you land?" Morgan started to stand with his bowl, and Emery jumped up to refill it for him. He sat watching her as she gently set another simmering bowl in front of him.

"In the bay of San Francisco. Thank God for the Mission San Francisco de Asis."

Carlotta nodded her head and made the sign of the cross. "Saint Francis of Assisi."

"They were kind to us, gave us food and clothing for our rags. My father quickly went to work with the livestock, mostly sheep and goats." Her tone was wistful, remembering those days. "There were thousands of farm animals at the mission." She nodded, and then her face turned serious. "My father, he wanted to find gold, so we went to Hangtown." Standing quickly, she added wood to the stove. "I would like to do the dishes." She took their empty bowls. "Carlotta, do you mind?"

"A chance to go to bed early. At my age, how do I mind?" Carlotta held onto the table as she scooted her chair out. "*Buenas noches.*"

"*Buenas noches,*" Emery repeated back.

"Good night, Carlotta," Morgan said.

Emery would finish the dishes and return to her room. His questions seemed innocent enough, but he'd likely continue with more. She filled the basin with the hot water from the stove.

"You know your way around a kitchen and are a good cook." Morgan hadn't moved from the table.

"Carlotta said you wouldn't like anything different from her beans and tortillas." Suppressing a smile, she pulled the rag from the steaming water. "I'll think of a way to repay you for your hospitality."

"Did your family pay the mission?" he asked.

She glanced over her shoulder. "No, but we all worked. My mother and little siblings in the garden. Everyone worked." She set a clean bowl on the drying rack. Feeling like he might be trying to make a point, she changed the subject. "How did you meet Carlotta?" *She could lead the questioning too.*

"Ahh," Morgan settled back in the chair. "She worked at the military encampment in Texas—some in the kitchen and then some in surgery."

"In the surgery?" Emery shook her head, drying the dishes.

"Some people have the constitution for . . . it. Blood never bothered me. Everything in the body is set in perfect motion. If you see how the Creator fashioned every bone and vein, the pumping of the heart, the air in and out of the lungs, it's a mystery that stands to be understood."

"Can man understand such wonders?" Emery held the dishrag, eyeing him.

"No, but we like to try." Morgan's eyes squinted softly at her as he bit back a smile. His expression was so kind, so friendly, Emery felt something strange down to her toes. She turned away quickly.

"When I was getting back on my feet, the war

was ending. Carlotta spoke enough English, and I already knew she had nowhere to go."

"No family?" Emery frowned.

"Two husbands in the grave and five of her six children fled somewhere deeper into Mexico. I'm not sure why she was left behind, but at her age, I don't think she wanted to go search for them."

"*Yo me ocupo de myself.*" The firm statement came suddenly from around the corner wall.

Emery held her hand over her mouth, suppressing a giggle. The old woman wasn't asleep but had heard them talking about her.

Morgan tilted a smile and Emery stepped close to whisper near his ear. "She says she can take care of herself." Only inches apart, she caught his eyes searching hers and flinching back. She chided her impetuous move. Quickly jerking on the apron strings, she pulled it over her head and dropped it on the chair. She needed to go to her room.

The warm meal and personal conversation had stirred within her a small, delicate joy. It had been so long since she'd had calm or comfort that it tried to slip in without notice. Suddenly he stood in the way of her exit. Sucking in a quick gasp, she turned to go around the other side of the table.

"Wait." He took hold of the band around her waist.

Emery felt herself crumble. For heaven's sake,

Carlotta was in the next room. She would scream if necessary. "Please." She begged. "Please don't." Still stupid and foolish, she should've seen this coming. Her eyes filled with watery terror.

He looked confused and dropped his hand. "I'd almost forgotten you still have the band and lock around your waist. When you pulled off the apron, I saw it." His voice stayed calm as he took a step back, pulling his hair behind his ears.

Her heart still pounded in her veins. "Oh." She looked away, embarrassed.

"I have a bone saw," he said.

Emery gasped and lurched back, her eyes frozen wide in shock.

Eight

A hundred thoughts flashed through Morgan's head. What had he done now? What did he say? Something upset her. One minute they were talking, amused at Carlotta's words, and the next, she moved away like her feet were on hot coals. He shouldn't have looked long into her eyes, but they were by far the most beautiful, rich brown eyes he'd ever seen. It seemed improper, but he knew it the minute the warmth of her eyes melted with his.

What could he do? There wasn't a day he didn't remember he was a man. And if he allowed himself to admit it, only an impetuous, lonely one would stare at a married woman. True, dinner conversation with an attractive, sweet, young maiden felt highly refreshing. And the way she'd innocently leaned close to translate Carlotta's words could have been his undoing. Yet all he'd done was reach to hold the band around her waist and stop her. The young woman had fallen apart, instantly riddled with dread and tears.

The mistake was identified. Touching the band had to have been the error in his ways.

Morgan stood next to his bed and pulled off his shirt, hanging it back in the wardrobe. Emery had very little interest in letting him cut away the metal band or lock. She'd hurried to her room and closed the door before he could reassure her he would be careful. Morgan shook his head, sure he heard the bedroom chair being dragged in front of her door.

Sitting on the edge of his bed, he leaned his elbows onto his knees. He'd held her the night he'd carried her to the room. She hadn't seemed terrorized then, but she was also mostly asleep and bound. He scratched his fingers through his hair.

Tonight's questions and conversation seemed to spark her goodwill. He'd succeeded in not mentioning the obvious. Why wouldn't she let him help her? Why wasn't she eager to get back to her husband's care? Morgan pulled off his boots and flopped back into his bed.

Could he make it another day without pressing her for answers? What if the Derry brothers returned early? Groaning, he dropped an arm across his face. "Lord, have mercy on my soul," he mumbled. A strange stillness surrounded him, like moments of being in the woods alone, with only his senses alert. The thought occurred to him: *Maybe he needed to quit worrying about his needs and be more sensitive to hers?* Wasn't that part of his doctor training? Have the sensitivity to set aside what you know—to care and really listen to what the patient needed?

How many fatally fallen soldiers had begged

him with hollow eyes to leave them be when he'd felt the tearing of his conscience to do a procedure. One that *might* help them survive. Could he stand back and just let them have their say over their death? How could he forget Private Barrows, who'd begged him to forego the amputation that might give him a chance to live? Morgan relinquished his training that day by not amputating his leg, and that very soldier was upright and talking as the medics rolled the wagon out of Texas six weeks later.

Morgan stilled. Had he just said his second prayer in the last two years? Pulling the blanket over his long frame, he rolled to his side. A sort of strange quiet truth lingered, and Morgan squeezed his pillow firm under his head. *Try to listen. Try to hear what she needs without asking delicate questions.* That shouldn't be too hard if he kept to himself, mining at the creek all day.

A protective rod stiffened in his backbone and Morgan pulled the blanket off and stood. Reaching above his wardrobe, he jerked his rifle off its perch. All things aside, he couldn't be gone all day and leave his cabin unprotected. Who knows who would come next? He popped the handle apart to check for bullets. He'd have to come often and check on the women. Snapping it back in place, he cocked it once. Blast it, the sound reverberated louder than he'd wanted. Did she hear a rifle cocked from across the living area and become startled? Good Lord, now what would she think?

Emery awoke the next morning to voices. Thankfully they were not outside her door, and she could easily recognize Carlotta and Morgan talking in the kitchen. The dizziness returned when she tried to sit up. As soon as Dr. Hastings went about his work, she could get something to eat to settle this seasickness. The wooziness mimicked the waves of a rocking boat in the bay. How long till her land legs would work again?

Emery pulled at the metal band and wondered, if she could rid this from her body, maybe she could be done with traces of the ship once and for all. Taking a few steadying breaths, she stood. Having Morgan Hastings cut it off seemed like the worst of her options. It was only an inch or two from her skin. *Have a true care,* she chided. How could she be so concerned with her own well-being while her sister was left on that ship? Emery smoothed back her hair, reaching for her new blouse and skirt. There must be a solution she hadn't thought of.

Dr. Hastings was willing to hand-carry a letter to her father. If her father could rescue Gianna, would Arnold Snider insist on getting his money back from him? Arnold Snider had paid for their domestic service up front in gold.

Emery finished fastening the buttons on her

blouse. She'd never minded the work in the big house in Hangtown. Miss Cassidy, their English tutor, had become a close friend—the only real friend Emery had known in California. Cassidy had made the work enjoyable. But everything changed when the Hangtown bank locked its doors. There were riots, and someone had viciously hurt Miss Cassidy.

Emery shivered as she remembered finding her. Her stomach rolled uneasily again. Arnold's wife, Finny, had to be close to delivering any day. The ill-mannered redhead announced to the entire boat more than once that she *would not* deliver a baby on a pirate ship with only two maids to help. Maybe they had all departed by now?

Emery waited by the door until she heard what she thought were the sounds of Dr. Hastings leaving. Closing her eyes, she leaned her cheek against the door. *Please, Lord, please Mommi . . . what am I to do?*

Sipping the last of her hot tea, Emery thanked Carlotta for breakfast.

"I see some blue sky." Carlotta nodded toward the front window. She neared the table where Emery sat. "Here, take these."

Emery looked down as Carlotta popped her feet out of her own *huaraches*. "I walk on the back strap. Too lazy to pull it on."

Emery stilled. *Was she ready for her to leave? Was today the day she should go? If the woman could loan her some money—*

"You like to cook, *sí?*" Carlotta broke into Emery's fretting.

Emery nodded.

"Then take these sandals, go out the front and stay back from the barn. There look to be a garden at some time. I'm too old to keep it up. All that bending and weeding." Carlotta frowned. "You go see what is there. You can cook again, *sí?*"

A faint smile lifted from Emery's face. She wasn't trying to send her on her way. She was telling her to go explore outside.

"Use that shawl." Carlotta pointed to the hook that held her aprons.

"*Gracias.*" Emery nodded. A walk outside in the fresh air would be agreeable. She slipped her feet into the sandals and took the cream shawl off the hook. Wrapping it tightly around her shoulders, she felt safe and warm. Breathing in the light scent of wool and fried tortillas, she smiled at Carlotta. "I'll see what I can find. You don't mind if I cook again tonight?"

"Oh, no, no." Carlotta crooned. "You cook, you cook." Carlotta flicked her hand towards the door.

Thankful that her toe pain had lessened without any attention from *Doctor* Hastings,

Emery gently took her leave from the cabin. A grandmother who didn't want children underfoot. She, the nuisance, was shooed from the cabin. The ground was damp as she walked toward the barn. Eyeing the cow and horse tucked inside, Emery stopped. What a simple, quiet, hidden refuge this place seemed. How could she thank the kidnappers?

Emery released a soft laugh. They had left her with agreeable people. Turning back, she eyed the covered porch, the refuge where she'd huddled on that first day. The same birds flitted and pecked outside her bedroom window. The quiet, the peace of this place was like the reverent moments when the monks sang at the mission. Almost touchable, the air felt fresh and clean, silent of greedy, crying seagulls, and the smell of fishy saltwater. Emery's eyes scanned long over the solid yard, enjoying the lush land more than the swelling bay that had felt like a death trap. The trees beckoned her admiration, so solid and appointed. A person could truly be happy, truly content here.

Walking around the barn, she stopped abruptly. That person was Morgan Hastings. This was his home, his life. He was the educated doctor who had served his country. This was his property, not hers, Emery chided herself. By comparison, the Marone family slept seven people in a canvas tent at their mining claim outside of Hangtown.

Emery sniffled in the damp air and pulled the cream shawl close. Shaking her head at her foolhardiness, she exhaled. It would only hurt more to let herself dream of such a fine home.

Pulling her skirts higher to avoid the tall, thick grass wetting her new skirt, Emery walked on until she noticed some coiled pieces of baling wire hiding among the weeds. *Weeds, yes, Carlotta, there were so many it was hard to tell what was a plant, or even once a garden.*

That evening when Morgan entered the cabin, she turned to him, holding back her smile. "I found your garden, Dr. Hastings."

"You did?" He spied Carlotta sitting at the table. "Her discovery is to your liking. I'd place a bet."

The woman flicked her hand at him. "I told you I'm too old for all that."

Morgan walked past his aging housemaid and turned toward the stove where Emery worked. "Are we having another Basque dish from the old country?"

Lean and tall, he stood close. His voice was curious, and he smelled like fresh pine. A strange heat, far more intense than what the stove produced, coursed through her.

"I . . . I . . ." Emery tried to remember what she was saying. "I found parsnips and carrots, onions, and different lettuces. Some of the fencings had fallen on the plants and actually protected them from the animals."

"Really?" Morgan turned back to Carlotta. "You said there was nothing."

"Ahh." She shook a wrinkled frown. "You only like beans and tortillas."

"No, I beg to differ." He smirked at her. "*You only like beans and tortillas.*"

Emery grinned, enjoying their banter.

"I'm not complaining." Morgan leaned closer and snatched a piece of carrot from her work area. "It seems incredulous to say this out loud." He chewed, watching her.

Emery wondered what the big word meant.

"But, I never entered the kitchen of my family home in Chicago. Never. I had no need," he continued.

Emery stopped stirring the pot and blinked. "Never?"

"Everything I was to eat was prepared and set before me."

Emery looked wide-eyed to Carlotta. Carlotta shook her head. "*No me extrana que me necesite.*"

Emery huffed and pinched her lips, not to laugh.

"I heard that, Carlotta." His brows furrowed, squinting at her. "No need to have a secret talk with Mrs. . . . ah . . . Emery. You said something in Spanish about how extremely grateful I am to have your help. Or how lucky you are to work for such an easy-going fellow." Morgan nodded proudly and sat at the table. "And if this kitchen weren't only three feet from the front room and ten feet from the front door, I likely would not visit."

"It's a lovely home." Emery wondered why she spoke up. Nothing he said needed defending. "Someone owned it before you?"

"Yes." Morgan looked wide-eyed at the savory stew and biscuits she put before him. "This looks wonderful." He picked up his spoon.

"Your neglected garden was once prized, I'm sure. The rows and beds are all planted in proper order. Likely fertilized with dead fish or eel."

Morgan looked up as he ate.

"Corn growing from the center, surrounded by pole beans. Squash served as a leafy mulch, preventing the weeds from blocking out all the light."

Morgan watched her, dabbing his napkin to the sides of his mouth. "I suppose if I want something besides beans and tortillas, I should pay more attention."

"You've made it into the kitchen, how difficult would it be to find the garden?" Emery lowered her chin and peered up at him. An awkward, strange silence hung between them. Should she be teasing him? Did he take it as chastisement? "Oh, and one other thing." She wanted to break the way he studied her. Carefully, she tempered her words. "I know little of how—" Emery shrugged. "But, I believe I saw motherwort, echinacea, and other herbs growing." Casually she took a bowl and ladled her dinner into it. "Would those be something helpful for healing, for medicine?"

His mouth twitched to the side. "Possibly." Swabbing his biscuit along the bottom of the bowl, his eyes met hers. "Tomorrow, can you show me?"

Emery hesitated, feeling embarrassed that her simple findings interested him. "Yes, of course," she said, casting her eyes back to her humble supper creation.

Nine

Morgan raised his eyebrows at the sight of the once tumble-down, weed-infested garden. Heavens, she must have been out here for hours yesterday. The rusty wire fence was propped back upright, though it looked unsteady in many places. He could easily fix that.

In her quiet, unassuming voice, Emery pointed out the rows of herbs and asked him if he liked beets. Locking his teeth in a frown, he shook his head no. As the young woman walked around the area, he couldn't take his eyes off her. Wearing Carlotta's sandals and shawl, she looked perfectly at home. Comfortable.

Had he seen her so comfortable before this? Her face was usually so wary and guarded. Today the sun warmed her deep chestnut braid laying casually along her back. Besides Ronald's fiancée, Olivia, Morgan had had so few up-close interactions with women. Studying her, he wondered if they all carried themselves with such grace and poise in the outdoors.

"I'm amazed at the work you've done," Morgan said, feeling a little guilty for admiring her *and* letting the garden go to seed.

"I hope you don't mind. I didn't ask your permission." She bent and straightened a floppy leaf. "I know it wasn't mine to tend." Her voice faded, and she pulled a thin green weed and tossed it to the side.

He watched her closely. "You sound sad."

"Oh, no." Quickly she stood. "I enjoyed this." Emery brushed the dirt off her fingers. "Sort of like looking for buried treasure." She offered a tender smile, and he had to look away. Her beauty and innocence made him hungry for something he hadn't known he'd wanted till right this moment. Did Mr. Snider appreciate the obvious, natural beauty she carried?

"I'll go back to the barn and get my tools." He cleared his throat. "We can shore up these sides and—" Morgan turned quickly. Hearing something from the road, his heart spiked. Growling, his face pinched red. "I left my gun on the porch. I hear a rider. Run, Emery! Run into the woods!" Before he could see the intruder, she'd raised her skirts and run as he'd said. Morgan looked past the barn for a view of the rider and then back at her. Her dark blue skirt faded as she moved in and out of the trees. Chiding himself for his stupidity, he jogged in front of the barn and stopped. Raking his fingers through his hair, his shoulders dropped. The short man atop his horse was Donald, the butcher.

"Hey ho, Morgan. Is Carlotta about? I got a big old fat beef tongue for her."

Morgan's mind wheeled, needing to go after

Emery before she got lost. "She's inside. Can you knock on the door? I have to go after something." He picked up the pace, jogging back toward the garden.

"Emery," Morgan called, running into the woods. "Emery, it's me. It's okay." Scanning the area, he looked down. Was that a sandal print in the mud? Disgusted, Morgan knew he was inept as a tracker. "Emery." He implored, looking left to right. His blood began to race as he ran, feeling desperation coming on. "Emery!"

Suddenly her flushed face peeked out from a grouping of tall oaks. "Morgan?"

With the use of his given name and seeing her safe, he permitted his lungs a steady breath. "It's nothing to fear," he said, winded, holding his hand out towards her. For a moment her face stilled and she didn't move.

"Who is it?" With rounded dread in her eyes, she took a small step forward.

"The butcher." Morgan met her in the middle, still reaching for her. Holding her skirt layers to the side, she stepped over a thick fallen branch and took his hand. As soon as her fingers were cupped inside his, his grip tightened, and he felt his body relax. He waited to speak, so many thoughts pounding in his head, but all he could feel was her soft hand in his.

"I'm keenly aware . . ." Morgan wanted to sound helpful, but his pulse was still erratic—

"that . . . that you do not want to be returned to where you came from." Needing to catch their breaths, he securely held her hand, not wanting to let go. Even with the unsightly scars that covered his skin, her touch somehow centered him to what was important. The moment appeared ripe, but he did not persist. He had to point out the obvious. "But I cannot hide you in the woods. If that had been Abner or Clayton, they would have had you in seconds. They are like hound dogs—it's their second nature." Carefully, Morgan covered her hand with both of his. "Please let me help you." He squeezed them. "You know me better now. Yes? I mean you no harm. No judgment."

In the silent damp woods, she looked everywhere but at him.

"What about the boardinghouse in Auburn?" He released his second hand and gave their grip a shake. "You would be safe there. Not having to flee into the woods at every sound."

Emery pulled away from his hand and gathered her skirt. Marching back through the brush where they'd come from, she shook her head.

"I have no money," he heard her say. "And I've been at your charity long enough." Tension seasoned her voice.

"No, Emery, you're not charity." Morgan tried to lengthen his strides to her quick steps. "You are a victim. This kidnapping was done to you by men I call friends. Did you have any say?"

"No." Shoulders squared, she hiked on.

"Wait." Morgan grasped her arm but let go as fast—the last lesson remembered.

"Emery." He pleaded to her back, and she finally stopped. "Just tell me what you want. What would be helpful?" The woodsy silence hung uninterrupted.

"Helpful is," she said, swiftly swiveling on her heel, her eyes boring into his, "these beautiful clothes." Emery brushed her hands along her sleeves. "Having my hands free." She held them upward. "A warm bath. A chance to doddle in a garden. A small kitchen to cook in, where people seem friendly, appreciative. Someone to graciously loan a pair of sandals, a lovely shawl." Pulling the garment tight around her chest, she blinked, and he prayed she would not cry.

Morgan tried to understand. "And that is enough for now?"

With dark silky eyes, Emery slowly nodded, and he almost leaned forward to take her in his arms. He stiffened. Who needed that embrace more. Him or her?

"All right." Didn't he agree with the Almighty he would try to back off? "I like having you here." Those words came out more honest than he'd expected. "The thing with Carlotta is that whatever she cooks, that's what we eat for a month. Have you ever had tamales every day for a month?" He felt he'd found a proper change of subject as they began to walk toward the cabin.

Emery shook her head as they approached the barn.

"You make a good variety of food." Morgan quirked a half-smile, about to place a hand on her back before he pulled it away. "How do you feel about beef tongue in your carne asada?"

Emery walked on and forced a small smile. His casual talk of food did not distract from the shaking that had started deep inside her. She nodded her thanks as they approached the cabin. Inside, she said she needed a few minutes and excused herself to her room. Her room? Feeling like an unwanted guest, she stood inside the closed door. This was not hers. She looked around the bare log walls, spying the chair, the simple bed. She'd always shared a bed with Gianna, and often a little brother or two.

Sitting on the chair, she tried to calm herself, but the shaking continued. Moments ago, she had been sure that Arnold Snider had found her. She would've run until her legs gave out if Morgan had not called for her. Standing, Emery removed the shawl and Carlotta's sandals. Walking to the window, she looked out as the insufferable shaking coursed through her body again.

Look again. The yard is free of any riders, she tried to convince herself while rubbing her arms briskly. Turning to the sound of Morgan and

Carlotta talking in the next room, she shook her head. What were they saying about the strange woman left on their doorstep? Morgan needed a solution for her. How long did she think if they didn't talk about her obvious presence in his home, maybe the outside world would go away? Perhaps she could just watch the little birds, work in the garden, and pretend nothing was amiss.

A ragged sigh came from the back of her throat. She needed to get to Hangtown. Her parents would be devastated, but she would limit the painful details, only conveying the threats and lies from Mr. Snider. Emery could do it, she could make her story convincing. Maybe her parents would find the will to leave America. It would mean a chance at life for her to be far away from this California. No one would have to know the shameful acts done to her. She would live at home and help her mother carry the load with the children, the family. It would suffice, and she would carry this nightmare to the grave.

Blowing out a breath, Emery wearily gazed through the window again into the yard. How would she get there? Dr. Hastings had done so much. The tension in her shoulders slackened. She would miss his presence, his kindness. Possibly he could pay for her to find a stage to Hangtown? Morgan might insist on taking her, but then how would she explain their acquaintance to her parents? She would need to go alone. Emery sighed. Feelings of hope and skepticism collided within her.

What if Snider had already found her parents and weaved his own lies? What if, from afar, she could see if Gianna had been returned? That's all that mattered. A fresh weight rested on her shoulders. Her parents were good people. Never had she been dishonest with them. How? How could she begin this tale, this falsehood? Looking into the eyes of her father, could she speak without falling into a hundred pieces?

Her back stiffened. She would have to. Their first-born child, the young, pure woman that they had sent off to work on a ship in the San Francisco Bay, was long gone.

Ten

"To find your way to Hangtown?" Morgan narrowed his eyes on her at the table that evening. "Yes, of course. I said I would be happy to take you." The words sounded believable, but something inside him wanted to rebel against what he'd just said.

"No, I don't want . . . ," Emery stopped, looking down, "you to take me." Nervously, she touched her tongue to her top lip. "I . . . I was hoping you would help me with the fare. Is there a stage or wagon I could travel on?"

His protest rolled in his mouth, chomping to be heard. "Yes, but nothing proper for a woman alone." He dropped his head to the side, scratching his ear. "I'm keenly aware that you want to keep me out of your . . . your dilemma, and there is no malice in me when I say that it is too late, Emery."

Emery glanced over to Carlotta. She shrugged, obviously agreeing with Morgan. Shaking her head, Emery dropped her elbow on the table and rested her head in her palm. "You know my abduction was dreadful," she mumbled. "Why do you insist on making this more difficult?"

Morgan jerked. "Me? Why do you insist on being vague and aloof? A woman who was abducted, kidnapped from her husband?" How could she think *he* made things difficult? "If that is even what really happened."

Emery rose so fast her chair scratched the floor. "I don't even know what aloof is!" She growled and turned to Carlotta. *"Por que este hombre no puede acuparse de sus propios asuntos?"*

Carlotta raised another shrug.

"Stop that." Morgan stood, pointing to Carlotta. "Don't talk to her when you know that . . . that I don't understand . . . most . . . likely that was about me."

"She say you don't mind your own business," Carlotta smirked.

Morgan flinched and rolled his eyes. Leaning his hands onto the table, he forced his voice to stay steady. "Mrs. Snider, the day you were not only dropped off but also tied and bound to my porch, you became *my business*."

He could see the flames flickering in her eyes. "I am my own person, Dr. Hastings. People are not business. I knew I was a burden." Her voice cracked. "And now you think you will have the say of how I will come and go?" She shook her head. "You posed as someone kind and helpful." Her chin quivered. "It was only a matter of time before you would try to control me."

Morgan jumped back as if an invisible blow had been made to his chest. He raised his hands in the air, and his mouth hung ajar. "I have no wish to control you, ma'am. That would be a feat beyond which even your own husband is capable."

Her face flushed, searing red. "Stop it! Just stop it! Stop talking about my husband!" She screamed, wrapping her arms around her ears. "I hate you!" Tears spurted from her eyes, and she ran from the room sobbing. Her door slammed, causing the cabin windows to rattle.

Morgan's eyes flashed left to right while his body stood frozen. "What just happened?" He raked his fingers through his hair and squeezed it behind his head. "I am hated for offering a ride to where this woman wants to go?"

Carlotta dipped her head. "Something always wrong with that one. She not allow you to take off that band and lock. Aye, aye." She frowned, shaking her head. "Whatever it is, she don't want you to know."

Morgan took in a steady breath and let it out slowly. Apparently, he'd missed all the clues. His disappointment in himself was not a new revelation, but he felt fresh waves of it from head to toe. Tomorrow he would take her to Auburn and arrange for her ride. At least she would be gone when the Derry brothers returned, and he could confidently and truthfully say he knew nothing of her whereabouts.

Emery had such a fitful sleep, it was no wonder she felt the rocking of her body again the next morning. Would the swaying, the memory of the ship never leave her being? Would she be able to face Morgan Hastings today after her display last night? Her stomach soured with the recollection. Like a limb snapping from wet snow, the weight of this ordeal was too much to bear. But today, there was a plan that seemed possible.

She tried to rise, but the dizziness increased. The room spun, and her body broke out in a cold sweat. She stood for an instant before she fell to the floor and crawled to the chamber pot in the corner. The contents of her stomach wretched into the pot, and she dropped her head on the cold wood floor. Her fit of anger had upset her to the core, but what was this, this sickness?

The other mornings had left her slow and feeble. Violent nausea pulsated through her body while she wretched again. "Oh, Mommi," Emery moaned and laid back onto the floor. The band bit into her side, and she rolled onto her back. She fanned her face with her hand and remembered helping her mother to bed many a morning in Pamplona. Her mother always rose up within the hour, a shy smile on her face, admitting to Emery, she was likely with . . .

Emery moaned and swiftly curled into a ball, coiling her arms and legs like some insect on the floor needing protection. "Could it be?"

Her throat constricted, and she could not contain her whimpers. Everything within her cried out, "No, please, no!" Her forehead rolled on the hard floor while she gasped for air. "Please, please, this cannot be." Her eyes rolled back in her head, praying it was only a nightmare. Her monthly flow had yet to arrive, she realized with horror. Laying still with ragged gasps escaping her, Emery remembered she was cursed. With shaking limbs, she reached for the bed and crawled in. Pulling the covers over her head, she soaked the pillow in bitter tears.

Morgan quietly entered the cabin. It was after noon. Searching around the small area, Emery was nowhere to be seen. Had she changed her mind? Would she ever speak to him again? Carlotta peeked around the corner of the kitchen wall.

"Is she in there?" Wide-eyed, Morgan gestured to her door.

Carlotta nodded. "I try to take her some tea a few minutes ago. She say she is sick and wants to rest."

Morgan wrung his hands. This was his fault. It was too late for today, but he would help her first thing tomorrow. Gently, he knocked on the door. "Emery." He waited and heard a faint, "Yes?"

"I'm sorry you don't feel well, and I want to apologize for how I spoke to you last night. I . . . I . . ." The muscles in his jaw tightened, knowing he'd failed miserably. "I will take you to Auburn in the morning. I will help you find a wagon or stage to Hangtown." Frustrated, he hated talking to a door. "These mining towns have a lot of transportation back and forth." He pinched his lips and placed his hand on the door. "I'm sorry if I made you fearful or seemed like . . . I wanted to control you." Morgan shook his head, unconvinced his words were understood. "Could you let me in for a minute? I need to say this to you directly."

"No," Emery replied, faintly through the door.

Later, Morgan sat at the table alone. Restless, he rubbed his hand over the rough wooden table. He missed her conversation and her cooking. He'd spent the day preparing himself for her departure and the reality of life getting back to normal. The problem was normal held little appeal.

He stewed over possible explanations for Emery's sudden illness. Obviously, this whole ordeal had caught up with her, just like dormant germs or disease. One minute you are fine, the next minute you are abed. Their argument certainly had made her blood boil, triggering her fallen state. Glancing to his medical box on the floor by the fireplace, it would be of little consequence to pull his past to the present.

He was a doctor; surely there was something he could help with—some knowledge as to what was ailing her. No food or water all day wasn't a good sign. Morgan chewed on the corner of his bottom lip. The bone saw he'd used for many amputations lay in that box. It could be used to remove the metal band. He dropped his head into his palm and rubbed his head—none of his ideas ever seemed welcomed. Rising, he banked the fire. Suddenly feeling exhausted himself, he walked past his soft chair and went to his bed.

Sometime in the deep darkness, Morgan awoke. Carlotta never stirred much at night. Listening, he wondered if he'd dreamt the strange noise? Surely Emery would not try to leave on her own accord. He told her clearly that he would be of help. Rising on one elbow, Morgan listened again—no sound of doors or footsteps heard. Groggy, he was likely dreaming. He laid back down. *Another scrape, a thump. What hit the floor?* Morgan struck a match to a candle on his nightstand to confirm he wasn't dreaming. A strange sound seemed to come from Emery's room. Could she be dressing?

Rising, he peered out his front window. Searching left to right under the shadowy moonlight, nothing moved. Listening closely, now there was only silence. He sat on the edge of his bed. A few more minutes of nothing and he blew out his candle. Laying back, Morgan watched the smoke swirl above him until his eyes dropped shut.

Slam.

Startled into high alert, Morgan knew that sound

was real, *and* it came from her room. Had she fallen from the bed or dropped something? No, it sounded more like the chair tipped over. Waiting for more racket, an eerie, strange creaking came into his room. Glancing at the exposed log roof, and the beam over his bed, something creaked again. Morgan blinked; he could have sworn the roof beam groaned. Was something on the roof?

There it was again! He sat up and listened. What the devil would make only that beam groan unless something was—

Eleven

Morgan flung Emery's door open and dove to where her nightgown and feet swung in front of him. Pushing her body upward, he strained to support her weight while reaching with one hand to remove the rope from around her neck.

"Dear God!" he ground out, trying to pull the rope loose. Panic and sweat poured over his body as he jerked on the rope while trying to hold her free from the tension. Had her neck already snapped?

"Emery!" Morgan bellowed, knowing her arms hung limp around his head. "Please!" he begged while finding a space where his fingers could dislodge the rope from her skin. As soon as he could jerk the last loop over her head, her body sagged into his quaking arms, and they fell into a heap on the bed.

"Emery." He panted, shaking her chin. Leaning over her limp body, he held her face and leaned his cheek close over her mouth. *Was that a faint breath?* Pulling his fingers over her neck, there didn't seem to be any broken bones, but that didn't mean her airway had not collapsed.

"Oh, God, help me." Feeling every muscle useless in his body, he pulled her straight onto the bed and tipped her chin upward. "Save her,"

Morgan prayed, rubbing her arms up and down in some attempt to revive her. Fighting his own racing pulse and light-headedness, he scooped her up and sat on the bed, cradling her in his lap. Resisting the urge to shake the air back in her body, he buried his face into her neck and mass of hair. In between his mumbled prayers, a low, gravelly rasp came from her, and her elbow suddenly popped him in the ribs.

"I hate . . . you," Emery moaned, scratchy and clipped.

Morgan lifted his head and gripped his hands tighter around her body. Embracing her tight across his chest, he closed his eyes. She was breathing. *I hate you.* Sweeter words he'd never been so relieved to hear. Genuine gratitude pulsed through his body. Her hands felt like ice as she weakly pushed from his embrace. Innately aware that he held her close and secure on his lap, he didn't care. Neither of them was leaving until her words would make sense of this dreadful act.

"Emery," he whispered, fingering some loose locks from her face. "Are you in pain?"

"My . . . my pain was . . . almost . . . gone," she whispered hoarsely. "I hate you." She moaned, turning away. "You never . . . mind . . . ," she winced, "your own . . . business."

He felt her body shudder and scooted them both back further on the bed. Pulling the blanket out from under her, he leaned forward and carefully covered her bare feet and old white nightgown. Still feeling dizzy, with his heart pounding, Morgan rested his head on the pillow next to hers, wondering what had just happened. What would push this young woman to such desperation? Should she be left alone? It didn't matter being in her bed was improper. This was his home and at this moment, he would have the final say. This was where he needed to be. Morgan turned to his side and rested his warm hand on her arm.

After a few minutes of numbing stillness, he saw her blink, and his mind came back into focus. He spoke the first thought he had. "When I was five years old . . ." His words seemed trivial, but he continued. "In the middle of the night, our milk house burnt to the ground. I watched it burn from my upstairs window. After the excitement was over, my parents had retired while workers on my father's estate kept buckets of water near to keep any sparks from spreading. Even though I watched them for myself, it didn't matter." He held his hand steady on her and pressed her closer. "I was sure the house would burn down next." He eyed the rope still hanging from the beam above the fallen chair. "Such fear and dread came upon me that I did the most unlikely thing. I left the nursery and found my parents' room. I opened the large door and I tapped my sleeping mother in bed and said, 'I'm scared.'"

"Can you guess what my mother did?" Morgan waited and looked to see if she was sleeping. Her eyes blinked toward the darkness. She turned away. Holding her neck, ignoring him, she faced the window. "Can you guess?" He nudged her with his hand, unfortunately bumping the metal band around her waist.

"No," she huffed.

"My mother, who'd always left our care to others, opened up her warm comforter and moved over. I climbed into her bed and she wrapped me in her arms, just like this." He pulled her closer, avoiding the band, and rested his arm on hers, rubbing his thumb across her hand. "Granted, the bedding was far finer and the bed, oh Emery, it felt like feathers upon feathers." The memory was still fresh in his memory.

"I am dead, Morgan," she rasped. "Though your story is touching, just like your presence, it has no comfort for me." She released a small cough. "*I will* take my life. If not tonight, then another way."

Morgan thought his breathing had stopped, or the room had frozen in time. He listened for a sound from above. Only God above could redeem this moment.

"You know I was a surgeon in the war." Closing his eyes for a moment, all the sounds and cries from the war were still there. "I saw grown men beg me for life. Some begged me for death."

Morgan swallowed the bile rising as he spoke. "But I am no savior, no god, Emery. I didn't see ten—" His tone lowered. "Or fifty, or even a hundred. I saw many hundreds die from disease, and bullets, and stabbings. Many even died from my surgeries, after I'd reassured them they would make it home to their wives and children." He pinched the narrow space between his eyes. "But I went to war for honor, duty to my country, and life for my fellow men. I believed even in death, they were all the same, but it isn't true." He sighed. "How can I explain it?"

Cautiously his arm rested heavily on hers. "Some of what we believe just isn't true. There was no honor in seeing body after body being thrown into a pit in the bloodied Texas dirt. There is no honor in watching a vile disease that reduces healthy bodies to bones. By God's grace, I will go on, even with the nightmares and injuries that plague me." Morgan tried to compose his thoughts and raked his fingers through his hair. "I'm not sure what I am saying."

He stopped, and she turned, looking back at him, and relaxed her shoulder into his chest. Without permission, he pulled his hand loose and glided his fingers along her cold temple and cheek. "Emery, if you want to leave this world on your own accord—you're right, there is little I can do. Would you do me one favor?" he asked while gently stroking her hair. Oh, how he wished he could remove her desperate thoughts and hollowness.

"I'm just self-centered enough to believe all things are my fault." He rested his arm and hand back over hers. "Will you tell me what really happened to you?"

Her body rose and fell with the deep breath she took. Finally she spoke. "I am not Mrs. Snider," she whispered.

Morgan stilled, holding back his frantic questions.

"I . . . I work for Arnold Snider." Her voice was barely a wisp. "My sister and I are housemaids. We worked for him in Hangtown." She moved away from his hold, adjusted the metal band, and pulled the blanket up, gripping it under her chin. "My father wasn't doing well with his mining." More silence interrupted her faint words. "Our work for Arnold Snider was to help the family get by." She coughed and cleared her throat. "His wife is expecting. One of his men came to us in Hangtown and offered my father a handsome pouch of gold for our help with her and their needs on the ship in the San Francisco Bay."

Morgan's mind ran ahead. The answer was obvious—the Derry brothers had abducted the wrong woman, and her sister was left alone on the ship. But why not . . .

Her body began to tremble next to his, and Morgan froze with a dreaded realization. The likely pit of her despair struck him like a sword. He finally whispered, "What did he do to you?"

Her head began to shake, and she pulled the blanket over her face. The gulps and sobs said it all. The pig had pressed himself on her, likely taking her innocence. No wonder she reacted to the thought of going back or being called "Mrs. Snider."

Red hot anger boiled through Morgan's being. He would use this very rope and hang the reprobate this minute if he could get his hands on him. His muscles tightened as he thought to fetch his gun. Another deep sob from under the blanket brought him back to the moment.

"Emery." He pulled the blanket from her grip. She turned her face into her pillow. "You don't have to look at me, just listen." Morgan held the blanket over her shoulders. "I'm so sorry. I feel wretched for what has happened to you." She curled her legs up and wrapped into a ball. Gently, he tucked the blanket around her and began to rub her back. No wonder she often looked fearfully at him. He leaned back on the bed and stared at the beams. *But to take her own life?* Morgan blinked into the darkness, trying to steady his erratic breathing. Inherently prone to want to solve things, yet hadn't he said, even as a doctor, he was of little use. "I wish I could go back in time and do . . . do . . . anything," he whispered.

"I wish I could sink that ship." She mumbled between broken breaths. Morgan rolled back closer to her side.

"I'll get the Derry brothers to burn it," he offered.

Emery looked back over her shoulder. "My sister is probably still on it."

Their eyes met, and he risked dropping a soft hand on her arm. "Then let's get her off." She watched him intently. "I mean it. If those bean-heads could do it, surely I can figure a way. Arnold Snider's never laid an on eye me. I could pose as . . . as a buyer of goods or a doctor sent to check his wife's health." Even in the dark shadows, he could see her shattered wet face contemplating his words.

"You don't need the gravity of my problems, Morgan." Emery turned her face away from him.

"Are your people, the Basque people, are they all on the stubborn side?" He carefully massaged her shoulder and spine.

She huffed, looking back for a second before she shook her head and looked away.

"Do you believe in God, Emery?"

The room stilled, and she finally spoke. "There is a letter there on the stack of things you bought me."

Morgan raised on an elbow. In all the panic, he'd not seen her things neatly folded in the corner with a paper on top.

109

"In my church, a mortal sin forbids me from forgiveness." She sighed, looking back at him. "I explained it in the letter. I know what I'm doing." Resting back on the pillow, her eyes drooped closed. "Yes, I believe in God, but there will be no eternity to speak of. Except for one of suffering."

"Hell." Morgan leaned over her, narrowing his eyes on her. "You believe you will go to hell for the inability to live with the wrongs done to you?"

She nodded. "I am not strong enough. I will face the consequences."

"No one is strong enough, Emery." Unable to temper his voice, Morgan pleaded while clutching her arm.

"Stop, Morgan!" she growled. "Don't you think I've thought about this from every direction? I am a woman. You could never understand this." She pushed from his touch and hovered at the edge of the bed. "He didn't just take my body. He took my life. My ability to have a future. My ability to look my parents in the eye, to marry, and have my own children. Not some filthy reminder of . . ." She shuddered and pinched her lips closed.

Morgan went to open his mouth but didn't. He'd only known her a few days, but their thinking stretched as opposite as could be. He'd never expected to make peace with his own ghosts, but the solitude of mining and his simple home had been a strange healing salve. Only a breath away from the abused young woman, Morgan rested on the pillow.

The truth exposed an acid of anguish and hopelessness that burned in her blood, in her heart. She was right; it was a deep wound, far from what he could understand. Her eyes in their deep pools were heavily laden with despair. He now realized the burdens she'd been carrying from the first moment he'd seen her. Morgan knew of no cure, no medicine for that.

Twelve

"*Aye, aye, aye! Que es esto?*"

Morgan felt something poke his shoulder, jarring him from a terrible nightmare. Cracking his eyes open, Carlotta stood above him. Blinking and yawning, he appreciated being awake, but why was his housekeeper in his room scowling at him?

"Oh, good Lord." Morgan inched back from where his arm held Emery against his chest in her bed. Scowling, Carlotta shook her head, her chin so low the loose skin waggled back and forth.

"No, it's not what you think." Morgan held his hand in the air, in some way to divert her chastisement for the improper scene.

Emery stretched and glared back at him. "I'd rather swallow rocks," she snapped before flinging the blanket aside. She tried to rise and wavered back, sitting on the bed.

"Could everyone get . . . out?" Her gravelly voice quaked, and her color paled. "Is that too much to ask?"

"You are still ill." Morgan pulled his long legs around and sat next to her. She released a low groan and turned away from him. *"Swallow rocks"* finally registered, and seeing her back turned to him, he felt the red rising in his cheeks.

His stories, his comforting touch, had found rejection and an abrupt end.

Standing, Morgan set the chair upright. "Excuse me," he said to Carlotta, who must have been oblivious to a rope dangling only a foot above her. Morgan jerked it back over the beam and yanked it off. How easily he had given her forbearance last night. Her confession was heartbreaking, but in the morning light it seemed that he who had done no wrong, now stood proxy as the enemy.

The room couldn't empty nor could the door close fast enough. Emery flopped back on the bed and tried to gulp down the swaying nausea. Without food in her belly to vomit, she curled under the blanket despising the day she'd been dropped off with Morgan Hastings. At least the do-gooder knew half the truth. Was he recounting the sordid details to Carlotta at this moment? Telling her that she was *not* married? A lowly servant wench kidnapped accidentally? Or that he thwarted her death, leaving her pitiful life to end another day? She glanced at the beams in the room; he'd taken the rope with him. What a pathetic savior, full of childhood stories and tales of battle woes. She closed her eyes, wishing for nothing but darkness.

With a loud knock her door swung open. "One day is enough, *niña*." Carlotta entered with her hands on her hips. "Either you come out and eat or I go after the doctor."

"What? Where has he gone?"

"To mine gold in his creek." She scowled. "He told me last night he worry with your sickness, and by accident, he fell asleep in your bed." Her wrinkled cheek creased with seeming indifference.

Emery rose slowly, watching Carlotta. "I'm not hungry."

"Fine, I go get him."

"No." She huffed. "I'll come out."

Later in the afternoon, Emery stepped carefully within the rows of the refurbished garden. A butterfly landed on a leaf and she stopped to watch. The orange and black swirls on its wings were beautiful. Blinking, she swung in the other direction. She didn't want to feel anything beautiful ever again. The peace and smells of the garden had already tried to touch her senses but to no avail.

With every slight movement, the pain in her neck and shoulders reminded her of last night. Morgan Hastings was a foolish man. A fool to think she needed to live. A fool to help her. Pulling in a deep breath, she glanced down. There was some time before she would begin to show. *Maybe,* she chewed the corner of her lip, maybe she was too hasty, too distraught last night. Now that he knew some of her past, could she allow Morgan to help? How far would she go to help save her sister?

A few minutes later, Morgan rode up on his horse and jumped down in front of the barn. He disappeared inside, and Emery looked out onto his land. There was no decency or courage left in her. Last night had proven that. Now, why did she want to avoid him at all cost? A shiver ran up her spine, and she stepped out from the garden gate. How humiliating to have anyone see you at your worst—and then hold you and tell you heartfelt stories. She knew full well she'd slept soundly, like a child, in his arms. She could add that to her disgrace. Embarrassed anew, she rolled her eyes as he came around the barn towards her. *Now what?*

"Emery."

She glanced up; he looked normal, as if nothing had happened. He was so puzzling, and it irritated her even more.

"How are you feeling?"

Loathing everything within my skin came to mind, but she waited, saying nothing.

"Do you want to talk about last night?" He took a step closer.

"I'd prefer not to." Emery stepped away. "Carlotta is likely done with napping. I want to help her with supper." She headed to the cabin.

"Wait, I have something for you," Morgan said, following her.

Another package waited on the porch. "Morgan." She shook her head. "I can't accept . . ."

"Shoes. They're only shoes, Emery." He pulled them from the paper. "I guessed your size." Morgan handed the simple brown pair with black laces to her. She reluctantly took them.

"They look fine." She paused. Her own self-hatred collided with her good manners. "Thank you." She pressed them in the crook of her arm.

"We should leave tomorrow," Morgan said.

Emery's head shot up. "Leave? Leave here?"

"To go to Auburn, yes. It's within a day of the twins coming back for you." He nodded. "I want to take you to your parents. We leave in the morning." Emery wanted to protest his confident posture for where she was going, but she knew enough about this man. Smart and assertive, his unsolicited plans were to help her.

She clutched the shoes. "I will be ready."

"And one more thing." He opened the cabin door, and she walked through. "I will sleep on the floor of your room tonight."

Emery paused just inside the door. Carlotta was rolling balls of dough into tortillas. A rebuttal brewed behind her eyes, trying to form in her mouth. She was not a defiant child, needing a nanny. Her nose twitched. *Who cares?* He could sleep wherever he wanted. After she'd inform her parents of the need to recover Gianna, she'd find a vial of poison and go for a long walk.

Morgan walked past her and broke her frozen state. He picked up something from the corner and set the box on the table. "You have it hidden under your blouse, but I could feel it last night." He gestured with his hand for her to come forward. "I can cut off the band and not harm you."

Carlotta's apprehensive eyes looked up at hers. The woman shook her head and went back to slapping the dough flat between her hands. Emery took a wary step forward. Pushing the band farther onto her belly, she stopped. If nothing else, she knew this band would eventually suffocate what grew in her womb. Morgan withdrew a small saw. The corner of his mouth twitched as he glared down at his scarred hand and stretched his fingers. What if his damaged hand did not work, as he said? Her bottom lip popped out, and she gripped the band. "I don't care. You can just leave it be."

Morgan's eyes flashed anger, and his tone charged the room. "It goes. Now!"

Even in light of the startling information, Morgan had enough of her absurdity. He grabbed a flat piece of kindling to hold the band from her skin. Should he saw the lock or the actual barrel band? He'd not gripped a saw since the ghastly war. Just the weight of it against his palm rekindled the brutal surgeries he'd done. Thank God, he was a miner now. This would be the last time he would use this near another living being.

"Put this between your skin and the metal." He sucked in a fresh breath. *No flesh, no bones, no one screaming in agony. Just saw the metal.*

Emery took the wood and set it on the table. Defiantly, she slowly unbuttoned her blouse.

"There is no need for that." Morgan frowned.

"It's my only one, and I don't want any blood on it." Her eyes narrowed on his. Was she testing him? As she held her arms back, it slipped off her shoulders, and his gut twisted wildly. The soft white chemise and corset he'd bought her laid in full display against her ivory skin. The way her eyes turned abrasive, there was little doubt she was tormenting him. Now he prayed his hand would remain steady. Emery placed the wood under the metal band.

"Move it a bit to the left." Morgan held back the tension he felt. "I will try to cut the lock first."

Carlotta leaned on the table to watch. Thankfully her presence broke the unwarranted hitch in his confidence. He refused to look at Emery's bare arms, mere inches from him. Morgan lifted the padlock and held it against the wood. Starting with small movements, his grip held the first fast cuts. Any slips would only land on the wood, but he needed more muscle to impact the thick metal.

"You all right?" he asked. Emery swallowed and gave a slight nod. Her eyes transformed to something softer. Morgan pulled the wood and lock taut and she held herself back as best she could. He put his strength into the sawing, and the minute it broke free, his fist gripping the saw in motion caught her in the ribs.

"Oh." Emery grimaced, holding her chest.

"Forgive me." Morgan dropped the saw on the table, grasping her arm as she swayed back.

"No, no." She straightened. "I was just holding my breath, and it startled me." Emery pulled the lock and wood from her waist. "I'm fine. Really." She shrugged her shoulder back, removing his hand from her bare arm. Before he could register the moment, she had pulled the band apart and freed herself. Taking the cue, there would be no celebration, no gratitude or pleasantries. He returned the saw to his case and stared listless for a moment. Walking his medical box back to the corner, Morgan found a paper on his desk to read.

Anything was better than seeing the woman re-dress in his kitchen.

Thirteen

The next morning Emery fought down the nausea with a few bites of dried bread. Carlotta seemed unusually quiet as she stuffed a bag with food for their trip. Morgan could be seen through the front windows hitching his horse to a small wagon.

"*Tal vez deberias venir?*" Emery asked if Carlotta would come with them.

"No, no." Carlotta swung her hand in the air. "I like to be here. Too old."

Emery stilled for a moment, watching her. "I'm not sure if I'll see you again, but I would like to thank you for your kindness to me." Her own sadness was tainting her tone. Carlotta shrugged her standard indifference.

"Morgan is fortunate to have you." Emery reached out and held Carlotta's arm. "*Gracias, amiga.*"

"Aye, aye." Carlotta pulled away. "You take my poncho. I have another." She pulled it off the peg and gathered the bag of food, then waited for Emery to meet her by the door.

Emery stood and took one pained glance around. If she wasn't so dead inside, she might falter toward sentimentally for this warm cabin.

"Those fancy shoes." Carlotta pointed, breaking the moment. "They fit?"

"*Sí.*" Their eyes met, a mutual gloom evident. Carlotta pressed the items into Emery's arms. Emery opened the door and let herself out. Taking a steadying breath, she watched Morgan place his rifle under the bench before looking up.

"Ready?" He wore a wide-brimmed hat and leather gloves over his hands.

Emery nodded and walked to him. If she looked back at Carlotta, the growing pain in her throat might spill out in another pitiful goodbye. Pinching the bundle in her hands to one side, she took Morgan's hand and stepped up onto the bench.

"We . . . or I will return in a few days," he said to Carlotta. The bench rocked with his weight as he took the reins and tapped the wagon forward.

Emery moved as far from him as she could. Clutching the food bag and poncho to her stomach, she tried to straighten up and watch the turns from the dirt road winding out of Morgan Hastings's property.

For heaven's sake, Emery dared not look at him. This man was far too close and assuming. Just like last night, waiting till she was settled into bed, then coming in to lay on the floor below her. His distraction hadn't helped a hundred waves of confusion running through her head. Maybe she could've fallen asleep, but watching his back rise and fall with sleep proved aggravating. Morgan didn't trust her to not do something rash again. Some sort of sleeping, gallant bodyguard he'd tried to prove himself.

The wagon dipped in a rut, and she reached to grip the bench seat. Emery groaned behind clenched teeth; just like last night, her mind would barely still. Would she lead Morgan to their claim on Eureka Creek? What would he say? A stranger inquiring about the Marones' daughters? He pulled the wagon left, turning from the nar-row road onto a much broader one. A large barn loomed in the distance. The smell of someone burning brush lingered in the air. *This must be the road to Hangtown.* She chewed her bottom lip. The Derry brothers had wound them on horseback through the trees and hills. Her mind had been blurring then, and now it was again today. She spied long mounds of dirt. Far off in the distance, a team of horses pulled a plow. To the far right looked like fields of matching trees. Things grew well in this land. A pinch of regret nicked her—her little garden would likely go back to weeds.

The wagon clipped along at a steady pace. For a few moments, Emery allowed herself a daydream of running into her parents' open arms. Covering a yawn, she pictured Gianna and her little brothers running to greet her with smiles and bouncing sibling chatter, like the son in the Bible who returned home after his poor decisions.

His father ran out to meet him, overjoyed by his return—maybe her mother or brothers would do the same for her. Arturo, her brother who wanted to be called Art, was growing fast into a smart young man. She pictured Maxwello with his thick wavy mop of hair. Would he want it cut by her like she used to do? That left the rascal of the family, Ferdinand, so full of energy and mischief. His stories and tales often would go on for . . .

"Hey." Morgan steadied her swaying.

Emery bounced awake, blinking at him. "Sorry . . . I . . ."

"You can rest on my shoulder. I don't mind."

"No. no." She drew the hair from her face and straightened on the seat. "I didn't sleep much last night."

"And this morning, you didn't look well." His jaw flexed. "Is it your stomach?"

"No." She frowned at him. "It's all the . . . the turmoil." She looked away from his scrutiny, brushing a loose strand of hair behind her ear. "Everything in me is unwell. All of me."

"Of course." He nodded. "The unknowns are plenty." Morgan tipped his hat as a driver and wagon full of goods passed them on the other side. "You worry about your parents? Are they strict or harsh with their children?"

"No. They are good and proud." She clutched her hands over the poncho. "Morgan, you are never to repeat what I told you. I . . . I . . . was faint in my weakness . . . and . . ."

"I know." He stared ahead, listening to the rhythmic clopping of the horse hooves. He rubbed a glove-covered finger under his nose. "Why do you hate me?"

Emery quickly looked away from the lines of hurt on his face. "I hate myself." She looked down at her hands, tightening into fists. "And now you know something I don't want anyone to know." Dropping her chin, she shook her head. "I hate it. I hate the humiliating truth of it all." She closed her mouth and tried to breathe through her nose. "I hate every inch of my body and the bitter taste that every day of life leaves in my mouth. I hate that I have no plan that makes sense. I hate that you should hate me; the absurd way I removed my blouse in front of you."

She pressed her lips together and closed her eyes. *But you are the . . . the . . . only hope I have. I hate that when you held me in my bed, I couldn't hold back my sobs. And with you there, I felt consumed by something serene.* Her ridiculous thoughts curtailed, she gripped the bench seat. Morgan had pulled the horse over to the side of the road; holding the reins tightly in one hand, he pulled them to a stop and turned to her. Pulling his hat off, and setting it on his knee, his dark wavy hair stuck close to his head.

Struggling with what he wanted to say, he

pulled off his gloves. "Emery." His palm brushed against her cheek until his fingers rested in her hair. "Listen to me."

She froze with his touch and intense gaze. "There is more to you than this one offense, this one wrongdoing. Don't let someone else's sin and depravity crush you. Don't allow his darkness to dim the light inside you or steal the life you were meant to live. You aren't doomed from this iniquity." Morgan carefully pulled his hand back. "When you garden, when you cook, or talk of the old country, the lovely young woman you are or want to be is still there. I've seen it for myself."

His words were gentle and sincere, and she wished with everything she had that those sentiments would remain. Each word was a piece of gold, spoken kindly, like him. If only it could be true. But he was unaware of the worst of her secrets. The devil's filthy seed was growing inside her. Her chin began to quiver, and she gazed out to the land of trees and green grass around them.

"I'm not saying today." He inhaled and pulled his fingers down the corners of his mouth. "You probably don't want to know what was going on in me while I held that saw next to you last night. I shook inside, holding back the very worst of my past. Even more than the burns, I didn't want to relive the pain of the butchering I did with that saw. Those memories of the war are still inside me and, I don't know how, but I've found a way to live around them, or maybe with them." He tipped her chin, and she met his tender eyes. "I don't know how or when, but I think you, too, can overcome the pain of your past. I believe you can. Pray to God, Emery."

Trying to settle the pounding in her chest, she gave him the smallest of nods.

By lunch, they had arrived on the outskirts of Hangtown. From where they pulled off the road, Emery set her bread aside. She felt too nervous to eat. Morgan had poured some water into a tin cup, drank half and then offered her the cup. She took a few sips while looking out over the wagon. Their familiarity was becoming routine, comfortable. But, decisions were easier to make when she was angry with him.

"Are we close to this Eureka Creek? Your family's claim?" He brushed the crumbs from his pants.

Scrutinizing a handsome brown buggy as it rambled by, Emery began to panic. *What if Arnold Snider was in Hangtown and he spotted her?* The trembling in her body confirmed she had no courage for this. She looked down at her uneaten lunch. "I wish I had a gold nugget for every time I told you I didn't know what to do." A sad laugh escaped. "I could make my own way and live quite comfortably."

Morgan lifted a small smile. "Your sister. We are on a mission to find your sister."

"How do I do that without being seen?" Emery sighed.

Morgan raked his fingers through his hair, giving her a side glance. "You don't want to go home?" he asked carefully.

Emery stoically shook her head no. "I want to know if she is there first. If she is not, then how can I be off the ship without her? Even if we get near Eureka Creek, some of the other miners could recognize me. Oh, I don't know. I know I'm making no sense."

"Is there a hotel in Hangtown?" Morgan rubbed his scarred cheek.

"Yes, the Bedford and the El Dorado. But the El Dorado is . . . is." She rolled her eyes. "I could throw a rock and hit the Snider mansion. It stands like a hateful reminder at the end of Main Street."

"Then the Bedford it is." Morgan tapped the horse forward.

Emery felt her stomach twist and, though it was warm, she dropped the poncho over her head and pulled it close to her chin, hiding her long braid beneath.

A few minutes later, they pulled onto the bustling Main Street of Hangtown. Emery felt her body cower and move closer to Morgan. If she wasn't mistaken, his firm jaw and the way he kept looking from side to side, displayed his own tension. Was he watching for the Derry brothers?

He pulled in behind a tall brick building and tied the horse to the hitching post next to the trough.

"I'll get us a room and you can rest." Morgan reached up for her, grasped her waist, and lowered her to the ground. *Us?* Before she could clarify the room confusion, he jerked his rifle from under the bench and walked around to the front doors. It was hard not to feel safe in Hangtown following a tall man carrying a rifle.

Emery's eyes swept the lobby, thankful no one was about at the moment. Morgan leaned over the half-door and spoke to the clerk sitting at his desk inside. Chewing on the corner of her lip, Emery peered out the front windows. She knew so few people here. The last time she was in this very hotel was with Finny, Arnold's wife. The poncho now hung heavy over her heated frame. Morgan walked to the stairs and gestured for her to join him.

"We're on the second floor." He started up the stairs, and Emery followed, daunted. Sure enough, they stopped at the fourth door on the left. This young doctor turned miner had only one key.

They were sharing a room.

Fourteen

Emery followed Morgan Hastings into the Bedford Hotel room. If the room wasn't so stifling, she would have thought she'd worked herself into the vapors. Pulling the heavy poncho over her neck, Emery accidentally scraped the tender place where the rope had chafed her skin. Wincing, she set the poncho on the desk chair.

"The clerk said there would be paper and ink." Morgan stood next to her, reaching inside a drawer for the paper. "You can draw me directions to the claim, and then you don't have to go."

"I need air," Emery huffed, turning away.

"It *is* warm." He went to the window and lifted it. "Are you feeling sick? Or distraught?"

Emery felt a small breeze and rubbed her hands over her face. "Should we be sharing a room?" The words tumbled out. "Though you like being my guard, I'm sure you've wasted enough time and money."

"Please grant me permission to talk about social deportment." Shaking his head, Morgan pulled his hair behind his ears.

Emery frowned. She'd never heard the word deportment.

"In a proper society, a woman never talks about money."

"I know enough, Morgan. Enough to . . . to know we should not share this room. But I'm not demanding." She held her hand up. "This hotel is expensive." The one bed loomed in the center of the room with fluffy pillows and shining bedding. "I guess I never thought this far—"

Morgan lowered his chin and squinted. "I have enough money for ten rooms for ten months," he explained. "If you judge me by my rustic cabin and simple life, that's from my choosing."

"I don't judge you," she murmured.

"Well, I judge you," he cautioned. "I will sleep on the floor again. You've told me you lack the strength to go on. But I believe it's just your past that is weakening you unto death." Morgan sucked in a breath and stared out the window. "Emery, you are stronger than you realize."

Emery rolled her eyes. *Strong?* His sentiments were oblivious and foolhardy. The strength to see to Gianna's care was all that she had left. Carefully, she sat at the desk and drew a crude map to their claim. "These are my parents' names at the top. Their English is difficult to understand. What will you say?" She handed it to him. "What will you ask?"

Morgan's eyes searched around the room. "You said you have little brothers still in your home?"

"Tent," she corrected. "We live in a canvas

tent." Their difference in upbringing and family money were now glaringly evident. "Yes, I have three younger brothers."

"Mmm, I am Dr. Hastings. I am doing a survey of the children's health in this area." He looked in the mirror that hung on the wall and rubbed his scruffy chin. "I saw a mercantile a block down." He turned to her. "I'll grab a pad of paper and any medicine they have."

"What if you run into the men who took me?" She gripped the back of the chair.

"I will tell them you ran away." Morgan shrugged, looking at her map. "From the fork in the road here," he pointed, "how far past the bridge?"

"I'm not sure. Maybe four or five miles? Look for a large fallen pine next to the road. You can't miss the creek, and you'll see other tents and people, men mining in the water."

He nodded, watching her. "Will you be okay while I'm gone? Will you rest?"

Emery could almost see her little brothers, her mother. A jealous longing pulled at her heart. "Gianna is my little sister, only seventeen. Please, Morgan, please find out if she's still on that ship in the bay."

Morgan watched her, waiting.

"Yes, I will be here." Exasperated with his meddling, she dropped her head to the side. "I'll try to rest."

A few minutes later, the door clicked closed, and Emery leaned against the windowsill to watch Morgan leave the hotel. Sighing, she chewed on her thumbnail. He stepped among the other town folk with his usual masculine confidence and walked towards the mercantile. His simple plan seemed possible.

Morgan Hastings was a surgeon and a doctor. She'd seen his medical tools. There was often sickness and death among the weakest along the camps. None of the immigrants had money to see a doctor. She waited while he entered the store and came out a few minutes later. Morgan headed to the back of the Bedford, likely retrieving the wagon for the drive out to Eureka Creek. Emery watched him ride away until she couldn't see the road curve out of Hangtown.

Turning away from the movement of Hangtown, the room felt silent and empty. Her beating heart was her only company in the stillness. What if he'd left her here? What if Morgan was on his way back to Auburn?

It shouldn't surprise her. He'd had no say in hosting a derelict woman with no explanation and mysterious circumstances, who'd tried to hang herself in his cabin. No one would blame him if he took the first road far, far away from her. Her neck tensed, and she lightly rubbed her hands over the tender muscles. How could she blame him? Sitting on the edge of the bed, Emery stared at the red and green carpet, the want or appreciation for anything numb. Her body and soul hadn't been worth even a shallow breath. Yet here she sat, back in Hangtown, alive.

An hour later, Emery rolled up from where she had fallen asleep. Standing, she shook her head, recounting the restless nap—dreaming of Gianna drowning in the ocean and seeing a boat come to rescue her but inside was Arnold Snider. Emery pulled the tie off her long braid and pulled her hair apart. Trying to shake off the awful dream, she fingered her hair loose with her hands and walked around the hotel room.

She rechecked the door. The lock remained in place since Morgan had left. Glancing down at the small desk, she looked at the two books sitting on the corner. Picking up the Bible, she went to sit on the bed. Anything to distract her from the waiting and reading was better than sleeping. Emery flipped the first pages. *"In the beginning, God created the heaven and the earth . . ."* She read on. Most of the words were the simple ones that Miss Cassidy had taught her and Gianna. She flipped the next page. *"And the Lord God planted a garden eastward in Eden, and there he put man whom he'd formed."*

"Humph." She looked up. God planted the first garden. Emery could see herself standing in Morgan Hastings's tousled garden area. After those few days of rain, the soil begged for her attention. Someone had taken great care and time to plan it out very well, and she'd only brought it back to life, to its original form.

Just like I do.

The quiet thought was hers—or was it? It didn't sound like her thoughts. She gripped the Bible in her fingers. Does God bring people back to life? Even those who are dead inside? Was she the run-down garden, trampled and useless?

Emery rose and watched out the window. How much longer would he be? The Bible still held in her hand, she waited in silence. *I only have one reason to live.* She prayed without knowing it. *To see my sister safe.*

But I came to give you life. You. What strange words interrupted her thoughts? She considered the book of teaching she held in front of her. Her mother had often spoken about God's light, God's ways, truth, and blessing. How would her mother feel about a daughter who would choose hopelessness and kill herself? Her stomach twisted. As their firstborn, she would never choose anything to hurt them. Frustrated, she went to set the Bible back in its place. It hovered in the air an inch from the other book. Was it still trying to speak to her?

I've come to give you life.

Emery shook her head quickly and dropped the Bible back where she'd found it. It was Morgan Hastings's voice in her head. That's all. The man had some nerve pulling to the side of the road, telling her she was strong and could live with this offense. Reaching for the bag, she found a burrito that Carlotta had packed. Something to eat would help these rambling dreams and whispering voices.

A few hours later, Emery watched the afternoon orange glow begin to set behind the buildings of Hangtown's Main Street. Her fretting led her to one conclusion, he must have returned to Auburn. It was obvious. The mining claim was only twenty minutes from Hangtown. With no other explanation, she needed to face it. Morgan Hastings, the kind doctor she'd reluctantly come to like and trust, had left her.

She looked down past the mercantile to catch a glimpse of where So Chen and her sons did laundry. It was a small storefront on Main Street that had back rooms where she housed different working ladies. Would So Chen remember her from when she'd tried to help Miss Cassidy? Would the tiny woman take her in? Emery suppressed a low growl and turned from the window. Likely not.

The Bible lay speaking without saying a word. How did her eyes land once again on the desk?

"All right," she huffed. *"God, please show me the way if you want me to live, and then show me how. Morgan is gone. Do I walk to my parents myself? Then slip away before . . ."* As Emery dropped her chin, shame and pain punched the inside of her belly. Grabbing the pillow, she sat and buried her face. How did she explain why she was off the ship and Gianna was not?

A knock at her door made her jump, and she dropped the pillow on the floor.

"Emery." It was Morgan's muffled voice.

She turned the lock and stepped back. Anger and relief boiled together inside of her. "Where have you been? Did you see her? Did you see my sister?"

He crossed into the room and dropped the tablet and pencil on the desk.

Without warning, Morgan looked full into her desperate face and said, "No."

Fifteen

Emery's entire being crumbled. With her long brown waves hanging around her face and shoulders, she looked much like she had the first time he'd met her.

"I'm sorry I was gone so long," Morgan said. Emery didn't respond, looking despondent a few feet from him. "My simple plan ended up becoming an all-day clinic."

"What is a clinic?" Her eyes narrowed on his.

"I found the tents you spoke of." He took the desk chair and sat. "A young man was working a pick into some rock. I explained I was a doctor, wanting to check on the children's health. He left for a moment and brought his mother back."

Emery's cheeks flushed red. "What did she look like? Did you ask her name?" She gripped her hands in front of her chest.

"It wasn't your people." He glanced at the tablet. "The . . . the Broadricks . . . I believe."

"Yes, yes, I know of them." Emery blinked, wide-eyed.

"Anyway, before I could fully explain, someone had brought me a chair. I sat on the dirt road between the creek and the tent village. Two or three children lined up in front of me. I asked them their names and ages and their parents' names. I felt quite inept for a few moments." A light smile forced its way onto his lips, but he shook his head. "Then, when the mother hovered near, I asked if the children suffered from any pain or maladies. That led to checking teeth, and rashes, and infections. One poor little toddler was suffering from rickets. I told the mother about the need for fruit and vegetables for the tyke. I'm not sure how word spread so fast, but just as I finished up with two or three, there would be another three in line. Two or three more mothers came with babes in their arms. This went on for hours. I finally realized one little blond boy had already been in line earlier." Morgan glanced at the scribble on his tablet. "A Peter. About six. Do you know of him?"

Emery shrugged, brows narrowing.

"Came to find out that the other children were helping to play along with his game, changing his name, and teasing me that I had seen a ghost. One girl would break out in the giggles, and Peter would try and jump on her to quiet her. Then a wrestling match began, and I was pulling youngsters off youngsters, not realizing they were all laughing and just being children. Such simple joy they carried. Their laughter was like medicine to me." He smiled, scratching his forehead.

"Humph." Emery frowned. "Morgan's medicine."

His eyes widened in agreement. "Yes, laughter is medicinal."

Emery's tolerant expression revealed little amusement or delight in his tales of an afternoon with the poor miners' children.

"Your family is no longer in the tent area." He watched her carefully. "A woman who brought me food knew of them. She said a few months back, they were able to purchase a shanty up the creek a few miles."

Emery clenched her teeth. "Payment from Arnold Snider and our employment on his ship," she huffed. "I saw the pouch of gold he gave my father." Emery turned so fast her hair twirled in the air. In five long strides, she stopped in the corner of the room. Sliding down to the floor, she wrapped her arms around her knees and hung her head.

Morgan understood his news brought her little comfort. Standing, he came and knelt in front of her and quenched the desire to brush her hair back. "I will go tomorrow. I have things to drop off at the tent village. I won't take long. There are two with rotten teeth and an abscess. I know enough to pull them and relieve the suffering."

Emery didn't respond to his explanations. She'd counted on him finding her family and giving her answers after waiting all day.

Internally, he knew the doctoring had brought new life into his blood. Only one little girl innocently touched the side of his face and asked a curious question about his scars. He'd forgotten the joy he felt in helping others, but Emery didn't send him on an errand for that. He should have left earlier.

He held his hand forward, wanting to touch her, comfort her. "I'm sure I will see them tomorrow." Resting his fingers on the floor, he tapped them on the carpet and finally spoke. "I didn't feel right leaving you all afternoon. Are you hungry? We could go get some food."

He didn't hear any sobs, but her cold silence explained her obvious distress. "Emery." He waited. "Are you hungry?" Reaching out, he gently touched her hair-covered shoulder.

"Don't touch me!" she twisted and flung his hand away as if it was being burned in a fire. "I know what you're up to." In between her brown tresses, her round eyes swam with red, watery anger. With no warning, she pushed against his shoulders, knocking him onto his back.

"Whoa." Morgan came up on his elbows, wide-eyed. "What did I do?"

Emery rose quickly, bending over him with a forefinger aimed for battle.

"I waited all day for news of my sister! Now you want to get food?" She mocked. "You think this . . . this . . ." Now her hand swung close to his face. "This kindness." With such a bitter tone, she spewed the word, and he thought better to stay prone. "You think your smart ways, your helpful ways, your . . . your soft brown eyes and caring voice, and whatever else you think, will work. Well, none of it does. Because I've seen it all before!" She growled, suddenly dropping her knee into his belly. Before he could react, she'd reached forward and grabbed his collar. "It won't work! Do you hear me?"

His body flinched with the need to defend himself from the badger that looked to knee his insides out the back or scratch his eyes out. But touching her had started all this. He forced his body rigid. "Tell me, I beg you. What are you talking about?"

"Men." Her eyes blazed. "Don't think I don't know—that I am naïve to all the ways men use women." Her fists clenched his collar tighter as her knee pressed down, constricting his air. "Sweet words, sweet trinkets, and then when his body is crushing mine he says in his two-faced syrupy tone, 'I will drop your sister off this ship if you scream. Accidents like that happen all the time.'" She panted, fuming red.

Shocked for a split second, Morgan quickly got it; this rage appeared from the hurt done to her. "Can you get your knee off my belly?" With short choppy words, he pushed her knee away. Emery stood like a flash of lightning and turned away.

Morgan sat up slowly, straightening his shirt.

His heart pounded against the fabric. "I've done something, probably many things, to upset you." He moved over and rested his back against the bed, contemplating what could be said to settle her down. "We've been thrown together in the most unconventional circumstance but it's my wish to help you—" Clearing his throat, he pulled his hair back. "You seem to see my assistance as something corrupt or imprudent." His knees bent in front of him, and resting his forearms on them, he clasped his hands. "I think it wise," Morgan sucked in a breath, trying to settle himself, "if I leave you some money. It isn't far to your parents'. I will go now and leave you—" The declaration hung like a thick blanket over the room. He rolled his eyes and scratched his hairline.

"Don't go." A small murmur came from the corner she huddled in. Emery rested her forehead against the brown wall; hugging her waist with her arms, she slowly rolled her head back and forth.

"I think it best, I do." Morgan stood and grabbed his small canvas bag. Removing his wallet, he went to the desk to set the bills down. The yellow tablet mocked him, making his gut twist. The children were such a delight today. He'd allowed himself a brief moment to entertain the thought of using his doctoring skills again. Enough of that, he didn't want to get involved, today it had just taken him by surprise. Picturing his quiet creek, he remembered he was content with the small life he had. Morgan turned to see Emery standing in the middle of the room, tears streaming down her face.

"Please, Morgan. Don't leave me." Desperation laced her cries.

He shook his head and pulled his hand down his jaw. "I'm just causing you more pain."

"But I know it's *me*." She paused. "All day, I'd rehearsed you finding them and I . . . I . . . hold these stupid, hopeful pictures in my mind."

"That's not all that pains you." Morgan knew little of women but even less of women who'd been taken advantage of. "I've wanted to tell you something. For some reason, it's bothered me." He wet his lips and pressed them together. "Rush Medical College is one of the first medical colleges in Illinois."

She nodded, listening.

"My brother and I both graduated from there and went to serve the soldiers in the Mexican-American war. There were two important things we took with us. One was a chloride of lime. After a certain distilling process, it made an anesthetic called chloroform."

Emery listened, but he'd likely lost her. "It was something we could give the men who had amputations. It would put them to sleep instead of them suffering or passing out."

She nodded slightly.

"The other thing I studied was inoculation." He fingered the paper on the desk. "More soldiers died of disease than they did from battle. With the inoculation, we punctured the skin and introduced the disease, like smallpox, for example." He rolled his lips in a thin line. "I did it to myself and two of the men who agreed to try this outlandish experiment. Two that you know, as well." Morgan paused, finally meeting her round eyes. "The Derry twins, Abner and Clayton." He waited, as she didn't seem to understand his point. "We lost over a thousand men in my camp to smallpox. The Derry brothers helped for hours in the sick tent and never became ill. They went on to save my life in the fire that should have destroyed me. We all agreed to come to this part of California to mine for gold. Their gold was taken from the Hangtown bank months ago, and they kidnapped you in retribution."

"And you feel . . . ?" She hesitated. "Responsible? Guilty?"

"I'm not sure. What is providence? What is the hand of God?" He exhaled, scratching the top of his head. "I thought at first, the men I helped were the cause of your pain and distress. I suppose I did feel somehow responsible, but now in this moment . . ." Morgan looked back to the desk where his doctoring notes lay.

"Just by being who God made me, I am."

Sixteen

Emery stepped back, shocked by her thoughtless behavior. She wilted down onto the edge of the bed. "I'm not usually so impulsive." She blinked rapidly and wiped her cheeks with the back of her hand. "I told you earlier that I do not judge you, and yet I just did." She hung her head and exhaled. "I . . . I am sorry. Please forgive me. I don't want to hurt you." Humiliated, Emery waited until he would look at her. "You are a good man, helpful to more than me. I've never known a doctor, personally. I suppose it is part of your nature. God bless you for the lives you've helped." The thought of him leaving still crushed her chest. After such a ridiculous display, she prayed her words didn't sound insincere.

"And I am sorry." Morgan rubbed his hand over his scarred cheek and the chin stubble. "I should have never lain with my arms around you in your bed or supposed I could secure your safekeeping by sleeping on the floor." He shook his head. "You could've walked from here anytime today and found another rope and tree. My best-laid plans to save you are futile. There is really nothing I can do."

Emery cringed inside. Why had she put this poor man through such misery? He wasn't trying to bed her against her will; more likely, he was trying to get rid of her. She rolled her eyes. "This afternoon, I'd thought that you'd left me and gone back to Auburn. I wouldn't blame you. If you want to go, I cannot stop you."

"Well, maybe you can." Morgan leveled a curious gaze at her. "With another knee weighted on my intestines or fist in my neck." He joked, and a smile arose from the corner of his mouth.

A tiny warmth stirred within her, and she had to look away. His teasing made her cheeks flush. "I think all this started because you asked me about food." Could she pray that he would forgive her and still help her? "I ate from the bag Carlotta packed. I'm not hungry. And you?"

"Full with the offerings of the mothers." He patted his flat belly. "One gal gave me a stiff duck. As I got out of sight, I tossed it into the brush. It was smelly and too far gone."

A softening in the air settled between them. With the sun settling in the west, they stood laced in the shadows. Morgan reached for the bills on the desk.

"I think I'll go downstairs and see about another room." Striking a match, he lit the lantern.

Emery stood, suddenly aware of her loose hair and ruffled appearance. "Please just stay." Pulling her hair back, she realized the words poured out before she could catch them. The way he bit his bottom lip and waited dropped another strange pebble of warmth in her being.

"All right, but you promise me, no jumping on me in the night?"

Emery huffed but cracked a small smile. "I promise."

An hour later, the room danced in dark shadows. Morgan entered and closed the door quietly. He rolled out a blanket in the far corner, away from the bed, and laid down. Emery listened with a strange interest. She'd apologized for her behavior, but it felt like his kindness leaned again to her favor. He hadn't left her, and for that she was thankful.

"And what of your brother?" Emery asked through the darkness. The nap had robbed her of her ability to sleep. "Did he also take this ick . . . noc . . . ?"

"Inoculation," Morgan said. "No."

His hands pulled back through his hair, and he left his arms resting on the floor next to his head. In the dark, she could only guess the look on his face was sadness.

"My brother and I took turns when surgery would let up. Some of the wounded were left where they lay. There were only so many runners to carry them to the surgery tent and so we would go to where they had fallen. A white strip of cloth around their wrist meant we had pronounced them deceased. One day Ronald was looking over a young man who was still alive. Unfortunately, the Mexican soldier who he thought was dead, was not. The soldier rose and stabbed Ronald through the chest."

Emery gasped. "Oh my goodness, I'm so sorry."

"Cursed war." Morgan exhaled. "I thought he was out assessing the men, but my brother was suffering, dying in his own blood." Morgan cleared his throat. "When he was finally brought in, we had a few minutes together." His tone was laced with regret. "Ronald wanted me to tell his fiancée that he loved her."

"Oh my." Emery squeezed her eyes shut. "He sounds like a wonderful man."

Morgan rolled to his side.

"Did you ever tell her?" Emery whispered.

"I wrote a letter, but I never went home. So face-to-face, no. It felt too early, too difficult to face my father, my old life, without Ronald." He suppressed a sigh. "I was in poor condition to resume anything normal after so many men had sacrificed their lives. It was reckless of me to travel on with some of the other soldiers and Carlotta to this new land of California, but the war was over and we all had unrealistic dreams and . . . I guess, a need to be far away from the suffering. My scars were a constant reminder, so I suppose there really was nowhere to go to outrun my past."

"I can understand that." She sighed, rubbing her forehead.

"Tomorrow, when I find your family," Morgan started, but a cautious silence seemed to have fallen between them. "If your sister is not there . . . I'm thinking that is what I'll find." He sat up and leaned back against the wall. "It's only been a week. Who knows what Snider could've done? How can we know when you were kidnapped, did they all leave the ship? Is he still planning on meeting with the Derry brothers?" His tone was hesitant. "I wish I knew where this meeting was to take place. In all the panic, did you hear where?"

"No. They had written it on paper and threw it on the bed." A shiver ran up Emery's back, and she nestled deeper into the covers.

"It could be anywhere," Morgan said somberly. "Let's say your sister is not home. What can I say to your parents? You said their English is not good."

"I thought a lot about this today. I could write a letter and explain that the ship is dangerous, and my father should retrieve her as soon as possible."

Morgan rubbed the back of his head. "And this letter would be from you. Would I explain you are safe and with me?"

Emery rubbed her eyebrows back and forth. This was the same question she'd asked herself from every direction. How is one daughter off the ship, and another is left on? "I . . . I . . . don't know."

"I've never been a father, and I've never had a sister." Grabbing his pillow, he held it to his chest and wrapped his arms around it. "But the same desire I have to see you safe and well, must be beyond imagination for a father."

Emery felt her insides tremble, knowing that he was going to tell her to just go home. Should she remind Morgan, he had not returned home either?

"He would listen to you, I'm sure." Morgan continued. "Maybe you don't recount every detail, just knowing that any of his children were not safe. He—"

"What about the gold?" She cut him off. Mr. Snider had already paid her father. Her poppi had already moved the family into a wood-sided home. One with walls to keep them safe and warm. "Is my father to pay this gold back?"

"Never," Morgan rasped. "The degenerate should rot in jail." Morgan tossed his pillow back on the floor and lay down.

Emery felt her emotions weaving in and out like thread on a ragged garment. This man lying on the floor had heard none of the details of what had been done to her, yet he related to almost everything she had suffered. They'd known each other a week, and he'd shown nothing but compassion for a complete stranger. She had to hold to hope that she would receive forbearance from her family, her own flesh and blood.

Emery blew out a breath and shoved her hand between the sheet and her pillow. Her fingers landed on the tortilla she had folded in half and hid for safekeeping. If she could get a few bites in before rising in the morning, maybe she could keep her food down. Emery closed her eyes. The talking had settled to silence, but her body would not relax. Morgan Hastings now knew more of the evil things she had endured. She suppressed a whimper trying to escape her throat.

But he didn't know everything.

Seventeen

Emery cracked her eyes open to sunlight, and to Morgan sitting at the desk. He wore a brown shirt with rolled-up sleeves and was leaning over the desk with the pencil and tablet. Had she slept too long? She tore a piece of tortilla and chewed it carefully while watching him. His hair was dark, with uneven waves that touched the top of his collar. He seemed to be writing something. She chewed another bite. Her dreams had varied from seeing her mother to finding Gianna. Still lying in the soft bed in the light of day, she'd no clear direction. Raising on one elbow, Emery waited. At least her stomach hadn't rolled to the top of her throat.

"Good morning." Morgan twisted in the chair, and she pulled the sheet closer. She'd slept in her blouse and pantaloons. Her only skirt lay at the end of the bed. Like he read her mind, he stood.

"I will get us a tray from the kitchen. Would you like some tea?"

Emery nodded. How could he be so principled *and* handsome? "Thank you." Her voice crackled. *She didn't ask that question out loud, did she?*

"I'll give you some time for morning comforts." Morgan reached for the door. "Say twenty minutes or so?" He turned back and grabbed the tablet. Emery nodded again and he let himself out. What man goes and fetches the woman's breakfast? Brings her tea? She rose slowly and stacked the pillows. Resting, she felt her chest rise and fall. Maybe this doctor turned miner would agree to marry her, and they could pretend this baby was . . . Emery groaned and buried her face in the pillows. What kind of nonsense had diseased her in the night? No man would want a woman carrying another man's filthy seed. She flung the covers off and stood, and then sat back down. Heart pounding, she tried to breathe slowly, picturing the little garden at Morgan's home. The dizziness began to subside. After another bite of tortilla, she slowly dressed.

Morgan put his order in at the Bedford kitchen and then headed back down the walkway to the mercantile. Glancing over the list for the miners' children, he entered and looked around. Baking soda for their teeth. Pliers for the pulling. Fruit for the babies. Morgan found the items and threw in ten bars of lye soap. Paying, he thanked the woman behind the counter and carried the box of items under his arm.

Hangtown and early spring seem to agree with one another. Stepping out of the shop, he thought of his isolation in Auburn and how it had been a necessity for his body and soul. He stopped, waiting while a large wagon crossed by the side street. But this place, the doctoring he'd done in the tent village yesterday, had put a pop in his step. There was no use in denying it. He felt needed again, he was . . .

"Doc!"

Morgan turned, recognizing the deep voice. "Farly." He huffed, watching the man jog across the street. Farly's threadbare felt hat couldn't be missed.

"What are you doing in Hangtown, Doc?" Farly squeezed his arm holding the box of items.

Instant irritation rose. Morgan knew this man aided in the Derry brothers' kidnapping. "Just doing some medical runs for the miner families." He would weed the man out, he knew him well enough.

"Oh, good," Farly said, looking side to side. "Do you have the gal?" Farly whispered.

"Does it look like I do?"

"Well, don't know if you heard word from Abner or Clayton."

"I haven't."

"Well, we took the wrong gal. So, Snider ain't gonna pay back our gold." He looked at his dusty old boots, shaking his head. "I, myself, was never sure. They had such a grand idea." Farly crossed his arms. "It was dark and she was in bed with him. How could we know he had a gal on the side?"

Gal on the side, Morgan felt his anger spike.

"After she passed out, we had to take the gag off to see if she was alive." Farly rubbed under his nose, looking around the street again. "When the pretty thing came to, she said he wouldn't pay a red cent for her."

Morgan tried to steady his breathing. His pulse coursed to drop his box and take a fist to Farly's jaw, just to shut him up.

"She never said she wasn't the wife, but she did tell the truth." Farley frowned. "He'll pay nothing for the wench."

"I'm not happy with any of you." Morgan had had enough. "And if you see the Derry boys, you can tell them. All of you can stay away from me for a long, long time. It was a ludicrous plan after what you all went through to survive the war." Morgan clenched his teeth, shaking his head. "You just about got yourselves locked up in a nice cold cell for the rest of your lives, with nothing but urine-soaked hay to sleep on." Morgan stalked away with disgust lining his face and stepped across the side street. Unbelievable stupidity. He was done with them. *A thousand men had died in agony all around them. How could they not value this freedom, this new land?*

Morgan circled back behind the Bedford and dropped the box in his wagon. Gripping the side rail, he leaned back and dropped his chin to his chest. He was a hypocrite, spending his days next to the quiet streams on his land—mining in isolation. At least the poor folk in the Hangtown tents had each other. He straightened and shoved the box under the bench seat. He was late with breakfast.

Emery finished the letter to her parents. After watching the streets the day before, she thought of one possible thing to say. She reread it to herself in English.
Poppi and Mommi,
I was removed from the Snider ship without Gianna. I am very afraid for her. The ship is not safe. She cannot be there alone. Please, as soon as you can, go and retrieve her. Arnold Snider will not hold her to the employment as I was also released.
Emery sighed, wondering if she could get more paper and start over.
I have found my own employment in Hangtown. I do not wish to dishonor my family, but I am of age, and I choose to work and support myself. I know you believe this is not right for a daughter, and I pray one day you will forgive me. I am a hard worker and I will be in touch soon.
Please go for Gianna today! Emery
She heard her name muffled at the door and opened it for Morgan to bring a tray of food in. Quickly she folded the letter, and he set the tray down. They both looked at each other like neither had the nerve to speak first.

"Do you know the man Farly?" Morgan rubbed his forehead.

Instant fear froze inside Emery. "Yes," she whispered, remembering the rough one who gagged her.

"I just spoke with him. They know they took the wrong woman."

Emery knew her mouth hung open, but no words would form past her throat constriction.

"Is Arnold Snider here?" she finally choked out. "Here in Hangtown?" The chill of fear ran up and down her limbs.

"I didn't ask him, but I think not. Otherwise Farly wouldn't be wandering about so soon."

Emery felt her body sway and stepped back to sit on the bed. "They know we are together?"

"No." His eyes narrowed. "I said I was here helping with the miners' children."

Emery blinked, trying to confine her rambling thoughts. "Will you still go today? I have a letter for my family."

"Yes, of course." Morgan turned to the tray and grabbed a biscuit.

She stood wringing her hands. "So, the kidnapping plan is over."

"Yes." He chewed. "That is good, yes? My friends have found the end to their folly." Carefully he took the teacup from the tray. "It's probably cold." He handed it to her.

The gentle warmth tingled on her fingers as she

gripped the china cup. Would this news change anything in her letter? Taking a small sip of the amber liquid, she felt a dash of comfort settle down in her. What if Gianna was already there?

"You look nice." Morgan's words broke into her thoughts. "The way you did your hair." He pointed, but then pulled his finger back, seemingly embarrassed.

Emery clutched her braid that she had twisted into a bun at the nape of her neck. "There were some pins left in a drawer."

"Without the men coming for you . . ." He looked over at the wardrobe. "It would be even safer if you wanted to return to Auburn. You could—"

"I have something else already." She stood without making eye contact and set her cup on the tray.

Morgan Hastings had done enough.

Eighteen

The once cordial air between them had stiffened, and Morgan prepared to leave for the miner shanties. Reaching out, Emery handed him the letter. "Please don't read it." Morgan nodded, and a wave of guilt hit her. "If you see her, Gianna, she has a rounder face than I. About my size, but even if she is there, give the letter to my mother or whoever you can." He held it up, but his eyes held a particular vacancy or a question he wanted to ask. "I . . . I will be here when you return." Emery thought that sounded reassuring, but his face held little expression as he walked out.

A few minutes later, Emery fussed with a napkin over her head while looking in the mirror. The faded blue square from Carlotta's food packing made a decent scarf. With it pulled and tied just right, she looked like any other woman in Hangtown. Moving to the window, Emery took a long look back and forth. Those men had taken her in the pitch dark wearing nothing but a nightgown. She could only hope she looked different. Trying to will each step forward from the room, she would set her sights on So Chen's laundry. Was it just desperation when she'd thought of it yesterday? Was it part of those quiet voices whispering in her head? Maybe it *was*

God. This three-block walk would be a blessing or doom. Closing her eyes, she tried to pull in one last full breath. Rolling her lips, Emery opened the door and walked from the Bedford Hotel.

Just past the mercantile, a dirty miner bumped into her and asked her to give him the time of day. Thankfully, as she kept walking, he didn't follow. So Chen's little storefront came closer and, if she didn't look down to the Snider house looming at the end of Main Street, maybe her courage would stay with her.

After pulling her skirt layers flat over her belly, Emery held her hand on the handle. A little bell announced her entrance. So Chen came around two large steaming pots from the back and stopped at the long front table. "What you need?" She was shorter than Emery remembered.

"Ah, umm, months ago," Emery could feel the steam in the air, "I suppose seven or eight . . . months, I came in the back with Mr. Emerson and the woman, Cassidy. I don't know if you remember?"

"Ya, ya." So Chen nodded quickly.

Emery didn't know if she remembered them or her. "I have been working for Arnold Snider. I do house cleaning and laundry, but I no longer want to work . . ." *Holy heavens, why did this conversation make her eyes pool with tears?* The steamy room must be getting to her. ". . . for him. I need to find work. I am strong.

And need a place to stay." Might as well get it all out. The only problem was the woman's frown was getting larger, and Emery needed to dab her eyes before . . .

"You got bun in the oven?" So Chen asked frankly, pointing to her waist.

That did it. She should bolt back out the door, but instead, her tears found release down her cheeks. "Yes, ma'am."

So Chen let out a quick grunt. "Wipe face and follow."

Emery did as she was told and came around the back of the steaming pots. "Lots and lots of work," So Chen said before she stopped and looked down at Emery's belly. "The man, he come to make trouble?"

"No, he won't . . . no trouble." Emery looked away.

"Good, no trouble. No Truitt anymore. On my own."

"Yes, ma'am." Emery spied one of So Chen's sons, tending the fires and working the large tubs with wringers. Two young women ironed.

So Chen continued to the back of the building where Emery had been before. Stalls with sheets separated the tiny sleeping areas. "This one has baby. Sleeps all day and cries all night. Don't like. *Whaa Whaa.*" So Chen imitated. She walked to the fourth opening. "You can put your things here." So Chen frowned. "No things?"

Emery held her mouth open. Did she have anything but the clothes on her back?

"Rice and soup and sleep for work. Yes?" So Chen nodded before Emery could answer.

"May I return this afternoon and start work tomorrow?" Emery already dreaded telling Morgan Hastings her new plan.

"Ya, ya." So Chen returned to the wash. "You come back and start tomorrow."

Emery nodded and looked to the back door. She had a job and a place to sleep. Letting herself out without any farewells, she tried to gauge her trembling nerves. What had she done now? Another mistake or a true blessing?

The sun and a light breeze struck her face. Had her prayers been answered? Then why did she ache inside? She fisted the front of her skirt layers. She knew she didn't show what vermin grew inside of her. The narrow-eyed little woman had keen sight or more likely keen insight.

She came around to the sidewalk heading back to the Bedford. *Please, Lord, one more request. That my sister will be found unharmed.*

Morgan tossed the empty box back into the wagon. The same tent children had come out again, delighted to see him—except the poor boy with the rotten teeth. He'd never heard such a howl, and he hadn't even done any pulling yet. The howl wasn't as bad as the begging. The panting and begging were too reminiscent of his days in the surgery and his hands began to shake. The boy's mother held him tight over her lap and wedged a stick to keep his mouth open, but there was no chloroform or whiskey for the panicked child. He pulled both teeth quickly and swabbed up the blood and infection as the boy choked on his cries. Removing the stick, the mother held him tight and pounded his back with the assurance it was over.

Taking a full breath, Morgan jumped up on the wagon bench and pushed his hands down his pant legs. It *was* over, and the moments of discomfort were far better than the infection taking his life. He tapped the reins. Now to find Emery's parents.

After following her directions, he tied up his rig, and hiked up a steep trail to where four shanties hung off the side of a thin trail. A woman came around the back and stopped with wide eyes.

"Excuse me." Morgan looked to the ground. "Do you know the Marone family?" He took a step back, wondering if she understood him. She seemed a bit young for Emery's mother, and before he could ask another question, she disappeared around the back of her shanty. Morgan took a moment to breathe in the wide-open afternoon air. The river bubbled quickly downstream below the shanties. Men were swinging spikes and boys were shaking sluice boxes working for gold. A moment later, two women appeared, and this one had the same soft round eyes and olive skin as Emery. Gray streaks peeked out from her bonnet.

"Mrs. Marone." The first woman pointed to her. Morgan bowed slightly. Should he introduce himself? "I was asked to deliver a letter." His eyes shifted between the two women hoping one of them understood him. He pulled it from his back pocket. "For Mrs. Marone."

Emery's mother reached out and took it from him, nodding with kind eyes. Emery had wanted it private, though without a wax seal he'd peeked inside and saw her writing was in Spanish, or was it Basque? Suddenly guilty, he said, "*Adios,*" and turned to head down the trail.

"Wait." The younger woman stepped down the trail. "Who sent this? The mother said it's from her daughter."

"I'm sorry." Morgan turned away briefly, then looked back. "I'm only to deliver it."

Morgan walked up to the second story of the Bedford. *Emery had made other plans;* he'd chewed on those words during the ride back to Hangtown. Of course, they didn't sit well with him. He'd hardly been able to speak when he left earlier. Knocking lightly, Morgan opened the door to see her standing by the window. Thankfully, Emery was still here, as she'd said.

"Well?" She chewed on her thumbnail.

"I saw your mother. I gave the letter to her."

"What?" Her eyes flashed. "You're sure?"

"Yes." He glanced at the floor before gazing at her. "Her eyes were pretty, soft and round like yours."

"Did you see Gianna? My father or brothers?"

"No, I . . ."

"What?" Emery pleaded, coming closer.

"There was another woman." He stopped when she tightly clutched his arm.

"She couldn't be your sister. She was maybe thirty or . . . I don't know, older than you."

Her other hand rested on his chest like he was a post to steady her. Her confused and restless eyes searched the room. "And no one else?" She whispered, still someplace far off.

"No." Before he thought it through, he'd placed his hand over hers. The heat of hers burned through his shirt. Emery looked down and slowly pulled her hand free from his grasp.

"I apologize. I . . ." she stepped away. "Almost couldn't imagine this . . . this moment." Soft, blurry eyes met his. "You have been an overwhelming help." She tried to raise a sad smile. "I'll never have the words to thank you."

"Do you want to thank me?" He notched his chin lower.

"I . . . I . . . do." Warily, she nodded.

"Promise me." Morgan grabbed her waist and

gave her a small shake. "Promise me, you will not take your life." His voice rumbled with intensity, but the reality of having no control over a person gripped his insides. He raised his hands, pressing her jaw and cheek with his fingers. "Promise me, Emery. Promise me on your sister's life."

She paused and looked away as tears slipped down her face. "All right." She met his eyes for a split second. "I promise on my sister's life, that I will choose to live."

Morgan closed his eyes, fighting the constriction in his throat. He let his hands drop to her shoulders and reached around her back. "Thank you." He whispered as he embraced her. "Then everything is worth it." His body stilled. Did her arms reach around him? Yes, her hands lightly touched his back, and her head brushed against his shoulder. Though weakened without the news of her sister she longed to hear, her embrace felt like she must care or trust him. Just so long as the threat of her taking her life was gone. Closing his eyes, Morgan soaked in the moment of his cheek resting on her hair. That was all the answered prayer he needed.

She pulled back from their embrace and met him with desolate eyes.

"I'm sorry, Morgan." Emery choked, wiping her face. "I have to go."

Nineteen

Morgan pulled back on the reins and drew his horse to the side of the road. It was the fifth time he'd stopped on the dirt road back to Auburn. Each time he thought if he could stop the drive a solution would come to him. An answer that would let him turn around, go back, and find the beautiful, confusing, and headstrong young woman who had found her way under his skin. But what had she given him for his trouble? A small consolation?

He could come back and check on her the last Sunday of the month. They would meet again at the stables of the Bedford. A month was an eternity for a woman who has a job she won't name, and a demented notion to not return home to her parents.

Morgan clenched his jaw for over an hour, rehearsing all the danger that lay in wait for a young attractive woman in Hangtown. Baffled, once again he tapped the horse forward. From the beginning, she had been vague and nonsensical. Why would he think that a few days with her or even saving her life, would change that? Morgan rubbed the crease between his eyes.

At least her parents were in the area and maybe she will have returned to them by the time he saw her again. That brought him some relief. A thin layer of gray clouds that were once far off now seemed to loom over him. The young woman was stubborn and impossible to understand. With little reason to turn around, he tapped the horse back onto the side road to Auburn. A few miles along, the splatter of a cold rain pelted his body. Fitting weather to match the despair of his dark mood.

A week later, Emery fell exhausted into her pallet bed. Gripping and rolling the tiny flat feathers in her pillow, she attempted to form some bulk for her head. Morgan had insisted she take the money he handed her and get the things she needed for her new job. A working dress, an apron, and items for her bedding were all she'd wanted to purchase. The few soda crackers she needed in the morning were gone, but so was the awful morning retching. Sleep. Emery yawned. She needed to quit thinking about him and find sleep.

The toddler in the curtained stall next to her would be home soon from sleeping at the saloon and likely keep her awake with the fussing and babbling. So Chen pointed out the dark circles under Emery's eyes. The laundry was tough backbreaking work. The wet sheets from the Bedford and the El Dorado broke in new muscles in her arms and back she never knew she had. Unfortunately, So Chen's soup twice a day contained more water than anything. Occasionally, her sons boiled a chunk of fish in with the rice. So Chen had said that for every month Emery stayed with the laundry, she could earn a dollar. *A dollar for carrots and potatoes and spices and . . . anything more . . .* She dozed.

The rattle of pots and pans woke Emery every morning for the next few weeks. At dawn, another day of hauling water, stoking the fires and hand-scrubbing the piles of laundry started all over again. Another young woman named Francine came and went from the back sleeping area.

On this morning, Francine stopped what she was doing and Emery nodded to her as she poured her coffee.

"You still look pale," Francine said, sipping from her cup. "You can take the ironing. I'll take the wash pots."

"Umm, thank you." Emery took a deep swallow and pushed on the front of her skirt layers. Every day she missed Gianna and truth be told she thought of Morgan every day too. The women at So Chen's laundry had all been kind.

"It should go away soon." Francine looked her up and down. "This town is no place for a lone gal and a baby." She huffed and rolled her eyes. "Guess I don't know any town that is good to a gal with child and no man."

Emery looked around the long washing establishment and set her cup down. "I'm thankful for a job. A place to stay." She gripped her calloused hands.

"Took two of mine to a place in Sacramento," Francine said matter-of-factly. "A children's charity home that gives them to good people. The place still got my son, Joshua. I see him when I can. Janny Long's boy, Thomas, is still there too. Nuns teach them schoolin'."

Emery felt like her insides were dipped into the hot water. *Could she do that?* She finally looked Francine in the eye. "How would I find this place?"

Francine lifted a crooked frown. "I don't read or write much, but tonight I'll try to tell you how to get there, and you can write it down."

So Chen entered, clapping her hands. "Work, work. Today we hang outside. Nice spring air. Good smell." She nodded at the ladies as they turned to start their tasks.

The last Sunday of the month, Emery awoke and shifted on her pallet trying to find a better spot for her stiff muscles. Maybe she could fall back asleep. When she'd asked for the day off, So Chen had said no problem. The short woman worked like a mule, but never ruled over her sons or the other women who came and went. Most of the women's requests were met with a nod and quick approval. Emery flipped to her left side and tried to close her eyes. They opened only a second later—this was the Sunday she'd agreed to meet Morgan at the Bedford stables.

The conflict inside her would never allow her to fall back asleep. Part of her being beat with excitement to see him. He was the only friend who knew what she'd been through. And what woman wouldn't like to talk to him, to enjoy his interest in them? How could she not appreciate and value his kindness to her? Emery chewed the tough skin around her thumbnail. Would it be too much to ask him to go back to the miners' shanties just to look? Just to make sure Gianna wasn't there? She flipped onto her back. Of course, her father had already gone for her sister. Lord of mercy, she would go mad thinking of her sister still on that rat ship. Emery rubbed her hands back and forth over her face.

She could not, would not lead Morgan Hastings on. She'd seen the hurt she caused in the deep brown hue of his eyes. By next month she'd likely be showing, and she would have to find an excuse to end their visits. Rolling her eyes, Emery growled in the back of her throat. Why was she so sure Morgan would even want to continue to visit her? She was a poor, outcast laundress hiding in the back of So Chen's laundry. Morgan hailed from a fine family, was educated and complimentary in face, stature, and generosity. After this, today, she could reassure him she was doing fine and pay him back. Then he would be able to go back to his safe, quiet life.

With such an exceptionally beautiful ride to Hangtown, Morgan had stopped at the closest field and picked a handful of wildflowers. It seemed strange for him, but he remembered how much his mother had enjoyed fresh flowers, before she passed away. Morgan wondered if his father would ever remarry. Maybe he already had. Their letters were so few and far between. The flowers bumped along on the wagon seat into Hangtown.

Morgan determined by the sun's position in the sky that he'd arrived at the Bedford stables long before noon. He had brought a basket of food from Carlotta, a thick Mexican blanket, and the wishful hope of a picnic under a tree with the lovely Emery. Securing his rig and looking around, it could be an hour of waiting and watching for her. What if she didn't come? Walking out from the stables, he glanced down the road he'd taken to doctor the miners' children. A strange desire arose to go back. At home, he'd gone through his medical journals for common ailments of children. Unfortunately, there was very little medical research on the most vulnerable group.

He'd found his papers on inoculations. Would they be something to help the little ones who died every day from smallpox and other diseases? He remembered the line of children that spring day, so many siblings. It was strange for his own parents to only have two boys and now only one left. So many hard-working folks needed large families to survive. Morgan came back and looked at his poor floral gift. The presentation was off; it needed a vase.

A church bell rang out. Emery jumped. Stopping a block from the Bedford, she clutched her blouse, the one that Morgan had bought her, and tried to control her breathing. Thankfully Hangtown presented a sleepy Sunday version of its usual bustling self. Except now, she noticed the stream of people coming down the stairs at the church on the corner. Feeling confident her family wouldn't be in attendance, she picked up her blue skirt and hurried to the Bedford Hotel anyway. She wrung her hands together and hesitantly stepped around the corner of the building.

Morgan, sitting on a stump, jumped to his feet. His smile made every fiber in her want to run to him. Eyes locking, he stepped toward her in his canvas pants and green striped shirt. His hair was a bit shorter and he looked good. Really good. Her heart stuck in her airway as Morgan said her name while reaching out to embrace her. Her arms came up and briefly patted his back before he released her.

"You look well." Morgan held her elbows and looked a little closer. "Maybe thinner." His eyes narrowed with a rogue smile. "Carlotta will help with that."

Emery turned side to side. "Is she here?"

"No, just me." Morgan held her arm and walked her to the wagon. "These are for you." He held the bouquet out for her.

Emery struggled to reach for the splay of lovely colors before her. "Morgan, this is too kind." She gritted her teeth to fight the tingling in her nose. Her eyes filled anyway as she took the vase and took a deep smell of the flowers. "They are beautiful."

"Hey." Morgan squinted, being his usual overly observant self. "Those are tears. Are you all right, Emery? Has something happened?"

"No, I . . . ," she dabbed her face with her sleeve, "need to purchase a handkerchief is all." Ignoring the strange homesickness, Emery forced a smile while tucking the vase in the crook of her arm. Reaching in her pocket, she pulled out a dollar.

"Which reminds me, this is for you. I'm a wage-earning gal now that—" Before she could finish, his eyes narrowed, and jaw hardened. "For all the many, many things you had to purchase for me." She tried to soften her words, but he looked as if she'd slapped him. "Don't look so angry, Morgan. I want to pay you back."

His tongue touched the corner of his mouth, and his eyes lost all their shine.

"Loud and clear, it's no."

Twenty

Morgan tried to smooth out his heated expression, but the tightness in his throat would have none of it. He'd looked forward to this moment for days—no, weeks. Honestly, from the moment he'd driven away, all he thought about was seeing her again. By his own confession, he knew little of women, but this particular round-eyed beauty could kill a man's expectations in a single sentence. "Put your money in your pocket, Emery." Morgan cleared his throat and looked around. "Can we go for a ride?" That suggestion seemed rational. His picnic idea seemed fit only for blushing school children, but he didn't care.

"Where are you taking me, Dr. Hastings?" Her voice held a light tease, and she closed her eyes, taking another long smell of the flowers.

"Would you consider allowing me to kidnap you?" he asked, his brows rising quickly.

"I would not." Her eyes flashed open, and she smiled, shaking her head.

"Then, a ride only. Do you have something in mind?" Morgan helped her into the wagon.

"Just away from Hangtown and the directions I gave you before." She settled her skirts closer and he sat next to her.

"You have not been to your parents, I would

guess." He pulled the horse out and left down Main Street.

Emery looked everywhere but straight ahead as the Snider mansion came closer. "No," she mumbled, squeezing the glass vase in her hands. Squinting from the sunlight, they rounded the road to the left and started up a small grade. "How is Carlotta?"

Morgan caught her sweet gaze. "Well. She asks of you. Carlotta would love it if you came for a visit." They traveled on, and Morgan felt the calm of simple conversation and having her safe by his side.

"Humm." Emery scratched her chin. "And what of the garden? Has it shown more growth?"

Morgan wanted to tell her to come see that for herself too. "I suppose it's fine." Without her love and attention, it would surely go back to weeds.

Morgan spied a grove of trees and brought the wagon closer. "Speaking of Carlotta, I have a basket of food." He pulled the reins and set the brake. "Maybe we can eat here?"

Emery looked around to the secluded grassy area. "Yes, that would be nice."

He jumped down and reached for her hand, but the vase and flowers extended toward him. As Emery pulled up her skirt with her other hand, she took a step out, but her toe caught on the siding. Without warning, she fell against him, and he caught her, suspended against his frame. Eye to eye, his arms easily held her tight. Waiting to see . . . anything? Any mischief, caring, or desire. Morgan smiled anyway because he felt all those things and more.

"Once again at my rescue, or at least the flowers." Her voice was soft and gentle, just like her body meshing with his. He realized she held the vase outward from her, and he slowly brought her feet to the ground. For the second time in his life, he'd held this woman close, and though the first time was all night long, this surpassed the last. His heart did a strange flip. Her small smile and round brown eyes allured him beyond reason. Like warm wax, she felt perfect pressed to him.

"So." He jumped back. "I have a blanket." Morgan reached in the back and brought it out. Kicking a few pine cones aside, he tried to settle his pounding heartbeat. Going back for the basket, Morgan rolled his eyes. What was wrong with him? His breath quickened. A second longer and he would have kissed her. Spreading the blanket out before them, they sat.

"My grandmother from Spain could weave beautiful blankets. So thick, they could be used as rugs." Emery ran her hand over the tan and blue textile. A large fallen tree rested at their back, and they both leaned against it. A sweet breeze brought a welcomed warmth to their comfortable site.

Morgan watched as the leaves rustled above

them. The new spring foliage sparkled like glitter between the sunlight. "It's a perfect day to be outside," he said and reached inside the bag Carlotta had packed.

"I hope this warm weather holds." Emery took the tamale Morgan held out. "It makes the drying so much easier at the—"

Morgan waited. "Easier to what?"

"Oh, nothing." Emery smiled quickly as she took a bite. Chewing slowly, she spoke, "Please tell Carlotta the food is wonderful."

Morgan chewed, swallowed, and looked long at her. "So, your job is something you won't come out and tell me about?" He leaned forward and wrapped his arm around his upraised knee. "But what would need drying?" He took another large bite. "And what would be easier to dry in the sun?" Tipping his head to the side, he swallowed the last bite of his tamale. "You work at the laundry, Emery?"

"Possibly." A squirrel watched them from the end of the long-fallen tree. Emery tore off a piece of tortilla and tossed it at him. "This is a lovely spot." She grinned, looking at him. "How is the gold mining?"

"Going well." Morgan wondered if knowing her past would always keep her wary of him. The laundry appeared a fair place to work. He would not begrudge her independence, something she clearly craved so dearly.

"Have you seen your family in Hangtown?"

"No." She looked down, shaking her head. "I haven't had time—or time to think about Gianna." Sighing, she rubbed her forehead.

"Have you seen the Derry brothers?"

"No, and I don't expect to." Morgan unsuccessfully tried to sensor his disgust of the simpletons. Resorting to kidnapping to get their gold back was still unfathomable. "They'd be wise to find work and make their lost money back honestly."

"I suppose Gianna is back home," she murmured.

Morgan transfixed on the slight movements in the swaying leaves around them. "Do you want me—" He turned to face her. "Do you want me to check? To ask?"

Emery moved away from her backrest and settled on her side, supporting her head with her elbow. "I can't ask any more from you."

"Yes, you can, Emery. We can meet again in . . . in a month. Like this." Morgan noticed the circles that surrounded her downcast eyes. "That will give me time."

"No." She rubbed the back of her neck. "I have to trust. I have to trust my father. I suppose I have to trust God." Emery yawned. "A full belly is making me tired." She covered another weary sigh. "I'm sorry. I'm a poor conversationalist."

Morgan patted the thick blanket. "You look

worn out. Just rest for a moment." Emery covered another yawn and slipped her head onto her flattened elbow. As soon as she stretched her shoulders and pulled her skirt flat around her, she was lulled into sleep.

Morgan watched the tired girl nap. If anyone deserved an uninterrupted rest, it was this young woman. She held the same beauty and grace when she slept, and for some reason she remained beautiful when she was riled.

Would he ever forget the first time he saw past the dirty nightgown and face full of thick wild hair? The crazed woman had been shackled and bound and didn't want any help from him. He could freely admit it now; he'd moved past pity and everything about her endeared her to him. Well, maybe not everything. Holding her body as it dangled from a rope around her neck was a memory he could live a lifetime without.

The squirrel came closer looking for another handout, and Morgan found a rock and tossed it, scaring the squirrel away. The war, the greed of man, had left so many bereft of heart and morals, but now he elected to be a recluse miner, and this broken one elected to hide away in the laundry store. Morgan studied her as she slept, feeling nettled.

Her body was perfect the way it felt against his. Desire to have her for his own warmed him, yet just as fast, it was cooled down by hopelessness.

He could offer her his name, a home, security, but she'd never hinted at wanting any of those things. Though he'd be a gentleman, would she never trust his caring words, his touch? Recalling her knee crushing his gut, he shook his head.

With a faint smile at her gumption, he reached out to pull a strand of brown hair from her peaceful face. With his hand hovering and her hair dangling from his fingers, how long before he wouldn't trust his gentleman's restraints? Slowly, Morgan drew his hand back. He was enamored with someone who never wanted a gentle touch, never a slow, loving kiss, and certainly never to be with him in the marriage bed. Could he only be a friend? The idea brought him no joy.

Morgan looked away and took a deep breath of the warm afternoon air. This day was still important. She'd shown up at the Bedford stables as she said. She worked, lived away from harm and had money in her pocket. Laden with fatigue, she felt comfortable enough to take a much-needed rest. The threat of Arnold Snider finding her was unlikely since he surely would risk an angry mob and hanging if he returned to Hangtown. What had she said? She needed to trust God. At least that sounded like a woman who'd discovered a measure of her faith.

Two birds flitted back and forth above him. Maybe he'd have to *trust God too?* God had seen him through the horrors of the war; had given him a quiet sanctuary to work and live in. *Oh, but this young woman* . . . He settled on his back, watching the blue sky above him. The peace of this afternoon, of being here with her, felt tangible. The beating in his heart was real, but he'd been a man of logic, facts, and evidence all his days. Only a few inches away, Morgan watched Emery's chest rise and fall with tranquil effort.

Why was there was no reasonable or logical path for their future?

Twenty-One

Emery exhaled an irritated huff as Morgan, without her directions, led his wagon into the back of So Chen's laundry store. The narrow building stood blocked by the waving of the long white sheets hung that morning. Emery forced her eyes forward. The man was smart and far too attentive. She clutched her vase of flowers. It had been such a peaceful, calm day and now in leaving, she hated to ruin the peace they shared. "Thank you, Morgan. Please forgive me for falling asleep." Emery chided herself for the rudeness and looked away from him quickly.

The entire day, she'd promised herself not to lead him on in any way. He said he was glad she partook of the perfect afternoon for a nap. Morgan set the brake and came around to her side. Emery looked around for workers from the laundry, anything to distract from what happened when she stepped down last time. Attractive and strong, he'd too many chances to hold her close. She pulled her skirts upward to avoid tripping. Two simple steps down and her feet were on solid ground. Quickly she released his hand and offered a hasty smile. "Thank you, again." She stepped back. Parting for good was like stabbing sewing needles in her heart. "Maybe sometime . . ."

"Next week." A warm hand lightly grasped her arm as she tried to step away.

"No. I . . . I can't ask for days off." She pulled from his touch.

"Then, next month." His voice followed after her toward the soft, waving sheets. "I know you can get time off. Please ask."

With her back to him, Emery stopped and closed her eyes. Would it do any harm? Could he see the bump from her belly? Her face heated red, and a cold wave of shame hit her, like stepping from the rowboat into the icy bay waters of San Francisco's shore. Glancing over her shoulder, she pulled in a deep breath. "I have to let my past go," she said through gritted teeth. "Please, Morgan, please . . . don't come." A tight cry escaped from her closed throat, and she hurried away. The back door to the laundry loomed ahead; four more steps and she would be inside, and find the little pallet bed for comfort.

Bending low, she set the vase of flowers in the corner. Her tiny quarters felt more like a stall in a barn without any privacy for the rush of pain pelting her body and soul. Squatting, she sat on the low pallet and held her knees. Would he leave her be? Emery dropped her head and covered her face for darkness. Morgan Hastings needed to leave her be. Maybe after she delivered and took the baby to the charity home, maybe then, or the next year, they could meet again.

Oh Lord, she didn't want to repay his kindness like this. She didn't have to look in his eyes to know he'd felt rejected head to toe. A low groan mixed with a hiccup spilled out.

"Did he hurt you? That the one who got yer bun in the oven?"

Emery wiped her face on her sleeve and looked up to see Francine standing in her open curtain. She shook her head no.

"Did he give you them flowers?" she asked.

Emery swallowed and nodded. "We're just friends." She rubbed the tension between her eyebrows.

"After I seen you come in upset, I watched him sit in his wagon out the side window. He don't look like a drunkard."

Emery shook her head no.

"He hits women?"

Emery wished Francine would leave. "No," she sighed.

"He's married." Francine sounded like a child who'd solved a puzzle. "He's got a decent face. Lots'a women like that to be sure. Brave to be bringing ya through town and such."

Emery dropped her head again to her knees in hopes she would go away.

"After soup tonight, I'll get ya directions to the charity home I told you about."

Emery looked up and nodded, "Thank you, Francine." Dropping her head again, she crossed her arms over her ears and hair, praying he had left.

The following weeks, Emery tried to convince herself she'd done the right thing to end the friendship quickly. Morgan Hastings was a godsend for those few days after her kidnapping, and her attachment to him was purely based on the destitute state she had been in. He had given her the only thing she cared about, getting word to her family for Gianna's safety. If she really cared about him, as she believed she did, then the right thing would be to thank him for his help and leave him to live an upstanding life.

Even though she'd slept through the loveliest afternoon she'd ever known, his smiles and questions asked for more. Many a dark night, to help her sleep, she pretended she was the spotless princess, and he, with his deep brown eyes smiling his approval, was the handsome prince. But then the rattles of the pots being filled with water broke into her dreams, starting the reality of another day.

Emery looked up from tying her shoes. So Chen's son, Lo, thin and short, stood in her opening. "I go catch fish. You help in bathing room or go deliver sheets."

Emery stood quickly and fingered her hair back

in a bun. "I can't help with the bathing area." She frowned. "They're all men who come and go."

"Okay." Lo bowed. "You do my delivery." He turned away before Emery could compose her rebuttal. Stepping from her sleeping pallet, she looked through the long building, hoping she could pass this off to someone else.

So Chen had customers in line at the front of the laundry store, and the other workers seemed to be missing this morning. Rolling her eyes, she snatched a basket off the floor and went to the folding table. Tossing the stiff square sheets into the basket, she tried to lift it. Heavy as the water she lugged, she dropped it to the floor. The water she'd only carried a few feet, this basket would have to be hauled from one end of Main Street to the other. Her back hurt just thinking of each step. Pulling half the load out and back onto the folding table, she was able to hoist the basket in front of her. Two trips to the El Dorado and two trips to the Bedford, she rehearsed to herself. So be it.

Stepping out from the laundry store, she heaved the basket up onto her hip. Looking toward the El Dorado Hotel, the Snider house loomed too close. The Bedford at least held some special moments with Morgan.

Emery turned on her heel and headed for the stately, tall brick hotel. A man bringing her a tray of food in the beautiful room filled her thoughts. When would that ever happen again? The way his face lit up when he talked about the different children he'd doctored. Emery sighed, adjusting her grip on the basket of sheets. They seemed like memories from years ago, another life.

Stepping off the walkway, she nodded to the mercantile owner as he swept his front walk. She rarely walked alone; it seemed odd to be about town, but the sun felt warm and, for the most part, Hangtown was a decent town. A wagon rolled closer, and for a moment seeing the man in the seat, her heart leaped. The man had similarities to her father, but it wasn't him. She dropped her gaze as it rolled by, praying that they were all doing well.

Coming around the Bedford to the back kitchen door, a short Chinese man with a long dirty apron looked her up and down. Obviously, she was not So Chen's son. Emery lifted a smile and pushed the basket forward. He stepped back and took her down the hall to the large linen closet, pointing to the shelves. Something Lo probably didn't do, she straightened the stacks and looked pleased with her tall equal lines of clean sheets. Just as she had nodded to the man and started to make her exit, he spoke in his own language, waving the knife in his hand toward the pile on the floor. Emery nodded and piled all the dirty kitchen rags into her basket.

Walking back down Main Street, more people appeared doing business and running errands. The blacksmith with a thick beard and heavy eyebrows stopped his pounding and watched her pass. The next trip down to the Bedford, she would go behind the buildings.

An hour later, the time came to face the El Dorado. Straightening her back with the load on her hip, she vowed to enjoy another walk without looking at the two-story display of dishonest prosperity the Sniders had called their home.

Finny, Arnold's wife, had fawned over every detail, all its shiny furnishings and matching draperies. Emery and Gianna had cleaned and polished every large and small possession the Sniders owned. Coming closer, it seemed someone had boarded up the windows. She wondered if Finny had had the baby. Considering her size while on the ship, surely her delivery time had come. Would they live in San Francisco now? Emery shook her head as she turned the corner to find the back door of the El Dorado.

Heavens, she'd failed at not thinking of Arnold and Finny. The fault lay with the imposing ornate house now a stone's throw away. She forced her thinking back to the job at hand.

A man slept on the ground. She walked around him. The El Dorado had a large bar that was filled with many patrons. Making her way up the back steps, it opened to a large hallway, and she stopped to look around. Following the most common path led to a room where an older woman was cleaning the floors.

"May I put these away for you, ma'am?" Emery asked.

"Just leave them on the table by the door." She looked up briefly, nodding to the table.

Emery stacked the linens and turned. Would this be a better place to work than the laundry? The woman didn't look like she would welcome the conversation, but there was no pile to take back anywhere she could see.

"Have a good day, ma'am." Emery walked back down the hall. The shoes Morgan had bought her tapped along the wood floor. A pinch of sorrow caught her unaware. She wondered how her mother fared. Certainly, a shanty had benefit over a tent. When she returned to the family, she convinced herself, her two hands would be a tremendous help to her mother. Yet her parents were the ones who told their two eldest daughters that their outside work money would help the family more. Maybe her parents would want her to continue at the laundry. The dread circled inside her, yet she held no malice. Her parents were as naive in this new country as she once was.

Stepping out the back door, something jerked on her skirt as she tried to turn the corner. Before Emery could pull it from his grasp, the sleeping man pulled on the basket too. "Help me get up, gal," he croaked.

Emery's nose was confronted with the vilest smell and, since he was already pulling on her, she turned her face away and tried to pull him to his feet.

"Now, you're up." She tried to untangle her basket from his wavering and groping.

"Hold up, now." The drunkard pulled her basket away and gripped her arms tighter, standing a head taller. "You wouldn't want an old feller to fall." Suddenly he pressed his dirty frame into hers and wrapped his arms around her waist. Her basket dropped to the ground, and she pressed her hands to his chest to get him off.

"Let me go!" Emery growled, now pounding her fists anywhere she could. The revolting man pulled her tighter, and she began to lose her footing with his weight sagging back on her body. "Stop!" Emery screamed before her knees buckled under the weight, and he fell on top of her.

Fighting to get her breath back, she pushed her arms in every possible opening between them, yelling, "Get off!" Faster than she thought him able, he took her wrists and pinned them above her head. "No, I said, stop!" cried Emery. Now a terrible fear blocked her ability to scream as his hand locked on the pin Carlotta had given her, ripping it and her blouse down the front.

"No, please, no." He crudely ground into her, as his shoulder tried to muffle her cries. In one last desperate attempt, Emery opened her mouth and bit through the fabric of his shirt and into his flesh.

Twenty-Two

The filthy man screeched and pulled his shoulder back. Emery squinted through the dust and could vaguely see someone looming near. The sound of a pistol cocking was heard above the swirl of dirt and her panting. The man froze and rolled off her. Emery's mouth tasted blood and she scooted back, spitting into the dirt. Laying on his back, the man's hands were in the air. Emery could finally take a real breath. A gentleman in a fine tailored black suit and thin mustache held his hand out to her as he held the gun and kept eyes on her attacker. Her arm shook as she placed her hand in his. She remembered him. Mr. Doré, the manager of the El Dorado. Swiftly, he pulled her to standing, and she came around behind him.

"I'z just having a little fun," the man choked out, holding his hand over his shoulder. Emery peeked around her protector's black suit. Bright red blood soaked into the drunkard's rancid shirt. "I thought she was one of those painted gals. Nothin' happened, but I'll toss her two bits and be on my way."

Mr. Doré displayed complete composure. "Empty your pockets."

The man scowled and pulled the coin out and handed his money to Mr. Doré, who then gave it to Emery.

Emery looked back at someone filling the back door and covered her ripped blouse with her hand.

"Reg, walk this reprobate down to the sheriff's office."

"Yes, sir." The big man walked past them, pulling his own gun out.

"Tell the sheriff, it was rape. And Hangtown should live up to its name, give him the rope."

Emery swallowed. *This one would swing?* Even if she's only been roughed up? Rape was what Arnold Sn . . . The dusty air began to restrict her throat. Against her own willpower, she narrowed her eyes on the Snider home and saw black spots start to cover the horrid spinning mansion.

"I don't think she needs a doctor."

Emery heard a woman's voice and groggily whispered, "Mommi?"

"I feel bad." The woman continued on, talking to someone. "I'd seen him out there when I was dumping water. When she dropped off the laundry, I should've walked her out. Usually, the China boy does all the deliveries."

A damp rag touched her cheek, and Emery willed her eyes open. The woman who had been cleaning floors earlier was speaking to Mr. Doré.

His expression wasn't happy as he pulled on his thin, waxed mustache. She'd been a burden as usual. Pushing off, she tried to rise from a small bed.

"I'm so sorry. I . . . I . . ." Emery held her hand over her chest. "I must go. They will wonder what happened." The simple room was well lit with sunlight and she tried to steady her heartbeat as she sat.

"I do remember you, *mon cher*." Mr. Doré stepped forward, tapping his cheek.

Emery looked up, catching his French accent, thinking it always made him sound regal and important.

"I helped the night we found Miss Cassidy in the basement of the Snider house." She rubbed her wrists, feeling the sting of where the drunk had crushed them into the rock and dirt. "I used to work as a housemaid at the Snider home." She tried to stand, hoping her legs would hold her.

"*Oui, oui*," he said, as they watched the cleaning woman leave. "She is bringing you a new blouse. I apologize for what happened to you." Pierre looked her over. "You seem a bit faint. How may I be of assistance?"

Suddenly aware of how ragged she must look, she held her blouse together and tried to finger her hair back in place. He didn't try to touch her or steady her, and for that she liked him.

"You have been kind and I owe you a very big thank you. How do you say 'thank you' in your country?"

"*Je vous remercie.* Or better just *merci.*"

"*Je vous* . . . re . . . ahh." She couldn't get the sounds to form.

"Well done, for your attempt." A broad white smile awarded her efforts.

The cleaning lady returned, holding a white blouse.

"When you are dressed, please allow me to walk you back to the laundry." He bowed and left quickly.

A few minutes later, Emery was walking alongside Pierre Doré, the distinguished manager of the El Dorado Hotel. "Who should I return this blouse to?" Emery frowned at the ripped one at the bottom of her basket. Morgan had bought it for her. Though fixable, it was foolish of her to wear it on a workday.

"It is yours," he nodded, as Emery spied the laundry store. Men do not like to be repaid. Hadn't she learned that lesson from Morgan?

"I cannot guarantee our respectable sheriff will hang the man as desired or banish him from this town. If you see the vagrant anywhere, you will come to me. *Oui*?"

Emery nodded. He was too young to be her father's age, but he carried a certain authority.

"Your family? They are still at work along Eureka Creek?" he asked.

"Yes."

"And being a laundress? This work suits you?"

"Yes," she said timidly.

Pierre Doré huffed. "Better days you've had, I'm sure."

Emery nodded wide-eyed. "You are correct." Her chin twitched. If the man only knew how this attack had brought back the memories she'd begged God to take away. A cold sweat dampened her skin. Only a few more steps remained as she tried to rehearse a proper expression of her thanks.

So Chen stepped from the laundry. "What? What's dis?" She raised her hands, and Emery wondered why her tone sounded angry with her. "Sheriff just here. He looking for you. I say no trouble!" So Chen pounded the edge of her hand against her palm. "I give you work and sleep. I say no trouble." Her tiny eyes glared.

"Madam Chen." Mr. Doré stepped closer. "Your young employee started no trouble, I assure you. She was attacked while making a delivery and—"

"No." So Chen shook her head quickly. "No good." She stepped back. "I too busy. I need workers. I no have Truitt. Truitt not here anymore." The small woman scowled. "I run business. No want make trouble."

Emery went to open her mouth, but Pierre spoke up.

"Are you to terminate her employment? Is that what you are saying?"

Emery gasped. "Oh, please."

"Have no fear, Miss." Pierre still held a steady gaze on So Chen. Nothing seemed to rattle this man today.

"No. no." So Chen's lips pursed. "She a hard worker. Good worker."

Emery's shoulders drooped with relief. What else could go wrong in one day?

"But no more trouble!" She barked at Emery and turned around into the laundry shop.

Emery felt an uncomfortable silence. She was a poor girl from a poor family. Mr. Doré stood unmoved in his refined black suit and shiny shoes. He finally turned to face her. "I've heard it said often that an angry reaction is more from fear. I'm sure the madam was worried about you."

Emery ran her hand down her face and closed her eyes. It might not be true of So Chen, but it sounded endearing, to say the least. Trying to remember the words for thank you. "Je vous . . . re . . ."

"Ha!" Mr. Doré flashed a wide smile. "Bravo, for such attempts." He nodded his approval. "The El Dorado has a large account here." He lowered his voice. "Don't let that little woman get to you. She's shrewd and probably one of the wealthiest women in all the territory. So," he said, straightening up, "I will come again tomorrow evening to check on you."

Emery went to say something, but he held up a finger. "She's deemed you a good worker, but if she threatens your employment, you will always have a job at the El Dorado."

Emery supposed the shock might have shone on her face.

"Even if I have to meet with your father and assure him of your safety, that would be my utmost priority."

Emery repressed a squeak, letting that idea fall away quickly. "Thank you again for all your help today." She stepped to the door and turned. "You'll never know how deeply your timing and rescue saved . . ." *what was left of me.* She kept the last words to herself. "My thanks again." Emery nodded and entered the shop.

Twenty-Three

Morgan threaded his fingers behind his neck, pulling his shaggy locks apart. A haircut and a shave were in order. Drawing his hand across his beard, he glanced down at the letter sitting on his lap. His father was leaving Chicago and coming to California. Morgan leaned forward and grabbed the poker. Tapping on the hot red and black coals, small sparks flew up. The distraction did not help the mix of his competing emotions. The shadows deepened in his cabin.

He had already read the date over and over. The letter was written more than three months ago. His father had wanted to take the wagon caravan across these newly settled states. That could take up to a year, depending on the weather and the route. Morgan set the fire poker against the rock and sat back. He should be happy. Happy to have family near. They were the only two left. Then why did his gut twist?

He leaned forward and set his elbows on his knees. Holding his head in his palms, he squeezed. *Expectations.* He'd lived his life with the family's expectations. His father's boys would have the best education, the best opportunities. A Rush medical doctor was a prized commodity, something to make his father proud. And now there was only one son left.

Hastings men didn't live in secluded cabins spending their days swirling rock and silt around a tin pan. Surveying the scarred skin on his hand he wondered if his father understood his need to give up medicine. A deft hand was a must for a surgeon. Without remorse, he'd no desire to do surgery again. He'd written these things in his letters home. Was he coming to prod Morgan back to life? Back to respectability?

Morgan stretched out his long legs; leaning back, he rested his head against the cushioned chair. The image of the little girl from the Hangtown mining tents came to mind. The way she'd gently touched his scarred cheek; the line of giggling children awaiting his care as if they were in line to receive gifts. *Blessed are the poor in spirit: for theirs is the kingdom of heaven.*

He glanced at his Bible lying on his desk. Wasn't that what he'd read just yesterday? He'd felt poor in spirit these last weeks. The only thing that motivated him was returning with supplies to the tent mining camps.

He'd rehearsed finding all of Emery's family. The day of the picnic, he could tell she'd wanted to ask him to check and see if Gianna was there, but the stubborn, independent young woman would never impose. And even though he could go on his own, what if her sister wasn't there?

Would he report back to Emery and risk her devastation? What if the news pulled her back into her low state? His gut clenched as in his mind's eye he could see her swinging from the rope attached to the beams of his cabin.

Releasing a low groan, Morgan shook his head. At least his father had no knowledge of her. His own injuries were obviously thwarting him from his training, but no scarring was as painful as the scars of the heart. Emery did not see a friendship nor a future with him. Why? Why not take the chance to know him better? What was so difficult about another outing? The woman was working to exhaustion. A Sunday drive and a place to rest. Why did her eyes crinkle with pain at the idea of meeting him again? Her desire to be left alone obviously made sense to her, but completely unsettled his thoughts and desires.

Grabbing the letter, Morgan huffed and tossed it on his desk. The mining had gone well this week. He stood up and stepped into his room. He could listen to Carlotta chide him about his low state or he could do something different. He pulled his shirt up and over his head and threw it on the bed. His hand traced the scarring on the left side of his chest. Had his scars become well-used excuses? Is that something his father might think? Shaking himself from his musings, Morgan decided a change of scenery was in order. Bringing fruit and supplies, and checking on the miners' children—at least that had gone well.

Emery pulled in a deep whiff of summer air and clean laundry. Dropping the basket between the long lines, sometimes she could pretend she was lost in low white clouds softly waving back and forth, catching her in their glistening folds. She ran her hands down the fabric, determining if it was fully dry.

Pulling the pins loose, she folded and dropped the linen in her basket. Dragging the basket down her row, Emery rose up and felt a pinch in her back. Her belly now protruded, and often her back would ache from hauling the water. She frowned, drawing another sheet off the line. As soon as she could get these down, there would be another load to put up.

Mr. Doré had come by twice in the last several weeks, and she was able to reassure him that she still had a job with So Chen. Missing the clothespin bucket, she bent to pick it up, wondering if cleaning for him at the El Dorado would be less backbreaking.

Emery had no desire to be caught out in public again. So Chen's shop was filled with different women who came and went, but she could stay within the safety here, never told to do a delivery again. No one asked her about the child within and Francine was the only one she cared to talk to. A large shadow crossed the sheet in front of her.

"Oh, heavens." Emery gasped and turned to grab the basket, holding it tight against her belly.

"Hello, Emery." Morgan came into view at her left.

"Morgan!" Her nose flared. "You scared my blood cold."

"I'm sorry." He grinned, his hair shorter and off his collar.

"I . . . I . . . can't visit." She pulled the basket tighter. Her heart pounded with the shock of seeing him; a strange flood of emotion tried to rise up in her throat.

"I just wanted to see how you were—" Morgan followed her around to the next clothesline, "—doing."

"I'm well, thank you." She looked over her shoulder. "But So Chen doesn't like any disruption."

"Then I'll come back on Sunday. We can take a drive or—"

"No." She panted, eyes flashing side to side. "I'm so sorry." She stepped quickly toward the back of the shop. Just as the open door offered her safety, he crossed in front, and the wicker basket slammed into him.

"What is it?" he said with flexing jaw. "You can speak to me no longer than a minute? I drove from Auburn and I think you owe me a bit more than this hasty dismissal." His eyes narrowed as he blocked the door like a brick wall.

Emery looked past him, praying So Chen wasn't watching. Ready to crumble, she stepped back from the basket pressing between them. "Morgan, please don't." She looked to see if anyone was behind her. "I did what you asked," she huffed. "I'm still alive."

Her reasoning didn't make an inch of difference in his hurt expression and he leaned closer. "Do you despise me? Can you just tell me what I've done?" His voice was firm. "I just want a Sunday drive. You didn't seem to be upset by that a month ago."

"You haven't done anything wrong." Her voice cracked. "I so appreciate everything, but I feel it's best we go our separate ways."

"*Why*, Emery?" His scowl deepened, and his eyes dropped to her blouse—the fabric, the hand stitching glaring from where she'd patched it together.

"Because I want to forget my past." She sucked in a shaky breath. "Forget everything. I can't do that when I see you. You know too much." She would beg for understanding if she had to, though his eyes held a hurt she would wish on no one. One of So Chen's sons stopped inside and watched them. Morgan's arms spread wide, hands gripping the door jamb, blocking anyone's entrance or exit.

"I don't care about your past." His insistent tone demanded her attention. "I'm not even asking for your future."

"Let me pass, Morgan," she blurted out, trying to look away.

"Have you seen your family? Do they know you are here?"

"No." Emery yanked his arm down and pushed the basket and herself past him.

"I've seen them." He turned, speaking to her back. "I've seen your sister. I've told them."

His words stopped her like an animal trap snapped around her ankle. *Please, God.* "Gianna?" Wide-eyed, Emery stepped closer. "You are sure it was her?" Before she could read his face, So Chen came from the back, rattling something in Chinese. The angry woman held the long plank of wood they used to stir the pots of wash.

"Go, Morgan!" Emery released the basket with one hand and pushed at his chest. Turning quickly, she held her hand out at the tiny woman who had a wooden weapon and fury in her eyes. "He will do no harm, no trouble," Emery begged.

Spinning back to make sure he'd gone, she lost her balance, and Morgan reached out to steady her arm. So Chen swung with a flash, and a blunt agony struck Emery's forehead before everything went black.

• • •

So Chen's face closed up in remorse as she dropped her wood plank. "Oh no, so sorry." The little woman backed up as Emery lay crumbled on the floor. Morgan was on his knees. Grabbing at the spilled linens from her basket, he pulled one under her head. "Emery!" He gripped her face. *Oh Lord, she was out cold.*

"I'm a doctor." He barked at So Chen and the others who gathered to watch. "I need clean water." Taking another sheet, he tore a strip from the end. The cut was deep, and he dabbed the blood from running into her eyes. "Emery. My dear, please. That whack was meant for me." Fighting a groan, he brushed his fingers gently across her cheek. A pan of water was set next to him, and Morgan dipped the other end of the cloth in it and wiped the blood away.

"We got a needle and some thread if ya needin' it. So Chen knows how to do a fair amount of skin stichin'." A young woman in a brown dress and thick white apron knelt next to him. Morgan rinsed the blood off the cloth. "Yes, that would be helpful, but I can do it." He took Emery's wrist; her pulse was good, steadier than his. A few stitches, while she was out, would work. The woman returned with the needle, and he asked her for a stick from the fire. Holding it to the side, he held the needle into the flame. "Ain't that gonna burn her?" the woman asked before she took the stick back.

"I was purifying the metal. To clean it." Morgan carefully threaded the needle, glancing up to see So Chen watching with an agitated frown. "Why is her blouse repaired?" Morgan asked the woman kneeling close.

"Just a dirty Joe from the El Dorado. She was fine by nightfall."

Fuming, Morgan tried to focus on what he was doing.

"I'm Francine." She knelt next to Emery and held her hand. "So you really a doc?"

Morgan nodded. "I'll also need scissors."

"I get." So Chen turned quickly.

"You called her dear," Francine whispered. "She say it ain't so, but you the one who got her in the family way?"

Morgan blinked twice, three times. The needle suspended above Emery's forehead. "Could you steady her arms, if she comes awake while I do this?" Those words sounded like another man speaking. Trying to clear his mind, his hand shook doing three simple stitches. Emery was . . . was pregnant? Morgan took the scissors held in front of him and snipped the thread. Dropping them in the water, he took the sheet and tore a clean bandage. Circling her head like he'd done to soldiers a thousand times during the war, his eyes searched her frame and landed on the round bump. The evidence under the folds of her waistband confirmed the woman's story.

Emery, the beautiful hiding laundress that lay before him, was pregnant with Arnold Snider's baby.

Twenty-Four

Emery awoke on her pallet bed and gently held her splitting head. Carefully, she tried to move her jaw, but her ears and cheeks and everything above her neck crackled and throbbed.

"She's awake." Francine hollered from the foot of where she lay.

The woman's words bounced like another wooden stick against her skull. Emery rolled her eyes, trying to move away without really moving. Warily, she fingered the cloth around her head. Morgan. Morgan was here, blocking the door, and So Chen was angry, with a laundry stick in her hand. Emery closed her eyes again as it all came back to her.

"How long . . . how long have I been sleeping?" Emery tried to sit up.

"Just an hour or so. He's waiting outside. The doctor."

Emery leaned forward, gasping from her stupor. "My basket. What happened to the basket with the laundry?"

"The basket is fine, silly girl, but your young man ripped up one sheet, some of it's around your head." Francine pointed. "I asked, but he never told me if this was his baby. I guess he was too busy stitchin' up yer busted head."

Emery stilled. "Francine, please tell me you did *not* ask him," Emery whined, feeling her stomach roll up to her throat.

So Chen's little body filled the space in front of her. She held out two dollar bills. "You go now." So Chen shook them until Emery reached up to take them from her. "Take that and no go to sheriff."

"I won't go. Why would I go to the sheriff?" Emery pled with a weak, despairing tone. "Please, I won't cause any trouble."

So Chen shook her head. "You go with my money. And no tell sheriff what I did."

Emery knew her mouth hung open. How could she promise the little businesswoman she'd never cause trouble when it kept appearing unannounced?

"Sorry, friend. I will miss you." Francine held a small bundle out. Emery felt every ounce of blood wane. Had they already packed her few things? The two vastly different women held out their arms and helped her to stand. The room tilted, and her head spun as she took the steps to the door. Just barely able to stay upright, she was too weak to find a decent rebuttal.

Morgan Hastings looked up from where he sat. Catching sight of Emery at the door, he jumped down from his wagon. Before she could focus against the bright sunlight, his arms were supporting her while she murmured weak goodbyes

212

to the women who helped her step up to the wagon seat. Wishing the right words would rise past this pounding pain, she'd muster the strength and refuse his help.

The man had cost her a job and place to live. With two dollars in her pocket, a bribe to pardon So Chen from trouble with the sheriff, and not a clear mind to speak, Emery realized she was indeed leaving. The sunlight made her eyes water, and she pulled her small bundle close on her lap. *Morgan Hastings, now look at what you've done.* The wagon rocked forward, and she gripped the seat as they rolled from town.

The following afternoon Morgan stood up as Carlotta left the second bedroom with a tray. "Did she say anything?"

"To me, *sí.*" Carlotta walked to the table.

Morgan shook his head. "It's been two days. I need to check her wound."

"It's fine. The bandage is off."

"Is it puffy or seeping?"

Carlotta put the dishes in the basin. "It's fine."

Morgan rolled his tongue around the inside of his cheek. Carlotta had clearly joined the forces against him. "I told you I'd only stopped to check on her. How could I know her boss swings washing sticks? She lost her balance and dropped the basket. I reached to steady her, and . . . it was an accident."

"You block the door, *hombre*." Carlotta scrubbed the few dishes.

Morgan rolled his head. He'd been rash and impetuous—so out of character for his usual demeanor.

"Did Emery tell you she is pregnant?" His voice lowered.

"*Sí*." Carlotta sighed, setting a dish on a towel. "Hard to miss."

Morgan pulled out a kitchen chair and sat, holding his head. He'd lost sleep rehearsing what he knew of her and hoped he'd put together her story correctly. The shame would keep her from her people, her family. That could be why she had been adamantly against going to them. Arnold Snider still could be found. The Derry brothers could track anything. Wanting vengeance, he felt he could lead the charge to have Snider lynched. Picturing the moment of justice, his mind flashed to Emery dangling from the rafters. This had to be why she'd try to kill herself.

"You let her stay till the *bebe* comes?" Carlotta asked.

"Yes, of course. Please tell her as much."

"Maybe you marry her." Carlotta shrugged.

Morgan stilled the words knocking his chest. "She doesn't care for me," he countered. "I think she's known enough pain for a lifetime."

"*Sí*," Carlotta murmured, hung her apron, and

turned the corner to her room. "Like someone else I know."

Morgan spent the next day mining in the creek closer to his cabin. A strange protectiveness still swirled inside him. Hourly he had stopped and listened then reminded himself the Derry brothers were not coming, and Emery was not a helpless victim tied and tethered to a metal bar around her waist. Any day he could find her gone. Though Carlotta said she slept for hours, he could reason that away easily after seeing her delicate condition and the crude sleeping quarters at the laundry shop. The heat of the late afternoon peeked through the shade and he licked his dry lips. What a waste of time. He'd already mined this area months ago. A refreshing splash was due after a fruitless day.

Dripping and refreshed, Morgan walked from the tree line into the field before his cabin. Catching movement from the corner of his eye, he stopped. Like a butterfly emerged from its cocoon, Emery worked in the shaded garden area and tossed a weed over to the side. Her long brown braid laid against her back. She'd returned to the place she loved, likely her only place of peace and comfort.

His heart fell to his stomach watching her like this. What would he say? Was she still angry with him? Walking to the barn, he dropped his mining supplies and raked his wet hair behind his ears.

Without any conversational direction in mind, his feet betrayed him as they stepped toward the garden.

Just her name, soft and contrite. "Emery," Morgan said, sounding harmless enough. She knelt with her back to him and continued weeding.

"How is your head?" Stepping around, he tried to face her.

"It's fine." She kept pulling and tossing weeds over the rusty wire fence. *Fine* was what Carlotta had already told him. How did he approach the real need? Had she suffered any repercussions in her confinement?

"You are welcome, if you'd be comfortable, to stay as long as you need."

Emery took in a deep gulp of air, exhaling as her shoulders trembled. Standing slowly, she brushed the dirt off her hands and skirt.

Morgan clenched his teeth. His eyes had gone right to the bump that rounded through her full skirt. Averting his eyes, they took in the purple and pink bruise on her healing forehead. "I understand a bit more, well, a lot more of what you've been dealing with. I'd like to express my distress also—my sorrow for what you must be feeling. But I want you to know you can trust me."

The blank lifeless stare she gave him could have split a mountain. He cleared his throat, shoved his hands in his pockets, and pulled them out quickly. "Do you understand that though you probably want nothing to do with me, I am at your service?"

Emery's head dipped to the side. "All ardent and crusading, I would expect nothing less from you." The sarcasm dripped from her tone, but Morgan felt no shame. Those terse words were a fair depiction of his strengths and his weakness.

"Maybe you can find some wayward forgiveness for me," Morgan said, as Emery knelt and continued to pick through the garden. "As a war surgeon, I wanted, no, I believed I could help those men risking their lives, taking sword and bullet for our country. At least I could repair them, use all my knowledge for good." He rubbed his fingers between his eyebrows and felt the afternoon sun on his back. "Emery, if you only knew . . . I just wanted to help. But to confront you at your employment was wrong from the Atlantic to the Pacific. It was wrong and badly handled."

"So now I am your newest cause. Another chance to right all wrongs?" She looked over at a place of dried dirt and crumbled up a dirt clod with her hand. "I regret to tell you, you will be sorely disappointed . . . again."

Morgan humbly contemplated her assessment. A bit like the Creator, who knows all hearts and minds, she did know him quite well. "I've had a bit of an awakening with God. Solitude will cause these strange occurrences." His tone was pensive. "When a body can let go of their own expectations and just be moved by the divine then there are no regrets. I am who I am before the Almighty. It doesn't matter that you are beautiful and innocent. Or even that the injustice done to you grows right under your heart. I still would have helped, whoever the person, whatever the need. I'm no saint, just stepping carefully the path laid out by God."

"And you have *no* expectations?" Emery took in a long breath and let it out, her eyes carefully reaching up to his.

He dropped his head and bit on the corner of a smile. "Well, I can't really say that."

"What do you want, then?" Her lips creased in a thin line, and she pushed off her knees to standing.

"You have a way with cooking." His tone was light. "Those Basque meals were amazing." His eyebrows notched higher. "Give me a list and I will go to town for whatever you need."

Her eyes scrutinized him and he was just about to beg for the request back so as not to cause any more offense.

"All right." She huffed. "I can make a list."

Twenty-Five

The next evening the three of them sat around the familiar log cabin table. Morgan waited impatiently to make eye contact with Emery without Carlotta's notice.

"Tuna and potato stew. Humph," Carlotta stirred her bowl, and Morgan reached over to squeeze Emery's knee. Emery jumped and narrowed a wide-eyed scowl at him.

It's very good, he mouthed, then took another bite like it was the only meal he'd eaten in weeks.

Emery shook her head and looked away.

"I was wondering about a goat," Morgan asked. "I know nothing of herd animals. Do you have to have four or six, or how does that work?" He tore off a piece of bread.

Emery shrugged. "It depends on what they're for."

"I was thinking of what you talked about before."

She kept her eyes on her bowl, striking her usual indifferent pose.

"The first time you were here." Morgan wouldn't be distracted. "For cheese and milk, and whatever else."

Emery chewed a bite and swallowed. "For just the two of you, I suppose four would do fine."

Morgan caught her dismissal but had another plan. "Also, what about a greenhouse of some kind? We had a large one in our yard in Chicago. My mother enjoyed it when the weather was cold." He glanced at Carlotta. "I'm aware the winters are not as harsh as back east, but I'd like to grow some plants and herbs for medicinal use. I could dry them and have them for year-round dispensing."

"So now you are an apothecary?" Emery's lips tightened into a frown and her tone caused an awkward silence that covered the table as they finished eating.

"You said something I need to hear again." Emery's words broke in with strained undertones as she placed a napkin on the table. Morgan bristled. He wanted to believe her cold attitude was imbedded in something else besides him. Likely not.

"During the commotion at So Chen's, I believe you said . . ." She cleared her throat, staring at the table. "That you saw my family. You saw my sister?" Her eyes flashed upward for a split second. "Did I hear that right?" Her voice held the thinnest thread of hopefulness. His wonderful last bite of stew tried to burn a hole in his stomach and Morgan drew back in his chair, wishing he could disappear.

"I went to the miner's shack area outside of Eureka Creek. The same place I'd dropped off your letter." He rubbed his temple. "The children gathered around, and I handed out apples and potatoes. Some combs and paper."

Her soft brown eyes turned dark. "And?"

"A boy named Ferdinand approached me."

Emery's eyes widened. "That's my little brother."

"I asked him to name the people in the home and there would be food for them too." Morgan ran his fingers over the rough wood table. "He named your mother and father, not you." He glanced at her—she'd been through so much, and would this make it worse? "He named Gianna, Arturo . . . I think Maxwell?"

"Maxwello?"

"Yes, and Ferdinand." Morgan waited for her reaction, but her face seemed to pale.

"But you never saw her? She is younger with a rounder face and—"

"He didn't name you. I'm sure his recollection was accurate."

"But I thought you said at the laundry shop you'd seen Gianna?"

Her face revealed something innocent and earnest. Like the cursed liar of Hades, he'd lied in the excitement of the moment. Standing from the table, he rubbed his hand over the back of his head. "I never saw her. Only your brother." Morgan couldn't look her in the face. It was right that she constantly disapproved of him. "First

221

I delivered the letter, then the box of food. If Gianna or your mother had come out, how would I have explained the letter? Did you want me to tell them of our acquaintance?"

Emery held her knuckles against her lips. "No." She stood and picked up the dishes and then set them back down. Her body wavered and her eyes filled. "Carlotta, I need a moment. I will be back to do the dishes."

Carlotta batted her hand at Emery and murmured something to her in Spanish. Sniffing, Emery swiped her wet face and went into her room and closed the door.

Like an empty, broken eggshell, Emery sat on the edge of the bed and stared out the window. The sun had set, and the faint shadows filled the hardwood floor. Fernando was only nine, but he knew enough English to repeat his siblings' names. Morgan had lied about seeing Gianna in person and yet she wasn't angry with him. Good thing she'd felt little of any emotion lately. Her back ached so she laid back on her pillow and pulled a blanket close.

It wasn't that hard, this plan she carried. Instead of waiting for her delivery time and asking Francine to go with her to Sacramento, she would go herself. With the money from So Chen, she had the fare to get there. She could find the charity home, leave the baby, and then return to Hangtown. She could walk the same road Morgan had and greet her family without shame.

The job at the laundry shop had been real and she was of age. Her parents would just have to understand. *And Gianna—her sweet sister . . .* Emery closed her eyes as they began to fill again. All she had wanted was Gianna off the boat and returned to the safety of their family. That would be the thought that would carry her these next difficult weeks. Covering a hiccup, she held the blanket to her wet cheeks and pictured them all together.

The next morning Emery woke to a pounding sound. Wrapping the blanket around her nightgown, she stepped out to see Carlotta standing on the front porch. They both watched Morgan with the cool summer morning breeze surrounding them. He worked building something with wood on two different sawhorses in front of the barn.

"*Señor* is up early." Carlotta huffed. "He already gone for the goats. They are in the barn. Now he works on their pen."

"I never asked him for goats." Emery sighed.

"I know." Carlotta glanced at her. "He wants to please you. Make up for your hurt."

Emery slowly shook her head.

"But that not his job, *sí?*" Carlotta eyed her, and Emery regarded her, confused by her words.

"You *señorita*, you only and *Dios*." Carlotta quickly touched her shoulders and forehead and chest in the sign of the cross. "He the only one who can heal the heart, *sí*?" Carlotta looked her up and down. "And this tiny one, the *bebe* will fill your heart with goodness."

"I'm not keeping him. Or her." Emery never met her gaze. She knew it sounded harsh to the old woman's ears, but even with goats and gardens, she would not live here. "After I take the baby to an orphanage, I can finally go home to my family."

"*Bueno*." Carlotta shook her head and turned back inside the cabin.

Emery watched Morgan measure the lengths of wood. Manly confidence poured from him as he sawed the wood and pounded nails. Her eyes flitted down to the corner of the porch, where the logs crossed. It seemed like years ago she'd huddled lost in that corner—scared and angry, wishing for a solution when she knew there was none. God had kept her alive, given her a job and place to live in Hangtown. Her work had kept her busy and maybe provided a bit of calm, routine, or who knows—thinking of Carlotta's words, healing. But returning here was like being back to the beginning.

She felt edgy and angry. Angry that Morgan could not mind his own business. Angry that the man was relentlessly good, caring, *and* smart head to toe. Emery rolled her eyes; that made no sense. Possibly she was angry and felt slighted that So Chen had run her out, and Morgan had been there again to rescue her.

Wearily, she took in a deep breath. The scent of the summer wildflowers and cut wood wafted lovely this time of morning. The quiet of this place, so far from the bustle of busy Hangtown streets was calming, attempting to soothe her discontent.

Was she angry to have a room to herself and a soft bed and pillow? No, more like thankful. What about her calloused hands, and healing hot water burns? Now these hands were set to the ease and creativity of cooking—full hearty meals that left the stomach satisfied instead of watery soup.

Emery pulled her blanket tight and watched Morgan saw through a thick post. Was she angry he wanted to please her? The goats and greenhouse were things she would enjoy *if* she could find any joy. Sighing, she looked out to the quiet trees. He'd made no demands—well, except for cooking. Irritated, she recalled the wrongdoing of lying to her at So Chen's back door. Something to the left brought her head around. With a small lighthearted grin, Morgan waved her over.

Her lips pursed tight, she was about to turn on her heel. Did he need glasses? She was not dressed, for heaven's sake. She took one last look at the corner where she'd found refuge months ago and then back at the tall, muscular man waiting for her to come. Maybe her softening was from the thought of her little brothers and how proud they were to show off any small handmade items. Surely the man had already seen her worst. What kind of imposter faked propriety now?

Barefoot, with the blanket over her shoulders and draping over her swollen belly, she walked out to him to display a speck of kindness for his gallant efforts.

Twenty-Six

Later that afternoon, Emery rolled up her sleeves and unbuttoned the top of her blouse. The inside of the barn held little afternoon breeze, but the shade was needed. Morgan worked, dripping in sweat as he finished the outside fencing for the goat pen. Taking up a shingle she'd found in the barn, she fanned herself and sat on a turned-over wooden box. Already her fast friends, the two little blonde goats came close to nuzzle her skirts. She rubbed them under their chins and around their little nubby horns. Round eyes with notable yellow lines looked up for more attention.

"Neither of you will fit on my lap. Stop now." She had to push their little hooves off her legs when they tried to climb on her.

"The little ones are attached to you." Red-faced, Morgan came in the wide barn door. "Now, for the last part." He entered the goat pen and took ahold of the plank of wood and pounded it away from the barn. The goats skittered away from him and tried to huddle with Emery.

"No, ninnies." She pushed their heads away from her. "Go outside, go!" She stood and tried to shoo them out. "There's grass for you to chew all day long. Go," she said, clapping her hands until they found the opening and left.

"You look hot," Morgan said, putting his tools away. "I have a perfect place to cool off."

"You go ahead. I should start something for supper." Emery stood, shaking the hay off the bottom of her skirt.

"We'll only be a few minutes." His eyes narrowed with a wry grin. "Not enough time for you to fall asleep on me."

Emery sighed and dropped her head to the side. "I didn't mean to fall asleep. It was rude of me and I apologize."

"You're forgiven." Morgan held his hand out toward her. "But you should see my creek. Come on." He turned with his usual confident steps. She dropped her shoulders and followed. They didn't speak during the walk across his yard and into the brush and trees.

Finally, he turned. "And I should apologize for staring at you."

"What?" Emery gathered her thick skirt and stepped over a fallen log.

"When you fell asleep during our picnic. You just looked so peaceful."

"Yes, I'm sure that was an oddity." Sweat started to roll down her back. "How much further?"

"Just down this trail." He held the low branches for her as she crossed in front of him. The air did seem to cool as the fully shaded creek appeared. Morgan sat on the bank and removed his shoes and stockings. "You'll want to put your feet in." He glanced back to where she stood. "Go ahead."

Emery looked around and found a rock to sit on. Something strange pulled inside her. To have such childlike abandon as to put her feet in the water, could she do it? She watched him out of the corner of her eyes and looked back to her shoes—*the ones he'd bought for her.* Shaking her head, she untied them and turned her back to him. Discreetly, Emery lifted her skirts and undid her stockings. Stretching her toes forward, the chill of the cold water ran up her skin. Pulling in a held breath, she held her hem tight and submerged her feet and ankles.

"Oh my, it's cold." She brought them out and wiggled her toes.

"Snow water," Morgan said, taking handfuls and splashing his face. "Thank you for your help today." He pulled his wet hair behind his ears, and she caught herself looking long at him.

"I didn't do anything." She dug her toes into the cold, wet sand.

"You entertained m . . . I mean, the goats all day." He'd almost slipped and said *me.*

Emery smirked and shook her head. Morgan stepped up the creek to where she sat and waited until she would look at him. "I'm sorry I let you believe I'd seen your sister. I know I hurt you."

Emery fingered a twig at her feet and then

tossed it in the water, watching it twist and turn down the creek. "I can't be upset with you, Morgan. None of this has been your fault. If anything, I should apologize to you." Leaning forward, she dug her fingers into the pebbles and sand, wondering how anyone could find gold in all of this.

"No, it's not necessary. Just know, I . . . I mean well. And I've chewed on what you said about being a crusader of some sort."

Emery pursed her lips and rinsed her fingers in the cool water. *Ahhh, she'd said that in anger.*

"It might have been the old me, before the war." Morgan reached forward for another scoop of water and drank it. "But I have more conservative lines in my heart and—" he leaned back and raked his hair. "I want to do more to help the poor. Especially the children. I keep thinking of the boy whose tooth I pulled. I should have left him with some powder for the pain. Part of the motivation for the greenhouse. Would you be willing to help me with feverfew, ginger or cloves, anything I can grow myself?"

"Of course." Emery nodded. In her mind's eye, she could almost see the little boy holding a painful, swollen cheek. Morgan could use the medicine for good, for those who had no money. He really was a remarkable person, but would she be here to see anything come to pass?

"When I'm back with my family . . ." A

sudden longing arose and the words caught in her throat. She missed them all painfully. "Oh my." Emery swiped the tears from running down her cheeks. "I . . . I . . ." She gulped down the tightness and pulled on the corner of her skirt, touching the water. "I pictured seeing you walk up with your box of powders and vegetables, all the children clamoring for your attention." She sniffed. "I mean to say, I will be happy to see you do your doctoring when you come."

"And I will be happy to see you." A sweet honesty felt true in his words before he held out his hand and she took it. In spite of the cool dampness, an immediate heat filled her chest as he pulled her to standing. A strange longing to be held caused her body to sway forward. Her extended belly was a wisp away from touching him before the humiliation of her condition startled her back.

"I'm sorry, but there was a sharp rock." Emery broke the moment and pushed from his hand and stepped back. "You were right, this was a lovely place to cool off." Sitting, she brushed the sand from her feet, quickly pulling on her stockings and shoes. Unassuming, Morgan stood close but looked away. Water soaked up his pant leg and dripped down his shirt. His quiet presence made her heartbeat quicken. If she could keep her eyes from his then the flush on her face would have a chance to fade. He extended his hand again.

"Thank you." She took it and Morgan pulled her to standing again. Recognizing the same strength and warmth from his grip, she focused past the awkward sensation in mind and body and released his hand.

Morgan turned and tied the laces of his boots together and tossed them over his shoulder. "Ready?"

"Yes." Emery nodded and followed him out the way they came. Watching him walk through the brush barefoot, she couldn't imagine why she'd teared up so fast. Likely from the picture that flashed in her mind. What if she was back home, helping her mother with the meals and housework? What if the young doctor could come to call? Would they talk like new acquaintances and find favor with one another? Would he want to meet her parents?

Sitting around the crowded family table between their simple English words, would they see his integrity, the kindness and forbearance he'd shown to her? Would he want to court her? Emery fisted her hands in front of her overly extended skirt layers. He should not.

Morgan Hastings should find a pure, lovely young woman from a fine family like his. Watching her steps, she pulled in a deep breath.

It would not be her; that fact, over silly girlish dreams, would keep the tears away.

Morgan waited after his long legs easily stepped over a fallen log. He extended his hand again to help Emery cross. Since she had teared up by the creek, he'd felt too dumbfounded to speak. It seemed to him there had been a moment of tenderness or goodwill between them, but now she quickly dropped his hand and looked stricken with sadness.

Had she already regretted her words to look forward to seeing him after she'd returned to her parents? Although she'd spoken of her plan to return home, he suspected she didn't want her parents to know about the baby. Dare he ask? No, it would be seen as needling. Wasn't it more than obvious she didn't like it when he meddled in her life?

For now, there was an amicable air between them. Just like today, when she'd helped him hold the posts as he pounded them into the ground. They talked about the milking and the making of cheese. As long as Morgan didn't ask anything personal, she'd stayed and helped. Free any moment to go inside and out of the heat, she'd played with the goats and made the day a simple delight for him.

Looking back, he caught her attention. "Thank you for today." He scratched his forehead. "I know I already said that. I just wanted to tell you again."

Her round brown eyes seemed to pull at his senses again until she nodded with a slight grin. "You're welcome."

Twenty-Seven

The next two days afforded the space from Morgan Hastings that Emery needed. Morgan was busy with drawing plans and making supply lists for the greenhouse. He offered to take a list of extra food and any items needed for the baby when he went into Auburn, but she'd given him a polite no thank you, and he seemed not to question more. Maybe his lack of needing to know her every move came from trying to turn over a new leaf, she thought one morning while entering the barn before it got too stuffy. Like her childhood years ago, she enjoyed playing and caring for the goats.

If Morgan only knew her own biggest leaf turning had to do with him. The more he stayed busy, and they didn't talk until dinner every night, something new grew lighter within her. Having her own space all day, she'd found herself eager to speak each evening of the plants needed for medicine and ask about the seeds he'd ordered from San Francisco. She was curious what new fruits or vegetables were for sale at the mercantile. She asked about the news in the paper and about the greatest needs in the mining camps. Sometimes reworking the size and placement for the greenhouse, he'd ask for her thoughts, and they would talk long after Carlotta had gone to bed. Then, usually with a yawn or two, he'd remind her of his full day ahead; he would take the lantern and excuse himself to retire. He would wait in front of his door until she was inside hers. Her quiet room often welcomed her into a new peace, but of late, the summer shadows dropped a strange loneliness in her being.

One day Emery rose early, dressed, and found a shovel from the barn. "Hello, ninnies," she greeted the goats as they clamored against the pen for a treat or her attention. Walking out to the area to the south of the garden, Morgan worked, thrashing away at the brush. "Good morning." She smiled.

"Emery, it's just after dawn." Morgan stopped toiling and wiped his brow. "Are you feeling all right?" He worked in his thin linen undershirt, his exposed skin glistening with perspiration.

"Yes, I feel fine. I came to help clear the area for the greenhouse."

The corner of his mouth lifted a smile, and he squinted at her. "That is very kind, but I don't need any help."

Rolling her eyes, she scanned the area. "Like *I* haven't tried that before."

"Ha!" Morgan's laugh broke open as he sliced the machete into a low bush. Turning to smile at her, he set it down. "Yes, you have." His eyes held a coy enjoyment as he walked closer and took the shovel from her hands. "But you are in no condition to clear brush." About to speak her rebuttal, his finger touched her nose, stopping her. "It will be miserably hot in less than an hour." He nodded once. "I appreciate your willingness to work, but this will not be good for you or the baby." Morgan looked down at her large bump. "I speak just as a doctor." His eyes flashed up, meeting hers. "Could I touch it? I have little experience in obstetrics." He handed her back the shovel.

Emery wondered what that word meant and flinched as his hand came alongside her thick waist. Had she granted him permission? She looked away, embarrassed that someone might see them. This was only Dr. Hastings in his self-assurance causing her airway to freeze solid. Looking down, he pulled his hand across the thick layers and over her belly button. "We only had one class for this in my college for surgeons. Your womb is a lot harder than I imagined," he leaned closer and pushed on the other side. Her chin could drop no further, and neither could her open mouth.

"Providence is endless." His brows narrowed before he brought up his other hand. "A perfect tub of water to float in. Every need met by you." Morgan cradled her belly, and his eyes shot up to hers. "I think I felt something? Did you feel that?"

Of course, she had. Many a night trying to fall asleep, the nuisance had kicked and moved. "No," Emery lied and pushed his chest back until he stepped away.

"It is fascinating." The strange man looked innocent and surprised all at once.

"I'll let you get back to the clearing." Emery looked in a circle, fighting the need to straighten her skirt layers, though he hadn't ruffled anything but her good sense for distance. She walked back to the barn and replaced the shovel.

"And now I can't catch my breath," she said to the goats, feeling her chest rise and fall. "Why does he do this to me?" Emery scratched the blonde and tan one who jumped on the pen.

"What is it about him? Just tell me, please."

Morgan had cleared the greenhouse area to his liking and desired a deep soak before supper. The dirt had likely embedded into the scratches on his arms and chest. They burnt with heat and dry earth. After a walk on the backside of his land, he found a favorite wide spot in the creek. Thankful to be completely alone on his own property, he stripped and sank into the shallow water. The cold bath made his eyes blink wide while it soothed the day's work off his skin. Maybe this is how Emery's baby feels. Morgan flipped, splashed and scrubbed his fingers through his hair until he could take the cold no longer. Shaking the dust from his clothes, he pulled them over his wet skin. Should he volunteer to help with her delivery? A low groan escaped. That would not be wise. She had Carlotta and would not need him.

Her plan to return to her family clouded his mind every day. When would she go? After the baby was born? He stomped back through the brush. The woman lived day in and out in his cabin, he'd a right to know. *Blessed assurance,* he should've never touched the baby this morning. It pulled his heart too close—close to asking her to stay. Stay and be his. He'd be a good husband, a good father, he was sure of it. Taking sight of his humble cabin, Morgan slowed. To bring it up seemed too great a risk. They had fallen into the first true friendship, something he only had the Almighty to thank for.

Sharing and enjoying each other's company, their nightly talks just reinforced the hidden truth—a beautiful, unburdened, caring woman had been in there all along. Glancing over to his cleared area, he huffed. Why had she been standing with her hand on that shovel, round belly poking straight out this morning? Trying to help him? Pulling his hand across his chin,

Morgan pinched his smile. His housemate was adorable.

Emery awoke the next morning and peeked out to see Carlotta in the kitchen. "Have you all eaten?"

"*Sí.*" Carlotta poured her some coffee.

Knowing Morgan was out working, she sat at the table in her nightgown. She had one dress and she could no longer close the buttons. Her skirt's waistband added more weight to what was left of her waist. If it was just her and Carlotta, a simple loose shift would be more comfortable for her girth and summer heat. Holding her warm mug, she stood and walked to the open front door. "I don't see him." Emery waited. There was no movement except the goats chewing the grass. "Has he gone to mine gold this morning?"

"No." Carlotta wiped her hands on her apron. "*Señor* is in bed. Not well."

Emery turned wide-eyed, staring at his closed door. "What's wrong?" Coming back to the table, she set her mug down.

"His skin burns, and he is in pain."

Emery bit the corner of her lip. "Does this happen often?" Stunned, she shook her head. She never noticed his scarring anymore. The heat and work must have irritated it. "What can we do? Does this pain last long?"

"He asked for some soda and a bit of water. I

make a little paste." Carlotta set the bowl on the table. "You see if he's awake."

Emery took the bowl and stood in front of his door. She cracked it open and saw mostly darkness. "Morgan," she whispered.

"Yes." A graveled sound murmured.

"Can I come in?"

"You'd better not," his tone pained. "I'm not presentable."

Emery looked at the bowl and sighed. "I have some soda paste. Carlotta made it. I don't care how you look." She cracked the door a few more inches. His chest was bare, but he had a sheet over his legs. Slowly stepping in, her eyes adjusted to the sliver of morning light coming from under his closed curtain. "Oh, Lord of mercy, Morgan," Emery exclaimed. "What happened?" She leaned closer, his poor skin covered in far more red patches than his burns were responsible for."

"I think I got into some poison oak yesterday." He choked.

"Oh, oh, oh." She cooed and cringed.

"I want to think that behind those lip circles . . . you are *not* laughing?" His swollen eyes glared.

"No, no, never. I . . . I . . . am so sorry." She couldn't help but scan his red and blistered torso; his muscular arms held wide open like they would crack off if he moved. "You don't know what poison oak looks like?"

"I do," he grumbled. "I just thought I'd take a

roll in it to see how it felt to be this miserable." His eyes dropped closed. "I've never cleared brush in my life or made a goat pen or a greenhouse. And I'm probably a poor example of a miner."

"No." Emery still cringed inside. "I . . . how could you know, if you've never worked the land?"

"Now, I feel stupid and emasculated." He croaked.

"Morgan, I'm sorry. What can I do? This paste should help. My brother Arturo has this same reaction." She flung the curtain open, and he winced.

"That does *not* help," Morgan growled, squinting at her.

Emery looked closer. "Your eyes must be burning. Let me get a cool cloth." She found a cloth in the kitchen and dipped it in the bucket of cool water. Coming back into the room, she gently opened it and set it across his eyes.

"Is that better?"

"Yes, except I can't see now. Where is Carlotta? Don't know if I can trust you in my chambers."

Emery rolled her eyes. This irritation now lent him to use poor sarcasm. She'd never been in his room before. There was stacks of books, clothes tossed on the floor, and papers strewn left to right. Looking back at his suffering skin, she drew her finger gently across his forehead, the only area on his face that looked unaffected. "Maybe I can finally steal your gold and be gone from this place."

"You and the Derry brothers would be very happy together."

"I don't think so." She gently adjusted the cool cloth and drew her fingers across his temple and into his hair.

She watched his Adam's apple rise and fall as he swallowed hard. Pulling her fingers through his soft locks was far too tender, but she didn't care.

"You can have my claim and everything I own if you keep doing that," he rasped. "My hair is the only thing that doesn't feel like a swarm of bees had their way with me."

Emery lifted his arm and sat on the edge of his bed, then placed his arm on her lap. Morgan slowly lifted his eye cloth and peered out at her. "Please don't mind my infirmity. Get comfortable."

"Thank you, I will." She trailed her fingers around the back of his ear, pulling more soft brown hair back. *Poor man, even his ears were rough and red.* "You're a bit of a grouchy patient."

"It comes with the profession of doctor." His breath caught and holding the sheet, he inched away from her. "We don't like taking our own advice or medicine."

Leaving the soft strands of his hair, she reached over for the bowl of paste. "Oh yes, Morgan's medicine," she sighed.

"I knew that wouldn't last." Morgan took his eye cloth and flipped it over.

"Half of this rash will be gone by tomorrow." Emery took some paste on her finger and dabbed it between his fingers and in the burning crease of his forearm. "The poison likes the warmest places." Why did her eyes rest on his belly?

He pushed the eye cloth onto his forehead and watched her gentle moves. Delicately, she continued to dab the paste around his neck and reached over his chest to do his other arm and up to his neck and ear. She could see the scarring on his chest under the rough red patches. Poor man. Emery dabbed more over his ribs. There was a tender care, an intimacy, and she enjoyed being the one to—

"Emery." He suddenly grabbed her wrist, almost upsetting the bowl of paste. "You need to stop." His elbow accidentally tapped her swollen belly. "And get out. I need you out of my room now." Morgan's long, red-patched arm pushed her away from the bed. Though she didn't understand, she obeyed the urgency in his tone.

Twenty-Eight

To avoid the afternoon sun, Emery entered the barn. Kicking a pile of hay, she stared at the horse. "I know, you don't have to say it." Flipping her braid from front to back, she turned back to the goats and tried to reason why she was talking to barn animals now. First, she talked to herself as she walked to the creek and back, then to the goats, and now the horse. Emery shook her head and turned in a circle.

"Don't look at me that way," she said, scowling to her little blonde, horned friend. "I could have you roasted over a spit." The sweet round eyes and narrow hairy face nudged closer. "I know it wasn't right." Dropping her head side to side, she rubbed her neck. No wonder he'd kicked her from his room. He should ban her from the house too. "I didn't want to be this way." Pursing her lips, she glanced down at her belly.

A lonely pregnant woman teasing a man, freely running her fingers through his hair, like some wanton hussy. Groaning, her shoulders slumped. Sitting there in her nightgown, could she increase her shame any more than she had this morning? Maybe if she held him down and kissed him. He could do nothing, not even resist. The man was pained and helpless, and she'd practically jumped on him. Oh Lord, the ridiculous scene flashed before her. Another groan escaped as her hand covered her face, her reckless behavior humiliating her from head to toe.

"Emery."

She spun and covered her mouth, praying he'd not heard her ramblings. Morgan stood slightly bent forward, his shirttails hanging loose around his pant suspenders.

Her face flushed three deep colors of red. "You look better." Her eyes barely flashed to him and then the ground.

"Thank you for your ministrations. I think they helped."

A weak croak rose up in the back of her throat, but she pushed it down. Maybe it meant nothing, and they could pretend she never sat on his bed, touching him. "The goats are well," Emery huffed, wondering why that made any difference. *Did it just get even stuffier in here?*

"I just wanted to apologize for earlier." He blinked and stiffened his shoulders. "I sounded rude and—"

"No, no." She batted her hand in the air and bent over the pen to scratch the goat's chin. "I realized too late that I was being rude." Emery chuckled, shaking her head. "Well, I didn't intend to be." She smiled at him, and his warm eyes seemed to draw her back to his bedroom. "You told me not to come in, and I . . . *humph* . . . just barged right in." Another strange chuckle came from her that sounded nothing like her. The nosy blonde goat came up to lick her hand. "Anyway, this morning's over and done with." She patted the goat and straightened up. "Ow." She clutched under her belly.

"Are you having pains?" He stepped inside.

"No. It's nothing." Rubbing her hand over her hip, the pinch faded.

"I've tried not to ask you," Morgan said gently. "But you said when you return to Eureka Creek, you might see me there."

"I did." The goat's hooves pounded on the pen. "Go on now." She flung her hand at them. "There's nothing for you." She glanced at Morgan. "I should have never started bringing them scraps, now they're little beggars." Maybe, just maybe, he would leave well enough alone. Before she could ramble about anything else—

"Are you going home to have the baby?" He came out with it. "Soon—or when your time is near?" He rested his hand above his head, gripping the wooden beam, and silence filled the stuffy barn. "If I made it sound like you needed to be here to help me with the greenhouse, please know it's not as important as what you need."

"I know." Folding her arms across her chest, squeezing her elbows, she tried to ignore the patch of red skin his raised shirt revealed. "But . . . uh . . . I've made up my mind. I had a lot of time to think, working at So Chen's." Her hand rose to scratch her chin. She refused to look at him. "I'm taking the baby to Sacramento. I know of a charity home that will take it. I have the address. It's on Oak Street. Oak Street in Sacramento." Suddenly her mouth turned dry, and she felt lightheaded. "I need some water. You're right, the heat can be difficult." Dare she drop those words and stroll right by him?

"I'll get you some." Morgan stepped back. "There's an afternoon breeze and shade on the porch. Sit on the bench. I'll be right back." He turned and walked away before she could refuse.

Emery ground out a low groan and walked to the bench.

Heaven above, she was going to have to tell him sooner than later. Why not now? The day couldn't get any more outlandish if she'd planned it. Morgan came out the door with a cup of water, his brows creased with thought, yet little judgment. Handing her the water, he pulled the cotton shirt away from his skin. Fanning it back and forth, Morgan closed his eyes.

"Anything to cool the skin." He smiled. His patchy red cheek creased painfully.

Emery remembered their lighthearted banter in his room. "You should go in, Morgan. Really, we can talk later."

"No, I'm fine." Sitting next to her gazing

out across the dry grass, he finally spoke. "In Sacramento, you will leave the baby? You don't want to keep it?" Morgan glanced over his shoulder to meet her eyes, but she looked away.

"I don't. I don't want to have anything to do with Arnold Snider." Just his name on her lips, even after all these months, made her gut twist. "I can leave it and not look back." Emery took another drink, the water catching in her tight throat. "And I know that sounds cruel." She notched her shoulder up. "But these towns are small, and people know people. Word could get out to him about me having a baby, and then what would I do? Hide and run my whole life?"

Morgan gripped the bench front and back and rocked forward. "What if you were to give the baby not to a stranger, but to someone you knew?"

"Like my mother?" She shook her head and allowed her shoulders to slump. "All I ever wanted was to see Gianna safe." Her soft tone laced with desperation. "Not to shame my family further."

"No, I meant me."

Emery flinched and squinted at him. "You can't care for an infant."

"Why not? Anyone can learn a new skill." He fanned his shirt from his skin. "I'm learning that I'm allergic to poison oak."

"You're not a woman. They will find a mother

and father for the baby." She rolled her eyes at his foolish suggestion.

"With me, you can go to your family and yet see the baby whenever you want. It is half of you. It could be a girl who looks just like you."

"No, that would never work." Emery shuddered. She would not picture little eyes with a tiny nose and mouth. Especially a little girl who had her features.

Morgan gently touched her back and made little circles with his fingers. "Would you just think about it? I would have Carlotta to help me."

What a risk-taker he was, beginning to knead the tight skin and muscles up and down her spine. She should pull away from his—*oh, the tingling in her lower back.* Like heaven had come down, she closed her eyes. *What were they speaking of?*

"I can think about . . . it." Now the back of her legs tingled with feathery delight.

He tipped his head, smiling. "Thank you." Morgan carefully held his arm around her, pulled her close, and placed a gentle kiss on her cheek. Surprised by his kindness, even forbearance, she leaned back and stared at him.

"My lips are the only thing that doesn't sting." His eyes teased, and he tapped them lightly.

Emery stared mesmerized at him and felt the strangest sensation swirling inside of her. Just for a split second, it felt like she was just a girl sitting on a bench with a boy. Desiring and wondering what her first kiss would feel like. The light giddiness was real, it was tangible, and for just a few more moments, its effects lingered. With no job on a ship from hell, no family to disappoint, no baby crowded in her womb . . . just a girl who loved a boy.

"I look hideous, I know. You're staring at my thorn patch of a face." Morgan winced, moving his jaw back and forth.

Emery blinked and moved from his hold. "No, I . . . I guess your idea just caught me completely off guard." Or *a girl could love a boy.* Except she was no longer a doe-faced teen. Standing, she brushed her hands past the round bump in her skirt. Womanhood and all its burdens had been thrust upon her. Squaring her shoulders, she swallowed the last bit of water and consoled herself. Her one resolve hadn't been challenged. Emery was resolute, she would *not* be a mother to this immoral remembrance.

Twenty-Nine

At dusk later in the week, Morgan brought his tools back into the barn. He'd completed the wood frame for the greenhouse. After rocking the walls and testing the roof, it seemed sturdy enough for the California winters. Dropping his gloves on the workbench, he stepped out and turned to admire it. Its size was a fourth of the barn, but it was something he'd built with his own two hands. Surgeon to the simple country doctor, now a miner turned carpenter. The glass windows would be his next challenge. Starting across the dry grass to the cabin, Morgan stopped and turned around. The brown covered package from the mercantile still lay under a canvas in the barn. Should he just get it and bring it inside?

The poor young woman he shared his cabin with often held her back and swayed when she walked. Even getting up from the kitchen table proved difficult for her to maneuver. Wisely Carlotta had told him to buy new flannel and two yards of cotton for the baby when he was in town last, but they agreed to leave it alone until Emery asked. The goodwill and ease between them had stayed strong, but she'd not responded to his idea to adopt the baby as his own. She had not flatly rejected it, either. Many a night, Morgan lay awake and wondered what had possessed him to make that offer.

If Emery wanted nothing to do with it and he was to raise the child, would that keep her from wanting to know him—ruin the opportunity to be more than friends? Blowing out a breath, he headed for the cabin door. Was he hoping to give her time to change her mind and keep the baby? Carlotta had said that if Emery didn't take to her own infant right away, likely she never would.

Morgan held the porch post and looked up to see the first star in the dark blue sky. What were the words he'd read last night in the Psalms? God would heal the brokenhearted and bind up their wounds; how great is the Lord who calls each star by name.

Closing his eyes, he raked his hands through his hair. Morgan certainly believed God could do anything, but stubborn women had a will all their own.

The next morning he found Emery on the east side of the creek, picking wild raspberries.

She turned as he approached. "I need to go back to town. I'm short four pieces of lumbered wood for the casings."

"All right." She nodded.

"Can I get anything else? Anything you might need?" His stomach did a strange squeeze. She'd a different glow of late, always soft and pretty, seemingly without a care in the world; the sunlight played off some coppery strands entwined with her coffee brown hair. "You only ask for food supplies for us." Morgan stepped closer and rested his hand on the back of her neck. *Would she ask for baby items?* "What about something for you?" He gave her a slight squeeze. "A lavender soap for your girly skin or maybe a new ribbon?" He grabbed the end of her long braid and tickled her ear with it.

"Noo." She shrugged from his teasing, smiling. "I don't need anything."

Letting it be, Morgan dropped her braid and stepped away. "You won't stay in the sun too long?"

"Yes, I mean no, Dr. Hastings." She popped a berry in her mouth and smirked wide eyes at him. Morgan tried to give her a stern look, but his face broke out in a wide smile. As he reached for the bucket, she pulled it away, and they laughed as she twisted from his touch. Forget it. He was going to take her in his arms and . . . his eyes bounced to her round belly, and when their eyes met, the moment was broken.

"You'd better be on your way." Her smile was gone and the light had faded from her eyes. In a split second, she'd pulled the bucket to herself and returned to the berry bushes.

Excusing himself, Morgan couldn't curtail the tension in his limbs, so he jogged back to the barn.

Had he lost his entire sense of right and wrong? Jerking the horse from the stall, he squeezed the bridle. Why had he gone to So Chen's that day? Was he so lonely he'd resorted to chasing a pregnant woman around these rustic mining towns? A woman who was clearly determined to stay bound in her past? Why couldn't he keep to his own business?

As he passed, five rows of little upstarts peeked out of the burlap and dirt on the workbench. Their late summer planting was working. Morgan raked his fingers through his hair and dropped his wide-brimmed hat on his head. He was a man who liked results. Unwittingly beautiful and reserved, Emery was working his patience thin. Yet he was one who'd spend hours to gain the tiniest flakes of gold from a wide creek?

After washing the berries, Emery laid them out on a dark towel to dry. Carlotta worked on a simple pie crust. They spoke back and forth in Spanish as they often did when Morgan wasn't around. Emery wondered if it was a bit of comfort for both of them. They decided to bake later when the sun went down. Emery sat. She hadn't slept well; even sleeping on her side, she could find no comfortable position. Taking the towel by the corners, she rolled the berries into a bowl and slid it to Carlotta.

"I'll get the laundry off the line and then find

some long grass to take to the goats." Emery nodded to Carlotta before she grasped the table and back of her seat and rose carefully. The cramping in her back lessened as she stood; the small kitchen chairs were of no comfort.

Emery tossed the pins in an old can. At least the laundry was not by the potful. Shaking her head at the hours she worked for So Chen, her back had ached even then. She snapped a dishrag and folded it, dropping it in her basket. With little effort, she hoisted the basket with dry items to her left hip and set them on the porch. A walk to the creek for the best tall grass, and her goats would thank her.

Minutes later, while searching for one thicker clump, Emery heard a branch snap and turned. Morgan was probably looking for her, ready to scold her for being out in the heat. Stepping out from the banks, a horse and rider came near. It was not Morgan, and the man approaching made her drop her grassy bundle. Abner? Clayton? Before his eyes bore into hers, she grabbed her skirts and ran.

"Morgan!" She screamed and wrapped her arm around her bouncing girth. "Morgan, help!" The horse came closer and almost knocked her over. The twin pulled the mount tight in front of her.

"Ma'am! Don't run!" He jumped down and tried to grab her. Emery spun around the horse, trying to find a clearing. Running and stumbling between the trees, she clung on to thin saplings before falling over onto her hands and knees.

"Stay away from me!" She panted, trying to crawl away. "I . . . I . . . know who you are." That crooked nose—would she ever forget? Breathless, she wondered if she could find the air to stand and run again.

"I ain't gonna hurt ya, Missy." Abner stood over her with wide eyes. "I thought you was the doc."

Emery felt her belly pinch so hard it almost brought her into a ball. "Get away . . . he's not here." She moaned. *Oh Lord, that was the wrong thing to say.*

"I ain't gonna take you anywhere. We's come to see the doc. Me and Clayton." Abner held his hand up. "I promise ya."

"Ahhh." Emery groaned, grabbing her side.

"Let me help yer now. Yer in a bad way." He reached forward.

"Stay back!" Emery panted, grabbing a thick branch by her feet. "I will beat you with this."

"Whoa now. I told ya, I ain't gonna hurt you."

"I wouldn't believe a word from your mouth." The branch shook in her hand as she pointed it at him. "Another scheme for gold?" She winced with another pain. "Come to put me back where you found me? Stupid oafs." Emery rolled to her knees and pushed off the ground. "I told you he'd give you nothing, certainly no gold for me."

Flames for eyes locked on him as she pushed down the moan that tried to rise from her waist straight out of her mouth.

"Now you don't have to do no name callin'," Abner frowned. "We done found out, we was wrong."

"You were more than wrong!" Emery screeched and gripped the muscles twisting in her side. "You left my sister on that ship!" With new resolve and the branch raised, a swift slam to the head would stop this conversation. "What would she do without me?" Her rage crackled. "Who would protect her?"

Abner held up his hands and took two steps forward. "I . . . I . . . didn't know you had a sister."

"Stay!" Emery pulled the branch back, justice wanting to knock his nose crooked in the other direction. Abner lunged for it. "Noo," she squealed as he grabbed her and the branch. Wrestling the branch between them, she pushed at his thick chest with all her might. Suddenly, he let go, and she fell hard onto her backside.

"Morgan!" Pain radiated up and down her back. She screamed his name again. "Morgan!" There was nothing else she could do.

Thirty

Morgan's stomach leaped to his throat, and he jumped down from the bench and tied the wagon to the front post. The other horse, weighted heavy with packs and mining tools, looked familiar. He flung open the door to see Clayton sitting at his table, sipping a drink with Carlotta.

"Hey, Doc." Clayton lifted a wave. "Carlotta was just telling me what's new here with ya'll."

Morgan ignored him and looked in Emery's room, finding it empty. "Carlotta, where is she?"

"Down at the creek, I think, or feeding the goats."

Morgan looked around again. "Where is Abner?" The two rarely ever separated.

"Ahhh, I think he was takin' the horses for a drink."

Morgan spun on his heel and ran towards the creek. There was no extra horse to be seen, but a distant screech rent the air.

"Emery!" Yelling her name, he picked up the pace. Just past the brown horse grazing, he saw her on the ground and Abner standing a few feet away. Red-faced and panting, Morgan raced to her side. "What happened?"

"I'd tried to—" Abner spoke.

"Shut up." Morgan pulled the brown wisps

from Emery's sweaty face. "What happened? Emery, talk to me."

She released a relieved sob and gripped his shirt until she could wrap her arms around his neck. "Please, help me," Emery panted in his ear. With his help, she tried to stand up. As soon as she stood, he could see the pain and strain on her face.

"Here, hang on to my neck." Morgan swept her up in his arms and started marching back through the woods.

"You can put her on my horse," Abner called after them before they said "no" in unison.

"What happened?" Morgan tried to settle his pounding heart.

"I . . . I . . . he scared me. I . . . I . . . didn't know if he was coming to take me." She gripped his full shoulders tighter. "I just kept screaming your name until . . . thank God, you came."

He pulled her upward and pressed her damp cheek with a kiss. "Are you hurt or just scared?"

"I fell while running. I don't know, my back's been hurting all day and now it feels like someone is pulling my skin apart."

"Where does this pulling pain you?" He rounded the corner to the barn and sat her on a wood box. Released from his hold, she tried to stretch her back from side to side. "It starts in my back and then pulls hard around my belly."

He ran to get the dipper from the water bucket.

"Drink. You're flushed with heat." He looked behind them. "Listen to me. The Derry boys aren't taking you anywhere. They likely didn't know you were here, so they didn't come for you."

She scooped the water and patted it on her face. "You're sure?"

"Yes, they probably thought I'd cooled off after all these months, and we could be friends again."

"Oh, now I feel ridiculous." Emery unbuttoned her top buttons. "I almost thrashed one of them with a branch." She tried to fan her blouse in and out. "Oww." She winced, holding her side. "Please, Lord." Dropping her head to the side, she groaned. "Not this."

"You've seen this before?" Concern lined his face as he knelt on one knee in front of her.

"Yes." She whimpered. "I don't remember Gianna's birth, but I tried to help my mommi when her time came for the boys." Distraught, she ran her hand down his face. "I can't do it, Morgan." She cried, holding his jaw, pressing her fingers behind his ear. "I don't want this child. I . . . I'm not strong enough. There is too much hate—"

He held her wrist and gently dropped his forehead on hers. "You'll never be alone. Not for a minute." He kissed her damp cheekbone. "I will help you."

"The only thing I want . . ." Her eyes pleaded,

inches from his. "If I die, tell my family I love them." Emery sucked in a tearful sob. "If you really want, you can raise the baby. You're such a good man."

Her words swirled inside his head. *A good man. Why couldn't she see him as* her *man?* "You're not going to die, Emery. I won't let that happen."

Her color heightened to a deep red, and she closed her eyes. "Please, Morgan." Her mouth opened with the pain, but no sound came out. Her deep brown eyes suddenly flashed on his. "Just say you will."

"Yes, of course." Standing, he gently rubbed her back until her shoulders relaxed. Peering over his shoulder out the barn door to his cabin, he shook his head. "I picked this place for peace and quiet." Suppressing a grin, his tone was light-hearted. "I should've known better." Morgan leaned forward and scooped her in his arms. "I think you are about to bring forth another guest."

Hours later, Morgan paced back and forth, listening and watching through the crack in the door. *"Ponte de rodillas."* Carlotta pulled on her arm, telling her to get on her knees. Emery moaned and turned her awkward body on the bed. She'd been laboring on her back all afternoon, and Morgan thought it must have brought a moment of reprieve to be on all fours. Just as he thought she was going to have a break, another pain started in her back and pulled her to her side.

Carlotta rubbed her back through her nightgown as Emery cried out. "It didn't help, my bones and skin are separating." In between sobs she yelled, "I can't do this! Please make it stop, *oh Dios, oh Dios*." She grabbed Carlotta's arm. "Please get Morgan. Tell . . . tell him to give me something . . . please, Carlotta."

"*Bueno*." Carlotta went out of the bedroom door, and Morgan jumped back from where he'd been listening. "She must be close?"

Carlotta shrugged. "By nightfall or dawn."

Morgan rubbed his head and turned in a circle. "Dawn? Good Lord." He frowned, pretending he hadn't heard the request for him. Reaching for the package from the barn on the table, he unwrapped it. "What do you want with this?" Unsure, he held up the fabric. "I could cut it into diapers or blankets. What size is a diaper? Do we have pins?"

His last question froze in the air as they stilled. Another long guttural moan came from the bedroom. Carlotta pointed to the fabric and drew a line where he could cut. "Where are those twins?"

"I sent them to town. I told them to buy a cradle and some baby gowns. They owe her that much." Scratching the top of his head, he frowned. "I should have told them pins."

"*Sí.*" Carlotta nodded, sitting at the table. "Oh, she wants to see you."

"Me?" Morgan touched his chest, faking ignorance.

"Do you know any other doctors she ask for?"

"Well, no. I . . . I . . . didn't think." He turned to wash his hands. "Studies have shown that the washing of hands has reduced the birthing fever, so com—" Another low groan radiated through the wall, making him freeze. "In college, I only observed a doctor helping with a birth. A clinical sort of class setting." Continuing to scrub, he rambled on. "With midwives and other womenfolk, there isn't much need to—"

"You going to take the skin off those hands?" Carlotta's droopy, aged eyes widened. "Or do you just want to diddle-daddle about nothing?"

"No, Carlotta." He scowled and dried his hands on a towel.

"You no need to worry. She kick you out soon." Carlotta poured herself some water and sat down.

Morgan went to Emery's door with his clean hands and hesitantly turned the handle.

"Emery?" He carefully stepped inside. The ragged haired young woman sat on the edge of the bed in her white nightgown, with her chin dropped to her chest.

She sucked in a breath. "Morgan, please." Whining, she held out her hand, and he took it.

Opening her mouth to speak, her face turned red, puckering up with pain. He could tell she forcefully held back the groan. Suddenly *he* was about to cry out as she crushed his fingers within her vice grip.

With the smallest release, he pulled his hand free and shook it in the air. "What can I do?" *Without holding your hand.* He moved his fingers; they all worked.

Emery panted and rolled her head side to side. "Help me to stand. I want to walk."

Timidly, Morgan took her elbow and wrist and walked her around some small circles. Ignoring the words of Carlotta, he said, "I'm sure you are close."

"I thought that an hour ago." Growling, she glared up from her bent-over state. "I told you I couldn't do this." She panted. "Do you have medicine? Please Morgan, anything to make this stop."

"Chloroform. I used it in the war as a mild anesthetic. Ronald and my father actually enjoyed the chemical sciences more than I did. I've got a medical journal that named Dr. Holmes from the Harvard Medical School for his contribution to its uses. Besides brilliant, the man was a great scientist just based on others' description, analysis, and anecdotes."

She stopped walking and sneered up at him.

"It *is* interesting." He flinched. "It entails a

process of distilling alcohol and bleaching power and afterward purifying the distillate—"

"Do you have any?" She brayed, eyes pleading. "Even alcohol." Her face began to twitch and turn red.

"No, neither." Morgan inched back from her flaring nostrils.

Her eyes widened and then pinched tight. Leaning her hand into the wall, a low groan started in the back of her throat and continued deeper until Morgan felt himself gripping her arm. "Come back to the bed." He turned her, hearing her grind out some low unpleasant words in Spanish.

"The American Indian women labor silently and find the squatting position helpful." Once again, he knew he rambled about something he'd only read. Maybe a bit of distraction would help. "Women don't remember the pain after the infant has been delivered."

"Is that so?" Her head snapped up, and her eyes carried flaming arrows. With his help, she carefully sat on the edge of the bed.

"Yes. In other countries, a woman labors without fanfare, delivers, straps the infant to her chest, and goes on about caring for the family. Meals, I suppose, household duties." He scratched his head. "Likely no heavy lifting or anything too strenuous."

Emery took another strained gasp and dropped

her head back. The vexation on her face made him quickly lean back.

"I said in other countries," he murmured. "For you, that . . . that . . . would not be so."

Her head tilted forward. "This is all nonsense and provides me no help at all!" She cried. "Get out!" Pointing to the door, her arm trembled. "Just do it, before I strike you. Get far, far away. I don't care to ever hear your babbling again."

Thirty-One

Morgan awoke at daybreak. He'd been dreaming of poison oak spread across his body again. Blinking, he brushed the drool and hay off his cheek. He'd slept in the barn? The Derry brothers were asleep strewn across the sides of the entrance. Morgan remembered. He couldn't take another minute hearing Emery in such pain, and the boys were only too happy to join him in the smelly barn. He listened, no screaming, but hadn't he asked Carlotta to come for him after the birth?

Morgan stood, brushing the hay from his clothes. Was everything over? Reaching for the water barrel, he splashed some on his face. A strange pounding knocked in his chest as he walked closer and carefully entered his cabin. The thick rounded walls were too quiet. The floor creaked when he peeked around the kitchen wall and saw Carlotta asleep in her bed. Lifting his sleeve to his damp face, he listened. Why hadn't she awakened him? Morgan blew out a faint breath and stepped quietly.

The stillness choked him, what could have happened? He carefully pulled the handle to Emery's room and leaned in. She lay flat on her back. Too motionless and too pale. A long line of sunshine lay on her floor. "Oh, Jesus." Locking his jaw, he stepped inside. Nothing but a small pink round face with closed eyes lay in silence deep in the folds of her blanket. Would Carlotta tuck the infant in the crook of Emery's arm if it was dead?

"Morgan," she whispered as her sleepy eyes blinked up at him.

His shoulders relaxed, and he lifted a faint smile. "There you are."

"Humph. You left me after you said you'd never leave me?" Her voice was dry and gravelly.

"But you kicked me out." He scrutinized her with a slight smile.

"I did." Emery frowned. "And I suppose now I should tie the infant to my chest and jump up and fix your breakfast." She looked down at what lay next to her. "It's a boy," she said cheerlessly.

"Can I see him?" Morgan sat on the corner of her bed and leaned over her.

"Go ahead. He's all yours." She pulled her arm and the baby up toward him.

He sat up straight and watched the infant move his head side to side. Did she mean what she just said? Feeling the babe's weight in his hands, a peculiar connection swirled in him—brand new life. What an amazing miracle. Laying the bundle on his closed knees, he lifted a silent prayer of thanks. Unwrapping him, the baby flinched arms left to right. "That's good. He's small, but his color looks good." His cotton diaper was knotted on the sides. He supposed Carlotta knew things his generation would never think of.

"He looks like a dried-up grape. With arms and legs." Emery pulled another pillow behind her head.

"Have you fed him?" Morgan touched his tiny feet and pulled his legs back and forth.

"No." She pulled her loose hair behind her ears, watching as Morgan gently pushed on the baby's belly.

"I think he has your coloring. And look at these little dark hairs. So much like yours." Morgan ran his finger along the base of the baby's head. The infant seemed healthy and formed without harm. The tiny baby cracked open round, dark eyes. "Oh, oh, look at him looking at me. Yes, little man, I'm the one poking and prodding you." Morgan smiled. "How do you like the world and my humble cabin?" The baby's tiny arm and fist bounced off his little face, and he curled his limbs up. "One of my professors said the human is the only species born early. Because of our skulls and brains." Morgan inspected the tiny fingers gripping around his thumb. "Think of the other animals. Horses, cows, dogs all are up and moving after birth." Morgan meticulously wrapped the baby tight. "But human infants need to be kept in a womb-like state. He won't walk for at least a year."

"I know a few things, Morgan. I am the firstborn daughter of a large family." Emery yawned.

Morgan nodded, unable to quit staring at the little helpless round eyes looking up at him. "What will you name him?"

"I don't . . . know." Sighing, she looked away. "I guess I don't care. You name him."

"Humm." Morgan held the baby up close and looked him over. "We . . . could name him after my brother, Ronald."

Emery turned, frowning. "I don't like it. It sounds too much like Arnold."

Morgan nodded, agreeing. "And I suppose Abner or Clayton is out?" Her frown dropped lower and he gave a light chuckle. "What about after your father?"

"No," she said firmly.

"Maybe a strong Bible name? Like Peter or James?"

"No." Emery sulked.

"How about Flynn? That was my brother's middle name."

Emery smirked and shook her head. "It sounds too close to Finny."

"Who's Finny?"

"Arnold's wife," she droned.

"Oh. Well, I'm glad you don't care." Morgan rolled his eyes. "It's making this so *easy*." He bent forward, dropping a kiss on the baby's forehead. "How about . . . Augustus?"

Emery shrugged. "It's a bold name for a little skinny plum." She dipped her head to the side. "I guess that's all right."

"It's my middle name." He glanced at her. "The name of my grandfather on my mother's side."

Something stilled in her sour expression. "It's up to you. I like it well enough."

Morgan nodded. "Baby Gus, have you the pleasure of meeting this beautiful woman formally? Her name is Emery." Morgan turned the bundle to face her and gave her a thoughtful expression. "May he call you Emery?"

Her eyes drooped, and slowly she turned onto her side to face them. "After what he put me through, he should call me Saint Emery."

Before Morgan could agree, Baby Gus let out a squeal, turning his face into the blanket. The tiny peanut quaked and let out another cry.

"The infant's nursing will actually help the womb with bleeding and closure." Morgan lightly jostled him as he stole a glance at Emery. "Just for your health and wellbeing." Baby Gus fussed louder.

"How could you have been a surgeon when you know *everything* about birthing and women? You certainly missed your calling." Sighing, she took the baby from his hands and settled it in the crook of her arm. "Do you suppose I could feed him without your advice?" Emery began to undo the top buttons on her nightgown.

Morgan stared soberly at his empty hands, then watched her loosen the gown and felt a strange warmth rise from his toes. "Of course, just by being born female, you know instinctively . . ."

"I think you should go check on your greenhouse or something." Emery tried to arrange the hungry babe closer and pulled her gown off her shoulder.

"Maybe I should stay." His thoughts rolled out as words. "In case you need anything."

"Morgan." Her tone was brisk.

"Yes, I'm leaving. I'll start your breakfast as you take a moment to feed baby Gus. And I want you to stay abed all day." Standing, he reluctantly left, gently closing the door behind him. He'd the strangest desire to kiss them both before leaving.

Morgan blew out a long-held breath as he walked to the kitchen. He was just thankful, that's all. After such a rough night, she seemed fine. The baby as well. *And* she was speaking to him. *And* she'd agreed to feed the tiny little thing.

This was going to be a good day.

Thirty-Two

Growing up in Chicago, Morgan had been blessed with many fine Christmas gifts, but today felt like no other day. The Derry brothers had brought the cradle into the house. It was a deep, dark pine with curved edges and a stand that allowed it to rock or keep still. In the bottom were five baby gowns and a tiny cradle cap. It was hard not to be amazed at the simple-minded brothers' excellent choices. He fought an unexplainable smile as they ate their fill of eggs, beans, and tortillas.

"Carlotta," Abner said as she poured him more coffee. "Now that Doc's got a family, I don't think he needs you. You would do well to come with us. Cook and—"

Carlotta scowled and shook her head. "I like a roof and my bed."

Morgan smiled at the banter. He wished Emery and baby Gus were his real family, but maybe Emery had only agreed to be the wet nurse. She was right, as usual. He would have trouble feeding and taking care of an infant.

"So you goin' back to doctoring, Doc?" Abner gulped his coffee.

Morgan wished there was something in his life that wasn't in limbo. "Just a bit here and there. I can supply some simple remedies for the children around the mining camps. Emery's got a gift for growing plants and herbs. If she stays." The moment and room silenced. These were the men that kidnapped her from that ship and dumped her on his doorstep. Should he still be angry or thankful? "I'm not giving up my mining claim as of yet."

The brothers nodded, and they all looked at each other wide-eyed. A healthy infant squall was heard from the next room.

"Got good lungs!" Clayton exclaimed. "That's a good sign."

Morgan glanced at the tray he'd prepared earlier. When he'd peeked in, they were both asleep. Carlotta read his mind and took the tray. "I go see."

Later in the afternoon, after mining, Morgan was ready to hike back to the cabin. He'd trouble focusing on much. The Derry brothers' muscle was appreciated as they dug deep and sifted the layered rock and dirt. They found some luck in a few areas, and Morgan was happy for them. Years ago, they were barely whiskered teens, leaving everything to fight the Mexicans. Now they had thickened out, worked hard, and talked just as hard. Their jabbering was distracting.

Morgan pondered how long he could hold their past stupidity against them. They'd lost their hard-earned gold in the Hangtown bankruptcy the same day Arnold Snider disappeared. Though they thought their plan was justified, they had kidnapped the wrong woman. They also had, unknowingly, removed Emery from her nightmare.

Morgan stepped from the cold water and began to replace his stockings. The twins would be on their way tomorrow, but then what would the next weeks hold? Would Emery insist on taking the baby to Sacramento and return to her family?

He blew out a tired huff. "I'm heading back," Morgan called to them.

"We'll be along shortly." Abner looked up from where he swung a pick into a large rock. "Tell Carlotta not to burn the beans." He laughed.

Morgan hoisted his mining bag over his shoulder and headed out. *Beans.* Funny, when that's all you know, that's all you expect.

Emery was an excellent cook. There wasn't one meal that wasn't different and flavorful. *With her knowledge of goats and cheese and milk . . .* he stopped. His desires, his expectations were always dangling, waiting to be snipped away. Something turned in his stomach besides hunger. The cabin full of people, the cradle awaiting the sweet baby Gus, Emery's company, and help around the place—it had turned his life around. He'd pulled away to this seclusion to nurse his past, and yet today his life was more purposeful than he could even imagine.

Morgan spotted a tall grove of aspens that curved in a way that looked like God's own chapel in the woods. Walking over to where the breeze danced through the high leaves, he dropped his bag. Standing in the middle of the trees, he bent one knee and knelt. Leaning his elbow on his knee and then his face to his palm, he prayed. "I surrender, Lord. I can't beg, I can't force anything. You see the cry of my heart. Please, God, take all this . . . this . . ." There were no words, so he looked straight up through the canopy of leaves to the blue sky, feeling the resignation inside. "Give me the strength and grace to accept whatever may come," he whispered. "Amen."

After washing up from the chores, he asked Carlotta how the afternoon went.

"Fine," she reported. The woman had less information with each year she aged.

The Derry brothers entered and clamored around the table. They finally sat and began to talk about the gold flecks they'd found and where they were off to next.

Morgan saw Emery's door open from the corner of his eye and stood quickly. Resembling the gentle young woman he remembered, she stepped out, dressed, with her hair braided. Her chin was tucked, touching the blanket around the baby swaddled against her chest. Below that, her swollen belly was missing.

His feet wouldn't move until he willed them to her side. "How are you doing?"

"Better." Her eyes flicked on his only for a second.

Her color had improved. "You must be hungry. Come sit in my chair." He touched her elbow.

Her eyes downcast, she glanced at his full table, and her lips twitched to the side. They were all staring at her.

"Let me show you something." Morgan stepped back and revealed the cradle sitting in his front room.

"Oh, Morgan." Her eyebrows drew together, and the strange pained expression wasn't what he was expecting.

"I didn't get it, they did." Morgan picked up one of the tiny gowns. "These will work, won't they?"

She slowly nodded, and her eyes began to pool. "It's very kind."

Though it sounded like the others had gone back to eating, Morgan had the worst desire to shield her from any more pain. Inept as to what she needed, he placed his arm across her back and softly embraced mother and child. Two thick tears rolled down her cheeks. "What?" He kissed her hairline. "Tell me," he whispered.

Her chin quivered against his chest, and she swiped her tears with the corner of the blanket. Taking a long sniff inward, she swallowed hard. "I don't deserve any kindness."

Morgan knew this undeserving pit she felt. How did he survive the war when so many fathers and sons did not? Not even his own brother. Honestly, there were no words to heal the depth of unworthiness. His chest rose and fell, and he gently gave her a squeeze.

"Let's see if Master Augustus likes his stately cradle." Morgan held his hands out, and Emery carefully handed the baby to him and he laid him down. They both stood over the tiny sleeping baby. "See here." Morgan bent over and pulled on a wooden dowel. "Now, you can rock it." He lightly rocked it side to side. "Then put this back, and it will hold it still." Morgan grinned. The sleeping baby's lip twitched. "I think he likes it."

Carlotta spoke something in Spanish, and Emery looked over, nodding. "*Sí.*"

"You speak Mexican?" Abner asked her.

"Some Spanish. My people are Basque," she answered.

Both brothers nodded, wide-eyed. "We hail from Kentucky," Clayton said. "Carlotta got a good pot of beans, miss." He lifted the spoon.

Emery took a last look at Gus before stepping over to the table. Reluctantly, she sat.

"Morgan tells us you are a good cook yourself." Abner nodded.

"Eh," Carlotta stood, shrugging her shoulder.

"You sit here, *señor*." She gestured to Morgan. "I'm finished."

Morgan sat. His tiny kitchen and table had never been so crowded.

"Does the doc tell ya stories of the war?" Abner asked Emery.

"No, not really." Emery covered her mouth as she chewed.

"Not many good ones to tell, eh, Doc?" Clayton blew out a sigh and scooped more beans onto a tortilla. "He did give us a poke with that sharp needle. Many men were getting the sickness and the doc told us it would help." Clayton stopped chewing and stared at him. "You were right, and we never spent one day in a sickbed."

Morgan gave them a brief nod, and Emery waited for him to spout off about the benefits of the new inoculations or some medical fact. Funny how he couldn't stop reciting information when she was laboring. The very painful experience she had yet to forget. Now, though, he seemed reserved and quiet.

For a moment, she watched him eat. The way he'd reached around her and held her close moments ago. Likely his brain was as big as his heart. Taking another bite, she didn't want any more sappy moments. The birthing was over, and despite her wish to die and stop the pain, she'd endured. The menace that had taken over her body without want or love now lay alive and well in the wooden cradle. Before Morgan had come in this morning, she'd unwrapped him from Carlotta's tight bindings. There was no flood of mothering, no attraction for his wrinkled body. He looked just like her little brothers after they were born.

Hungry and gasping, he didn't take to the breast right away. Carlotta had warned her that, at first, he might need to be coaxed. Emery glanced up to where Carlotta started more hot water on the stove. The elderly woman had stayed with her into the night, eventually cutting the cord and giving him a light bath. She'd helped Emery with a rag for the bleeding, tucked her in, lay the baby in the crook of her arm, and said good night. Emery was exhausted and wide awake all at the same time, laying alone in the dark, feeling distant from everything she'd ever known. The small hitches in the infant's breathing added to the feeling of separation. She was a reprobate in every way. God had seen her through more things than a lifetime should remember. Now the excruciating physical pain was over, but there was no thankfulness to be found. What kind of woman would reject her own offspring?

Carlotta hung her apron on the peg, and Emery blinked back to the moment. "I will do the rest." She spoke to her in Spanish. Carlotta walked into the front room and spied the cradle. "He looks good." Carlotta stepped back to the kitchen and patted Emery on the shoulder. "Long night—I go back to bed. You come if you need me."

Emery caught Morgan watching her. He looked about to say something but held it back.

She glanced back at Carlotta. "*Sí, señora.*"

Thirty-Three

A familiar, yet new peace settled over his cabin in the days after the Derry brothers pulled out. Even the interrupted sleep was becoming a familiar routine. Baby Gus seemed to express his hungry squall every three hours through the night, but Morgan didn't mind. Emery appeared to find ease with the feedings the infant needed. The day before, when Morgan came in for the noon meal, she nursed the baby in his soft chair with a poncho that Carlotta had made out of an old sheet. It was discreet, yet allowed her to speak with Carlotta or him as they came and went. Once when Emery pulled baby Gus over her shoulder to coax a burp, Morgan caught her giving the wiggly baby a quick kiss on the cheek.

Morgan went back to nailing the new window casing to his greenhouse. Could he allow his soul to find this calm, this peace, lasting? Now that Emery was no longer pregnant, would the deep gorge between his heart and hers build a bridge? A loud, clanging noise of a wagon pulled into his front yard, and he set his tools down and jogged closer. A frantic-faced man jumped from the seat. "Are you the doc?" he panted. "Somebody told me—" Choking, he could barely pull in a breath. Carlotta and Emery peeked out from the open front door.

"Yes, what is it?" Morgan asked.

"My daughter, she . . . she . . . fell from the barn rafters. She landed on the boot scrape."

Morgan ran past the women and grabbed his surgical bag. "I'll be back as soon as I can." He met the man, and they both jumped onto the wagon seat. "How bad?" Morgan held the bench tight as the man snapped the horse down the lane.

"It's bad. Blood everywhere. At first, she talked to us for a few minutes, but now she's out cold." A pained groan escaped his mouth.

"Did you remove the wedge from her side?"

The man grimaced. "Yes, sir. It was the biggest hole I'd ever seen." Mouth ajar, he shook his head. "And no amount of nothing seemed to stop the bleeding. She might be bled out before we get back."

"Her name, her age?" Morgan ducked, as a low branch flew by his face.

"Margery." The sweat dripped from the father's forehead. "But, I always called her Biscuit." He pulled the horses to the right before they entered Auburn. "She's eight, but can eat those biscuits by the plateful." The worried face glanced at Morgan. "The Halls from the mining camps— my second cousin, he said there was a doc livin' near." Morgan watched as the simple white-sided house came into view. The father pulled the horse to a quick stop in front of the barn, and they both jumped down. He ran inside the wide barn door to see a pale, distraught woman bent over the child. The blood had soaked a deep, dark red through the child's entire dress.

"I'll need soap and water for my hands," Morgan said, commanding. The man ran from the barn. "And you. Please get all the clean sheets and put the water on to boil." He laid two fingers to her neck. Her pulse was slow and irregular. Two teen boys huddled in the corner. "You have a kitchen table?" he asked. They nodded in unison. "Stay close, I'm going to lift her carefully and carry her inside to the table."

They all did as told, and the parents converged at the kitchen table around the lifeless little girl. Morgan reached for the stove, poured the steaming water into a bowl, and dropped his instruments in. After thoroughly washing his hands, he took his scissors and cut away her dress. Her wound was laid open to her ribs. Both brothers moaned and ran from the kitchen. The father grabbed the mother as her knees gave way. "I might need only one person to help. Whoever has the constitution for surgery." Morgan set his instruments on a clean towel. The father led the mother to the settee in the front room and came back. "The name's Jacob. Whatever I can do."

Morgan began to clean the wound and determined that her organs had been spared. Like he was a war doctor yesterday, he threaded the needle and began to intricately stitch her back together. "She lost a large amount of blood." Just like the men in battle, that was one thing he could not put back. Morgan rechecked her pulse, leaving bloody prints on her neck. "She may not make it." He glanced at Jacob as he dabbed the area as the blood seeped out.

"I'd told her to stay off those rafters." Jacob's mouth twisted; his words hung between anger and desperation. Morgan nodded and began to check for other broken bones. A large knot protruded from her forehead. "I'm sorry." Morgan frowned. "I'd imagine she's a lively one." Morgan lifted her eyelids, checking her pupils. "But it may be the very thing that can bring her back." He gathered his instruments and put them in new boiling water. "But . . ." He glanced at the front room, where the mother was rocking, maybe praying. "You might want to gather any family to bring comfort."

Morgan finally noticed the little kitchen and glanced down at his hand. Taking a clean sheet to tear for a bandage, he'd never stopped to think he couldn't do this. Funny, months ago, he'd decided his scars would prevent him from using his abilities. Like they didn't belong to his arm, he stretched his nimble fingers in and out.

"Thanks, Doc, for all ya done." Jacob went to pull his billfold open.

"No, no." Morgan held his hand up. "Let's wait and see if she does awaken." Morgan motioned for the father to support his effort to bandage the wound. "I'll go to town and see what I can find for pain. Carefully put her to bed and have someone stay with her." He washed his hands and dried his instruments. "You should know, sir, I was a surgeon during the Mexican-American war. I . . . I . . ." Morgan searched for the words. "I did what I know, what I would have done for my own child." Morgan studied the man for a few seconds. How difficult to be a father, to carry the weight and responsibilities for the very lives of his family.

"I'll have my son give you a ride home." Jacob stuck out his hand and shook Morgan's with a thankful grip.

"I'll be back to check on her soon. If the child runs a fever, keep her cool and away from those fresh stitches." Morgan turned to leave, saying a prayer for the girl's recovery.

Minutes later, Morgan swung down from Jacob's wagon. Emery stood up from the bench on the porch. Had she been waiting for him? At her sad but caring smile, something stirred inside of him. Missing baby Gus in her arms, his houseguest was still a vision—a beautiful, enchanting woman offering comfort and longing that matched with the feeling of coming home. He couldn't take his eyes from hers.

"What happened?" she asked.

"She's still alive. But she'd lost a lot of blood. I can't say. It's too early."

A gentle touch rested on his forearm. "How did you do? Did your hands work well?"

"They did." Setting his bag on the bench, he wiggled his fingers. "I never gave it a thought until I was done with her stitches." He shook his head. "I suppose my training is inked in my brain."

"Word will spread of your abilities." Her eyebrows raised.

"Not if she dies." He raked his hand through his hair, and Emery's shoulders dropped. Fighting for the moment to last, Morgan wrapped his arm around her back and nudged her close to his chest. "What, what are you thinking?"

She rested her head under his chin and her hand on his chest. "There were five children who died on the ship to America. I remember the grief, the inconsolable mothers who were left without their child to hold." She pulled back and looked up with darkened eyes. "I don't know. I just don't know if I could . . . forget it." Emery stepped back. "I'm sure you're hungry. There is marmitako on the stove."

Walking into the small cabin, Emery glanced down at baby Gus in his cradle and then passed into the kitchen. Ladling the stew into a heavy bowl, she set it on the table. Morgan stopped at the cradle and picked up the baby. Coming near, he showed her the lazy, sleepy eyes cracking open. "He's changing, I can see it."

"It's only been two weeks. Here." She took the bundled baby. "Eat." She stepped around the table, swaying the baby. "You woke him up, Morgan."

"Forgive me. I hadn't seen him all day. Or you." Reaching for her skirt, he gave it a tug. "Sit and join me."

Emery pulled out a chair and sat.

"Today, I thought it would be strange to hold those instruments again, but I didn't give it a second thought." He took a bite and chewed, nodding his approval. "It was more of what you said earlier—to be a parent and lose your child. A heart would break into pieces for a lifetime."

Emery turned away from the baby. Looking across the kitchen, she sensed where he was leading.

"You are a good mother," he said. "And I would be a good father. And together—"

As she stood, the scrape of her chair on the floor disrupted his words. "Morgan, please."

"Please, what?" His voice clipped. "Do not tell me you are still thinking of taking this child to an orphanage?" Getting up, he took his bowl to the basin. "I love him. Wouldn't you want him to be with someone who loves him?"

Emery stepped away, started to turn and shook

her head. "I don't know what I want—I . . ."

"What is wrong with me? Just say it!" Morgan's eyes flashed.

"Nothing." The baby began to fuss, and she bounced him up and down.

"Your family? You want to return to your family?"

Emery rocked her head to the side, feeling her own frustration at her weary indecision and his confrontation.

"Then do it." Without warning, Morgan stepped close and took the baby from her arms. In five long strides, he crossed over his bedroom threshold and closed the door.

Emery's chin dropped, and her arms felt like feathers about to fall from a high tree. Shock and anger battled within her, and she marched to his door. "How dare you! You are not his father!"

"And you have yet to say if you are his mother!" boomed from the other side of the door.

She tried the handle and found it locked. "Open it at once, Morgan!" The silence from the other side of the door was like poison in her gut. She knew he'd been confronted with his past today, except a child's life hung in the balance. She tried to temper her voice. "Stop this, I mean it. You are being cruel and . . . and . . ." Hot tears flooded her eyes. Suddenly her chest ached with pressure, and she gripped her swollen skin under her bodice. Augustus was *her* baby. He had no right to keep her separated from him. Her tears spilled over. This healthy child was hers to hold.

A stiff rod rose up her backbone. This was *her* baby. She was the mother. No one would ever separate them. Emery pounded the door with her fist. "Open the door, Morgan!" She wiped her face dry. "Give me my baby!"

The door swung open with a swish of air, and Morgan glared at her holding wiggly Gus. "What did you say?"

"I said, give me *my* baby." She growled, gritting her teeth before reaching out.

"*Your* baby?"

"Yes, my baby." Her nostrils flared, and her hands reached across the threshold.

"He belongs to you?" Morgan asked.

"Yes, this baby belongs to me."

"Very well." Morgan placed the bundle in her arms. "I would never keep a mother from *her* child."

Emery stepped back, pressing baby Gus to her chest. "And I never will let myself think so highly of you again."

The glare before she turned could stop a stampede.

Thirty-Four

Morgan tossed and turned all night. Would Emery and baby Gus be gone when he awoke? As if yesterday hadn't been draining enough, then he'd decided to provoke a mother into claiming her child, but had he gone too far? Rubbing his dark hair back and forth, he sighed. A cool morning breeze entered his room as he sat on the edge of the bed. Had Gus cried in the night for his feedings? Morgan rose slowly and pulled his clothes on. He would have to know. Her indifference or rejection was painful, but he didn't want her walking back to Hangtown.

Carlotta worked in the kitchen, starting a small fire in the stove. Morgan opened the front door, watching the bright sunrays crest above his land. He tried to allow the illuminating beauty sink into his bones, but he felt weary and heavy. He turned back and stood in front of Emery's door.

"Hey." Carlotta frowned at him. "She just get baby to sleep. What do you need?"

Morgan stepped back and stared at his feet. She was still here. That's all he needed to know. "Yes, of course, let her sleep." He sat at the table and blew out a long breath. "I'll mine up the creek this morning, then head over to check on the little girl in Auburn."

Carlotta served him a plate with bean, egg, and cheese *Molletes.* "*Sí.*"

Baby Gus woke Emery with his usual snorts and squeaks. She blinked back her restless night and sat up to unwrap him. Changing his diaper, his legs and arms swung energetically in and out. "Yes, good morning to you, Augustus." She admired the sound of his manly, bold name. Instantly a dark shadow hovered inside her. He'd no last name. It didn't matter for a child dropped off at the charity home. His new family would name him. Emery brushed her fingers across the soft velvet folds under his ear and neck.

Last night for the first time, she'd allowed her mind to trace the steps she'd take to leave him at the charity house. Would the headmistress of the home be kind or stern and judgmental? What if it was a man sneering down at her? Gus turned his bright little face and tried to latch onto her finger. The last vision she allowed was looking into her cherub's trusting, round eyes one last time before she handed him over.

That had started the tears in the middle of the night. Would baby Gus wonder where she was, the feedings, the cuddles, her voice? Then the sobs began. She loved him. It was such a powerful thing, this attachment, this desire to keep him and look out for his wellbeing. *My baby,* she had growled at Morgan. Fresh tears dripped down, and she tried to catch them before they landed on the baby's face.

Morgan had pushed her. It was wrong and yet so like him. He could never leave well enough alone. Even with her new resolve to raise an illegitimate child, there was little joy or comfort. She knew keeping Gus would open another dark well she didn't want to face, but this baby was hers. Emery changed his gown and wrapped him in a fresh blanket. Pulling him into her arms, she stared into his sweet face, and he contently gazed back at her. How would she protect her infant, and one day her child from a painful horrid past? He would grow up without a last name. This was the scariest thought—the future of unknowns would be hard for both of them, and yet it was the rightest moment she'd ever known.

The day was overly quiet as Carlotta explained that Morgan had left early to mine and then to check on the child he'd doctored. Emery folded the last of the clean diapers as baby Gus slept in his cradle. The black medical bag that occupied the corner was missing, and Emery sighed. The dusty, vacant spot seemed to match the internal feeling she carried. His actions, and his words often held a challenge, but also a confidence greater than his long frame. Strangely, she'd come to rely on it, and now the home felt hollow without him. Trying to focus, she walked the fresh stack of diapers back into her room and peered out the window. What would she say now? After the bitter exchange from last night, could they return to the kindness they had shared? Likely not.

Living with his devoted intentions while she stayed aloof continually hurt him. All his soft hugs and long looks demonstrated that his affections had been growing. Blowing out a long sigh, her eyes shifted to the newly built greenhouse looming on the right. Another point of shame and regret, she'd led the man on. He'd given up his time, home, and food, and allowed her to plant and tend the garden—for what? So she could raise another man's baby, and they could live like brother and sister all their days?

The bed taunted her. It was only a few steps behind her. He'd already slept with his arms around her one fitful night, but sleeping wasn't her worry. Could she . . . ? She rubbed her forehead back and forth. Could she try to give herself over to him, his wants? A severe pain rolled in her stomach, and she wrapped her arms tightly over her waist. As a husband, of course, he would not be cruel or hold her by the neck and threaten to drown her sister. If they married and he was patient, could she . . . *one day?*

A low moan creaked from the back of her throat. What young woman wouldn't enjoy his brief kisses on her cheek? Each one had felt safe and gentle, but her mommi had said a husband's needs are different than a wife's. Emery glanced at the stack of clean diapers, knowing clearly what that meant. Maybe the man should labor in unrelenting pain for hours and push an infant from his body. That would surely slow his *needs* down. At the image, a sad chuckle escaped, and she quickly covered her mouth.

Before the evening meal, Emery heard Morgan ride up to the cabin. She watched from the window as he walked his horse into the barn. Feeling nervous, she still had nothing worthwhile to say. Would her choice to keep the baby make him better, or worse?

She circled the front room. "He's back," she said to Carlotta in Spanish. "Would you like me to start supper?"

Carlotta shrugged. "Soon. If it is well, we will see him. If it did not go well, then we won't see him for a while or not at all."

Emery's eyes narrowed.

"In the war, some found liquor or cards. *El doctor* found a place to disappear."

Emery chewed the corner of her thumbnail.

Soon after feeding Gus and burping the sleepy infant, Emery laid him in the cradle. "Carlotta, can you listen for the baby? I want to see if I can find him." Emery knew she had nothing to offer, but the long silence of his absence was more than she could bear.

Heading toward the creek, something caught

Emery's attention from the corner of her eye. Morgan sat on the ground with his back against the barn. When he looked up, his face was drawn and pale.

"Oh, Morgan." She crouched down. "The child?"

Fine lines etched his face. "The girl didn't make it." He raked his fingers through his hair.

Emery held her eyes closed and prayed for God's strength. She'd pouted and selfishly thought of herself all day while the rest of the world swirled in suffering.

"I . . . I . . ." She went to touch his knee and pulled her hand back. "I know there are no words to bring you relief, but I know you were a comfort to those poor parents. You tried. They can rest assured that everything possible was done."

Only a few birds squawking overhead could be heard. He intertwined his fingers behind his neck and lowered his head.

"You must be hungry. Please let me fix you something." Emery wrung her hands in her skirt, waiting.

Morgan shook his head, never looking up.

"Listen to me." She scratched her forehead. "I'm sorry for the harsh words last night. You were right to push me." Heart-wrenching in every direction, she looked to the sky. "You're right about most everything." Her voice trailed off. "I'm not going to take Gus to Sacramento. I've decided . . . to raise him."

Remaining face down, he nodded twice and began to rub his hair back and forth. "This fateful day has given me the push I've needed." Morgan looked out upon the land and held his temples. "I pledged to stay away from doctoring. To stay out west, finding my peace and healing in the simple life of a miner." Morgan blew out a held breath and stretched the fingers on his scarred hand. "You were right. The family and their people all thanked me for trying. There was no blame, only gratitude." A bittersweet tone joined his sober expression. "But I should have never gone to the mining camps to doctor the children. I did that to myself."

"No, no, you didn't." Gripping his knee, Emery held it tight. "You did that for me. I am to blame for all the things in your life that you never wanted. Please, Morgan—"

He grabbed her wrist, pulling her hand away, and stood quickly. "The Derry brothers, Silas and Farly . . ." He stepped around her and brushed off his pants. "They're all heading to the Oregon territory. I think I want to try that next."

Emery staggered back. *Oregon?*

"Carlotta may have a fuss, but since the two of you get along well, maybe she would agree to stay with you and Gus."

"Stay with me?" Her tone soured.

"I've thought about it." Morgan started to walk around the barn. "You could have the cabin with Gus and your garden."

Emery froze. What was he saying? Did he want to leave? The scent of fresh-cut wood from the greenhouse wafted through her senses.

"Morgan." She pleaded, but he kept walking. Quickening her steps, she met him on the porch. "Listen." Emery pulled on his arm until he stilled. "Please, I understand not wanting to be tethered. To want to make your own way. But this is your home and today was just a bad day." He would not look at her, and she could feel their tiny thread of kindred attachment unraveling.

Desperate, she shook his arm until he turned. "You know I tried to kill myself." Her shameful declaration choked with emotion, and his eyes finally dropped to meet hers. "I . . . wanted . . . to leave it all behind. I did. I almost succeeded." Swallowing hard, she ran her hand down his sleeve. "Please, we've been through so much and . . ." Her own words would not form any rational thoughts. There was only the truth pounding from her heart. "I . . . I do love you, but I know that all I do is . . . hurt you."

His tongue touched his top lip, and he blinked, looking away. Silently, he turned to go inside; a frigid, hollow air lingered where he'd been.

Thirty-Five

Emery frowned, patting the fussy baby's bottom at the table, and wishing she'd never sat through such a strange silent meal. As soon as Carlotta rose to start the dishes, Emery was faced with a problem. Usually, Morgan offered to take the baby while she helped clean up. Tonight, he seemed to find his solace and his silence more appealing than even baby Gus. Frustrated, she cleared the table with one hand. All three of them turned toward the door as another rattling wagon pulled up.

"Now what?" Morgan said abruptly as he stood and strode to the door. Carlotta and Emery watched from the kitchen as he lifted the lantern to see. Emery prayed it wasn't more town folk seeking a doctor, the timing glaringly off. Morgan stepped back from the door, and Emery noted Carlotta's worried expression. "It is late," she said to Carlotta in Spanish.

Morgan stepped back further, a wide-eyed, perplexed expression causing his mouth to fall open. "Father and . . . and—?"

Emery unknowingly gripped Carlotta's arm. The widest bell gown with soft purple and white stripes crossed the entry. Emery gasped. The young woman was stunning in the layers of shiny sheen accented with tan trims and laces. A small triangle hat with matching decorations sat posed on her golden locks. Emery had never seen anything so feminine and extravagant. One more step forward and her royal presence filled the cabin's front room.

"Olivia? Olivia? Is it you?" Morgan stood back, face riddled with shock. Finally, his father reached around her, and they shook hands. "Sir, what are you doing here? I . . . I . . ." He looked back and forth between them. "I can't believe you are . . . are both here in California." With jaw hanging open, he set the lantern on the table and carefully hugged the delicate woman. His father came to her side and they shook hands again. "I did receive your letter," Morgan stammered. "But it was weeks, maybe months ago and said nothing of Olivia. Miss Bradstreet." Morgan held his hand to his head. "Did your father come also?"

"Timely correspondence is a bit difficult," his well-dressed father said. He was a tad shorter and stockier than Morgan, with his salt and pepper hair clipped close. "Dr. Bradstreet passed over a year ago. With the loss of Ronald *and* her father . . ." The senior Dr. Hastings glanced at her, and Olivia's chin tilted down, and her eyelashes fluttered, looking at the floor. "Miss Bradstreet developed a brave soul and left Chicago to travel with our rustic group."

Morgan's mouth hung ajar. "Dear Olivia." He

reached and squeezed her gloved hand. "I'm sorry to hear of your father's passing."

Baby Gus's squeak cut into the tender moment and all eyes seem to suddenly narrow on Emery and the baby in her arms. "Oh, Lord," Emery whispered.

"And who are these ladies?" His father nodded at them.

"Please, forgive me." Morgan cleared his throat and filled his chest with a deep breath. "Dr. Maxwell Hastings, may I introduce my . . ." His eyes flitted over Emery and onto Carlotta, "my housekeeper, Mrs. Carlotta Rodriquez."

"Pleased to make your acquaintance." The elder doctor bowed at the waist, and Miss Bradstreet smiled before her fair blue eyes shifted narrowly to Emery and the baby.

"And this . . ." Morgan blinked, shifting his feet, "this woman is . . ."

"My granddaughter. *Mi nieta.*" Carlotta's deep brown facial wrinkles pulled upward for a moment. "*Mi bisnieto.*" She tapped the baby bundled in Emery's arms.

"What are you doing?" Emery asked her in Spanish.

"*Su marido,*" Carlotta frowned. "He died."

Emery froze. What just happened? Her imagined husband died? Besides being an unmarried woman living with an unmarried man, now she was suddenly a granddaughter

302

and a widow? She glared at Carlotta and pulled Gus onto her shoulder. The bold woman had lied without a flinch.

"Do you speak English?" wide-eyed, Miss Bradstreet asked sincerely.

Speechless and upended by Carlotta, Emery nodded. "*Un pequeño.*"

"I think that means a little, so I'll suppose we'll have to learn some Spanish." Dr. Hastings nodded at Miss Bradstreet. His smile was kind, like Morgan's. "We do apologize for the lateness of the evening. This town of Auburn is small, and there were no rooms to be had."

"No, no." Morgan rallied. "I have two rooms. And . . . father, you can stay with me. If Miss Bradstreet doesn't mind sharing with . . . with . . . Emery." He pointed at her without making eye contact.

"Poor thing." Miss Bradstreet leaned closer to Morgan. "Is it not custom to wear black for mourning in the West?"

Emery rolled her eyes and brushed the crumbs off the table with one hand. Miss Bradstreet and Morgan had an obvious familiar past. This was the woman engaged to his older brother. The three of them, his real family, were now filling the small cabin.

"We should offer food," Emery rattled off in Spanish, then shook her head disapprovingly at Carlotta, her newly appointed grandmother.

• • •

Emery paced back and forth in her small room. The baby would cry out off and on throughout the night. The woman would do better to sleep in Morgan's soft chair than in her bed. And what about nursing Gus? She'd found an easy way to prop him with a pillow near her breast. Sometimes she fell asleep and awoke to a sleeping baby with milk dripping down his chin. It all seemed a bit too indecent for the refined young Miss Olivia Bradstreet. Before she could settle her thoughts, a bump was heard at her door. The handle turned, and Morgan stood with the cradle in his arms.

"I thought maybe he could sleep in this tonight." Morgan glanced back as Miss Bradstreet followed him in. He set the cradle on the other side of the bed. Emery took a deep breath and scooped the sleeping baby off the bed and into the cradle.

"Oh, Emery. May I call you Emery?" Miss Bradstreet asked.

Emery tried to steady her thoughts as she tucked the blanket tight around Gus.

"It is my English?" The soft-spoken woman turned to Morgan. "Does the lady know what I'm saying?"

Emery allowed Morgan to feel the uncomfortable silence. "*Sí.*" She nodded and faced them. Though her heart pounded with the awkward situation, she tried not to glare at him.

"Ah, yes," Morgan stepped closer and bent down to touch the baby's cheek. For the first time, he looked long at Emery. "She does understand quite well."

"Oh, wonderful." Olivia brought her hands together. "I don't want to be any bother." Olivia set her reticule, gloves, and a white garment on the chair. "Please tell me how to stay out of your way. I know your child is your first priority."

"He is." Emery pulled up straighter. "You may sleep on this side."

Olivia's straight teeth shined through her soft pink lips, a small dimple appearing. "How delightful. You do speak English. And so well." Her admiration smiled up at Morgan. "Perhaps she and I could be friends? Yes?"

Morgan lifted a wry smile between them. "Sure," he said unconvincingly. "Olivia, do you have what you need from your trunk?"

"Yes, sweet Morgan." She clutched onto his arm. "I just can't believe we finally made it. Here I am standing in your humble home." Pulling on his arm, she raised up on her toes, pressed her full gown into him, and kissed his cheek. "After losing Ronald and then my father, the months of relentless travel, I'm just so thankful to be here and to see you." She rested her head on his shoulder while Morgan met a dark glare in Emery's eyes. Embarrassed by watching their intimate display, Emery quickly looked away.

"Goodnight, then." Morgan patted her arm before he pulled away and closed the door.

The poor woman smiled nervously. "There was a wonderful couple who traveled with us." Emery thought she saw her hands tremble as Olivia started on the buttons below her chin.

"Do you need help undressing?"

"Oh, bless you. I do. Thank you, ma'am."

Ma'am. That was a first, but perhaps appropriate for a widow with a baby. Emery took on the hundred pearl buttons down her back and waist. Her gown swished with layers, hoops, and bustles as Emery helped her step out. "Did you wear these gowns on your travels here?"

"Oh, no." Olivia smiled and covered her chest with crossed arms. She turned from Emery in her chemise and pantaloons and slipped the white gown from the chair over her head. "I found out the hard way. They are far too heavy." The refined young lady began to pull the pins from her hair. "In hopes of seeing Morgan, though, I just wanted to look as he remembered me."

Emery stepped back. Even in a simple smocked and laced white shift, the woman was exquisite with her golden hair smooth and fine, hanging loose around her shoulders. Forging a smile, Emery bent over the cradle and checked on Gus. Her brown braid fell around her shoulder. Huffing, she tossed it back. Of course, Miss

Bradstreet wanted to look the part for Morgan. He'd lost a beloved brother and Olivia had lost her future, her betrothed. They carried a wretched camaraderie, a past that no one else could understand. Emery turned her back to her, dropped her skirt and blouse, quickly pulling her plain nightgown over her head. The gown had places her milk had dried on the fabric. Embarrassed, she quickly blew out the lantern.

"Good night, then, and thank you for your gracious hospitality." Olivia lifted the sheet and blanket and laid down.

"*De nada. Buenas noches.*" Emery did the same, turning to face the cradle. Why did she say goodnight in Spanish? Blowing out a tired sigh, her finger traced the rim of the cradle. Why did she bristle, feeling their happy family reunion unnerving?

The lady needed a place to stay. Wasn't that the same gift Morgan had bestowed upon her? Why had she told Morgan she loved him today? After all these weeks, why had he left her coolly with no response? Was he really going to leave?

Emery held her eyes closed, wanting to sink down deep, far and away from this beautiful woman next to her and far from this chaotic day. *Now* her throat constricts? And why, oh why, did she need to press the sheet under her eyes, dabbing runaway tears?

Thirty-Six

Surely Miss Bradstreet did not sleep well as Gus found his diaper full and his stomach empty twice in the night. Emery tried, but couldn't get comfortable. Between a baby who snorted and cooed off and on, and her fear of waking Miss Bradstreet, the night was an exhausting disaster. In the pitch darkness of night, she gave up trying to nurse the noisemaker in bed, taking him to the chair to feed. Now the sun was up, but maybe Miss Bradstreet could sleep for another hour or so.

Emery laid on her side, lifting Gus from the cradle. Swinging his head back and forth, she slipped his happy flailing arms under her breast and nestled him in. At least she could see what she was doing, and he latched on without fuss. Just as she would doze off, the nursing would stop, and she'd open her eyes, finding baby Gus gazing up at her, content just to study her. Oh, this sweet baby, he was often so happy and alert in the morning. How could she not just ogle him back?

The bed rocked with Miss Bradstreet, and Emery grabbed the sheet, pulling it up to her chin.

"Oh, you're awake," Olivia whispered. "I hope I didn't keep you from your sleep." Rubbing her eyes, she laid on her back. "I went from being a woman who rarely left home to traveling across the wilds of America. This roof and bed are a welcome reprieve." Olivia pulled her hair back and nodded over her shoulder to Emery. "Oh, you have the baby in there," she smiled. "Am I in the way?"

Emery lessened her grip on the sheet. "No, he is very happy tucked next to me."

"Little angel." Olivia sighed. "I don't ever mean to compare, and your loss is far greater. A husband, your home."

Emery stilled as the young woman's eyes began to fill. "My Ronald and I had only our promises to each other." She chewed on her shaking bottom lip. "I envy your little reminder of your husband, the love you shared."

Like someone dropping hot coals in her bed, Emery jerked up. Pulling Gus loose, she quickly tugged her gown closed. "It wasn't like that." The truth rolled out as she set Gus on her shoulder. Slipping out of bed, Emery turned to the wall and patted his back.

"I'm sorry for my reaction. I know we don't know each other." Embarrassed, Emery glanced at Olivia and back to the wall. "But it sounds as if Ronald, just like Morgan, was a caring and just man." Shaking her head, she wanted to shake those false ridiculous tender sentiments from the room.

A needed, calming breath came to Emery with a new thought. "California is new territory. The war left many bitter, and now the gold has taken over the souls of many men." She turned to face Olivia. The innocent woman didn't need to hear Emery's spew of bitterness. She tried to soften her tone. "I'm not sure you will like it here. The circles of people you are used to are—" Suddenly the air would not reach her lungs, and a strange notion filled her head. Emery looked long into Olivia's soft eyes. "Are you here to marry Morgan?"

Olivia sat forward, quickly held her hand over her heart, and lifted one shoulder. "No, I . . . I had no idea. He chose not to come back to Chicago. He . . . he . . . could easily have been married." She smiled nervously. "When I saw you standing in his kitchen," a light laugh escaped, "I'd wondered if you were his wife."

Emery realized she fretfully patted baby Gus, but he was sound asleep. "I am not." Her stomach dropped; it was not a question posed to her. Laying Gus in the crook of her arm, he smiled in his sleep, distracting her. "Would you like help dressing?" Emery put Gus in the cradle, hoping to quickly exit this conversation.

Olivia slipped out of the bed and stared out the window. "Yes, thank you." She carefully looked over her shoulder to Emery. "Was your grandmother your help for the delivery?"

"Yes, Carlot . . . she was a great help." Emery pulled her skirt and blouse off the wall peg. "Morgan slept in the barn with his friends." She buttoned up her blouse, feeling like it was a lifetime ago.

"A doctor with no constitution for a female bringing new life in the world." Olivia smiled and looked back out the window. "What shall we do with him?"

We. Emery sighed, loosening her braid and pulling her fingers through her long brown hair.

Morgan sat at the table with his father, still blinking to make sure he wasn't dreaming. They'd talked openly about the war and the situation that caused his burns, and even the moments around Ronald's death that had been too much for a letter. After a long silence, his father finally looked up and patted his back.

"I'm anxious to see your place here." Maxwell sipped his coffee and ate his eggs. "Do you suppose we could stay on a bit? You could show me what you know about mining."

"Gold mining?" Morgan could not have heard him right.

"I know." His father patted him on the back, chuckling. "Doesn't sound like something I'd do in my lifetime, but . . ." He pursed his lips and nodded his head. "I've agreed to invest in a gold mining venture not far from here."

"Really!" Morgan scratched his head. "You?"

"Well, I know they want me for my money. No one's asking me to drill lines or pound rock." Maxwell took another bite, and Morgan tried to remember if he'd ever seen his father make a reckless choice in his life. The man had aged but in a good way.

"You inspired me." Maxwell nodded. "I realized I didn't have to die in the house I was born in." He frowned. "Your mother has been gone for years. Losing Ronald and reading in the letter that you'd seen enough pain and suffering . . . It just hit me one day when I was leaving work. I don't have to have my nose in medicine my entire life. I'd given enough to the college."

Morgan shrugged. "I have to applaud you." His smile was approving. "It's rugged, but it's a hardy territory—without the long winters."

"And you like it?" his father asked.

"I do. Only a few will find riches, but I like the hard work, the land, the quiet, and simplicity."

His father's face grew somber. "I didn't know or see the details of the war until we spoke. Everything you went through—I understand it was too much to write. Your burns will always remain, but they don't have to define us." Maxwell's eyes were tender.

Morgan nodded. *Us.* His father had no scars, but his own internal grief was something only a family could share.

The door opened, and the women stepped into the room, drawing all the conversation to a halt. Olivia wore a less ornate dress of deep blues, dipping the wide bodice off her shoulder. With a soft coral scarf around her neck, slivers of white skin showed underneath. Her hair was tucked behind her ears with soft twists down her back. Emery held her head down and went into the kitchen.

Glancing at Emery as she passed a few inches away, his stomach soured. What kind of cad was he? The poor young woman was weeks past her confinement. He should have bought her a new dress or something better to her liking. The stark discrepancy between the two made his teeth clench. Standing, he greeted Olivia.

"How did you sleep? Did the infant squeak and yelp through the night?" Before he could adjust his tone, Emery flashed terse eyes on him.

"No, no." Olivia sat as Morgan held out a chair for her. "I'm sure I was the one who kept poor Emery on the move. She has been a wonderful help to me." Olivia lifted a small smile, and Morgan felt his mouth go dry. Would Emery tell her the truth, the real reason she lived under his roof? Did she tell the proper young lady how he'd found her at So Chen's, desperate and pregnant with nowhere to go?

Emery slid a plate of eggs and tortillas in front of Olivia.

"A bit of American and Mexican." Morgan scratched behind his head.

Her dainty smile softened the room, and she picked up her fork.

"So my father and I are going to traipse around my property this morning," he said to Emery's back. She continued to work at the stove.

"Oh, I would love to see your land, Morgan." Olivia dabbed the corners of her rosebud mouth. "I won't be a bother, I promise."

Morgan nodded once, wondering if she would fare better inside. She'd always been delicate, but maybe he didn't know her well, either. He felt something twist in his gut. Their strange presence at his table—a shock mixed with a touch of delight—but why couldn't he put his finger on his discomfort?

Possibly his father's announcement that he was investing in a mine nearby? What kind of turn had the staunch, learned man taken? Was he fearful he didn't know what he was getting into? And truly, he didn't. And why would Olivia, practically a debutante in her own right, leave the city, the Bradstreet life? Their money and homes had raised them into the upper echelons of Chicago society.

The travel, the risks were so great for a young woman. Her loss of Ronald surely matched his own, but having this young woman sitting at his table made as much sense as having one of

Emery's nubby-headed goats drinking coffee with him. Morgan hid a smile; her sculptured face with the two bumps of her golden hair above her ear could be a match for one of Emery's favorite goats. Muddled at such a bizarre thought, he quickly looked away as she carefully set her mug down.

"Thank you for everything, Morgan," Olivia whispered. "Seeing you alive and well." Her head dipped to the side. "It's hard to explain, but such great comfort." She squeezed his wrist. "A true blessing from above."

Morgan nodded and went to take the last drink from his mug. Before it reached his lips, Emery swiped it from his hand, poured it into the compost bucket, and dropped it into the sudsy water. Before he could pull his lips together, she had given it a good scrub and rinse.

Now, what had he done?

Thirty-Seven

Morgan and his two guests laughed around the table as Carlotta walked by with a basket of wet laundry. Emery knew she should follow her out to help, but she hesitated. To ask Morgan to listen for the baby felt strange, like too great an imposition.

"I certainly did not possess the grace of serving that Emery does." Olivia laughed. "Emery, you must hear this story." Olivia bent from her chair and reached toward where she stood, touching her sleeve.

"My ladies aid group was helping with the medical society fundraiser." Olivia shook her head with a smile, a dimple appearing. "I was positive they would put me on decorations or table settings, but no." She smirked. "I was asked to serve. A complete fish out of water." She slid her hand down her cheek, covering her mouth. "Then to make matters worse, I came to my table and sitting there are these two handsome brothers. Both distinguished Rush medical students." Her eyes widened at Emery. "These brothers . . ." Her gaze shifted to Morgan. "You know, every girl longed for their attention."

"Ronald picked your table." Morgan cut in.

"He told me later." Like a sweet child, she

patted Morgan's hand. "So here I was just trying to deliver two glasses of water. Ronald said something, teasing me without cause." Olivia dipped her head to the side. "I went to set his water down, but accidentally set it on the fork. The water spilled out all over his place setting, running down onto his lap!" She shook her head, her cheeks flushed. "Like some clumsy oaf. Ahhh . . . all my shameful disabilities out for all the world to see," she whined, dismayed. "It was a wonder he even spoke to me after that." Rolling her eyes, she pressed her temple.

Emery forced herself to smile at the story. *The woman's worst humiliation was spilling water on a man's lap?*

"Likely the moment you caught his attention above all the rest," Morgan's father said.

"Maybe so." Her sweet smile, a second later, held a flash of pain.

"About today," Morgan cleared his throat, disrupting the somber sentiment they all shared. "The heat gets overbearing late in the afternoon."

"Yes, yes." His father stood. "Let's get going."

Morgan met Emery's eyes. "Would you like the cradle back in the front room?"

"Yes, thank you." There was so much more she wanted to say, but nothing felt connected between them. Impatient, she followed him into her room.

"What are we doing?" she whispered as he lifted the cradle and baby Gus. "As Carlotta's poor granddaughter, I'm to live a lie now?" Her eyes flashed on his as he stepped closer.

"I don't know," Morgan rasped softly, shrugging with the weight in his arms. "You *are* good at keeping secrets."

"That is cruel and unfair." Her back stiffened. Morgan shook his head and walked out the door.

A few minutes after Emery bid them a safe morning, the trio left the cabin. Blowing out a long breath, she noticed something sticking out of Morgan's messy papers. Reaching down, Emery held the small frame with a tintype of Olivia Bradstreet. Morgan had kept her picture. Did he look at it each night?

After a long moment, she replaced it as she'd found it and stepped around the chair and stood over where baby Gus slept. What kind of misery is this? Sinking into the soft chair, she held her elbows to her knees and sighed, dropping her chin into her palms. Forcing her mind to stop racing was like stopping mice in the barn. After a second or two, her thoughts would scurry around in more circles.

For heaven's sake, she had no claim on the man. He hadn't asked her to marry him in formal words. Hadn't she rehearsed what it would be like to become his wife? Her body stilled; she wasn't ready. Well, maybe in heart, but not in body.

Rubbing her temples, Emery closed her eyes.

He was attractive, and she found him desirable, but that wasn't it. It was her frayed existence. When would she find the strength to return home? Her mind wandered ahead. What if it was with Gus on her hip and Morgan's baby in her belly. How would she explain that to her parents?

It didn't matter, she pouted. The elder Dr. Hastings would never approve of her. More than ever, it was glaringly obvious that Morgan was born into another world—the privilege of a fine home and family, his education and training, like no one else she would ever know. The way they talked alike. *Finding Morgan was providence,* Olivia had said. They all used words she didn't understand. Emery watched baby Gus grunt and wiggle. A true cry of distress from him brought her out of her twisted thoughts.

"Yes, I hear you." Picking him up, he curled his head and body backward in a good stretch. "Your mommi is a rustic. I suppose even a lying rustic, now."

Morgan's point was well taken. She laid Gus on her knees and changed his diaper. "With dirty fingernails from the garden." Poking around, she found her nursing poncho tucked in the side of the chair. "Her friends are goats and an eighty-year-old woman." Emery popped her head into the poncho's opening and unbuttoned her blouse. Gus let out a bellowing cry. "Whose little baby boy has no manners." Gus latched on, and the room grew quiet. Emery could feel her chin quiver. Her little boy, Augustus, would have no advantages in life. Pulling on the opening, she watched his eyes droop with nursing satisfaction. Would her shame pass on to him, or would his own illegitimacy be worse? Could she do anything right by this innocent one? "Ahhh." She groaned, wiping a loose tear before it wet her cheek.

Her days had been both beautiful and dreadful since meeting Morgan Hastings. Full of care and kindness, and yet it was not who she was meant to be—whoever that was.

Emery sank further in the soft chair. Things were changing for Morgan, and it shimmered in his eyes as he spoke with his father and Olivia. There was a link to his past, to who he was meant to be. She no longer needed his rescuing and safeguarding. Without her misery, Morgan could be free to follow his own path.

Had God also seen her to the other side? It was hard to imagine she had been so desperate she'd wanted to end her life. The months had somehow dulled the sharp, piercing pain she once felt.

The truth remained without question: she loved Morgan Hastings. And though she was innocent in the ways of the heart, it was hard to think of being apart from his gentle, confident disposition. He'd been her gracious lifeline, her safety.

Her mind drifted to the stories of Jesus. A

savior, a healer, a man who could repair the broken parts of His people. Yet the stories her mother had read from her Bible also talked about laying down your life for a friend. Jesus's sacrifice brought Him no gain, but was always for our abundant life, our benefit.

If she really loved him, the room seemed to still with an airy peace, *would she do what was best for him, for Morgan?* After every kind thing he'd done for her, she could do this in return. A new tightness caught in her throat as Emery lifted Gus over her shoulder to burp. She'd been used, abandoned, hidden, and now she was living another lie. Regardless of Dr. Hastings or Olivia's arrival, it was time to stop.

Sitting up straighter while patting Gus's back, something alive rose in her. It was time, time to do the right thing. No more hiding behind in the depths of her shame. It wasn't fair to Morgan, and it was *not* fair to her little boy. Enough was enough. Morgan's words that she was "good at secrets" goaded her anew. Plagued with lies and secrets was not the life God had meant for her.

After a few hours of mining downstream in his small creek, Morgan checked on his father. "Remember what you are looking for will sink to the bottom. Gold is heavier than dirt and rock." He watched him working with his gold pan. "You've got it."

"This is a lot of stooping and swishing." Maxwell smiled up at Morgan. Setting his pan down, he took his handkerchief and wiped the perspiration from his forehead.

Morgan nodded, looking over to where Olivia sat on a rock in the shade. "She must be done waiting for us. I can't picture her sitting out here much longer."

Olivia, in her soft yellow gown, watched two little butterflies flitted from bush to bush. Taking in a deep breath, she popped open her fan and fanned her face.

"I did rebuff her plan to come out West." His father looked pensive and picked through his pan. "She asked that I not tell what happened. It was important that she tell you herself."

Morgan looked at her twice. "You refused to allow her to come to California?"

His father nodded yes. "In a matter of speaking, when the time is right, I'll let her tell you." He dipped his pan for another swirl of water. "Because she obviously did make it." He watched his pan. "You and I both know, she is charming, intelligent, and refined. And now we know she has a bearable constitution for the adversity of wilderness travel."

Morgan had a hundred questions. The sight of her sitting on a rock by a creek was amiss. She'd always been amiable and delicate, like a soft flower from a vase.

"I can tell you, she respects you a great deal." His father nodded before he looked back to the creek. "You haven't told me." His father continued. "Do you have any prospects for marriage?"

"Prospects?" Morgan huffed, that word was interesting. "I suppose it's just like the gold, always hiding and a pinch out of reach."

"Ha!" His father's tone was amused. "You're my only child now, but I didn't come here for you to fulfill my wishes." Maxwell dipped more water in his pan. "But I'm sure you can understand I want to see you happy and with a woman who will love and respect you." He smiled up at Morgan. "Give me Hastings grandsons."

Morgan forged a smile.

"You would do well to give Miss Bradstreet a chance." His father nodded, wide-eyed.

Morgan had to give him credit for finally getting to the point. "She has shown herself far above what any of us thought her capable. She's past her year of mourning. You and Ronald have many of the same qualities."

"Father, we were nothing alike." Morgan looked away.

"No, not in personality, but both my sons exhibit great courage and sacrifice."

Morgan saw his father's nose flare. "Such pride I've had in the two of you. Neither of you gave me a moment of regret. I now have even greater admiration for you, son." Maxwell winced and stood slowly. "All this crouching, the back of my legs feel like burning coals." He smiled and slapped Morgan on the back. "And for what?" His brows crinkled. "Did I find anything worth this effort?"

Morgan squinted. "It all adds up." Opening the small tin of gold flakes, he added the tiny specks his father had found. "And it helps to keep your expenses low." He grinned and glanced at Olivia. Morgan would've shown his father his favorite place in the creek to cool off, but Olivia stood, frowning.

He studied her from the corner of his eyes. No one would deny the woman was lovely in body and soul. She glanced up and caught him watching her.

"Miss Bradstreet." Morgan recovered. "Are you done watching two tired gold miners?"

Olivia smiled and nodded.

He walked closer. "Now, we pray that Emery is the cook for supper." He held out his elbow, and she took it. "Carlotta, in her senior years, is missing an imagination, and she has deep esteem for the cornmeal tortilla and beans." He grimaced. "Seven days a week."

Thirty-Eight

Morgan and his father had taken their warm bowls and bread out to the front porch to eat. The sun had ducked behind the trees, and the shade made a lovely canopy as they ate and talked.

"This is wonderful stew, Emery." Olivia took a bite at the kitchen table. "Your granddaughter has a flair for the culinary." She nodded to Carlotta.

Wide-eyed, Carlotta took another bite and shrugged.

"She said she likes my cooking better than yours," Emery rattled off in Spanish.

"Eh." Carlotta sneered and batted her hand at Emery.

"It's so wonderful that you two have each other in this time of loss." Olivia blinked through her long lashes. "Emery, have you always lived close to your grandmother?"

"Ah, no, not until just recently." Emery pulled a piece of bread apart. "Carlotta is from Mexico. Since the Americans took the land—I understand it is called Texas."

"Yes, the war." Olivia sighed, looking down. "So tragic to both sides, the loss of so many men. I can't imagine."

"My people are Basque. We come from Spain

and southwestern France. Have you heard of the Bay of Biscay?"

"No, I apologize. Geography was not my strongest suit in school." Olivia looked back and forth between them. "And now providence has brought you both to California."

"*Providencia.*" Emery exhaled.

Carlotta's usual frown seemed to deepen, like a heavy weight that she hid behind her tired eyes and customary indifference. Emery felt a wave of guilt to think she almost gave Gus away. She had her family a town away, Carlotta had no family to surround her in her last years.

"My *abuela* has seen more than you or I would wish for a lifetime." Emery blinked, looking to the table. "During the war, she worked in the surgery. That's how she came to meet Morgan and travel to California." Emery pondered and spooned another small bite of stew. "Can you imagine, your people, your village overrun with cannons and guns, most people dead or run off? Yet, in spite of her age and gender, she used her smarts. She could follow directions, cook, and learn the American man's ways." Emery scratched her chin, watching Carlotta eat. "Could you tend to the men who fought and killed your own—do what you could to help them live? I would think my hatred would burn a hole in my flesh." Emery felt the dark shadow of truth. Adapting is not for the prideful, but for the resilient. The woman had such courage. "But Carlotta survived and even prospered."

They watched as Carlotta's head dipped. "I can die in peace." Carlotta touched her forehead, chest, and each shoulder in the sign of the cross. "I will see them again."

Emery felt her chest swell. She would be proud to have this woman as a grandmother.

"It seems we've all been tested beyond what we thought we could endure," Olivia said, and a long silence followed.

Emery bit hard on the inside of her lip and asked gingerly, "Olivia, do you think you could do well here?"

Before she responded, her shoulder bumped up an inch. "I, like all of you, will survive, I suppose."

Emery saw Olivia's soft blue eyes pool and pushed past her own stomach's constriction. "Morgan." She bit the corner of her lip. "He is a good man." Her empty bowl stared back at her as the mixed thoughts became words. "He would never be cruel or malicious." She risked a glance at Olivia's watery eyes. "I know he is not your Ronald."

Olivia's head dipped a tiny notch, and a tear rolled down her cheek. "I've always admired Morgan." She dabbed her cheek.

Emery knew it. With their connections, despite all that had happened, they were meant for each other. This would work well for them both. Before the sting could get too far into her skin, she wanted to break the crushing moment. "How do you feel about goats?" Emery forged her a wry smile.

"I can say I've never had a feeling about a goat." Olivia chuckled, dabbing her other eye dry.

"Do you like gardens?"

"I suppose I like them better than goats." Olivia huffed a sad laugh.

Carlotta kicked Emery under the table. Emery jumped. "Ouch."

"*Casamentero?*" *Matchmaking?* Carlotta sneered at her.

Emery wiggled in her seat. "My grandmother is from the old country, and she thinks it's improper for us to talk openly about this." Her eyes narrowed on Carlotta. "Yet years of matchmaking happened around many a Spanish table. Families often brought their children together for the good of all." Emery glanced at Olivia. She was quiet but didn't seem offended. "Morgan may never return to medicine. He enjoys a simple life. Funny how far it is from what you all were used to."

The men's laughter could be heard from outside, and Emery looked back out the door. Would Morgan be upset at her meddling? Her stomach soured. She'd spoke up this far.

"I will be leaving soon." Emery squeezed her hands together, her tone hushed.

"Eh?" Carlotta scowled.

"As lovely as this visit has been—" Emery held Carlotta's gaze—"I have other family to see."

"*Eres estupida.*" Carlotta growled and stood up.

Emery didn't like being called stupid, but Carlotta never had minced words. The old woman shuffled around the corner to her room. Emery faced Olivia and lifted a small smile. "She would like for me to stay longer, but I feel I'm in the way."

"Oh, dear. I worry that is my fault." Olivia sighed. "I think Dr. Hastings was so thrilled to see Morgan. We should have made other arrangements."

"No, Morgan would want you all here." Emery knew that was true. "He has been overly gracious while I delivered little Gus, but now I must go." The words burnt her throat, and she stood to gather the dirty dishes. Swallowing hard, Emery vowed to keep her emotions at bay. "I will ask him to take me tomorrow."

"Oh, so soon?" Olivia stood next to her as she poured the steaming water into the basin. "I was so hoping to get to know you better. Perhaps you'll promise to come back soon?"

Emery flashed a quick smile, and her heart squeezed. "I think I hear the baby."

Turning towards her room, she clutched the apron to her face. Baby Gus was contently asleep on her bed as she closed the door. Holding the fabric to catch her moans and tears, she sank to the hard floor. Her teeth clenched to hold back the sound of her cries.

The image was too much. A visit? Her fingernails dug into the wood bed frame. To see Morgan and Olivia here? Married and happily tending to their new love. While what—she pretended to wish them well and act as if *her* time here never existed? Emery wiped her face hard and dropped her forehead into the bed. What would be the harm in that? *No harm if she enjoyed torture.*

She'd yet to forget that wretched ship, the rat hole floating in vile perversion, and forget being jerked from her cabin in nothing but her nightgown, the spawn of Arnold Snider already left inside her. She flung the apron over her mouth to catch another sob. Could she forget being dumped on the porch, or the caring brown eyes of the tall young man with scraggly dark hair? The way he spied her with annoyance and compassion? The way he cut her ropes and sawed her metal vice away? Their crazy moments in the Bedford Hotel, how he got word to her family, likely recusing her sister from Hades? Could she?

Dropping her head back, the cabin beams blurred above her. Would she ever forget the rope twisting around her neck, mimicking the straggling hold Arnold Snider had on her? What about the same man who pulled her from darkness and stayed with her into the night? Weakly, she pounded her fist on the floor. Could she forget all that and come back and pretend to be happy for them? Emery curled into a ball and covered her head. Earlier she'd been conflicted to point out the possibilities for Olivia, even sounding generous to the humble life here with Morgan. By evening, the thought of visiting them shredded her insides loose. Maybe she would tell one more pitiful lie. It was important not to raise any suspicion with the dear Miss Bradstreet. *Yes, I would love to return for a visit with you, Olivia.*

But neither legs nor arms, soul nor spirit, life nor death would persuade her to return to this place and see them in their new life together.

Thirty-Nine

Emery watched the evening shadows fall as she sat on the chair in her room and finished nursing Gus. The infant bobbed off her shoulder. He'd likely be awake for another three hours. Wishing only to find sleep herself, she laid him on her lap, refastened her blouse, and pulled his blanket tight around him. Olivia would want to retire soon. Emery stood and looked around. Maybe she could talk to Morgan tonight.

The idea of returning to her home on Eureka Creek brought little joy. The inevitable conversation with her parents sat on the top in the long list of the things Emery never wished for in her life. The sight of the baby, the things revealed, would devastate her parents. Trying to stand taller, she opened the door. The three of them turned to her.

"There you are." Morgan smiled as he and his father stood. "I didn't think you'd gone to bed yet. We were just about to have Olivia sing for us."

"She has a beautiful voice." Dr. Hastings nodded his agreement.

Emery held the baby close and gave them a half-smile. "That would be wonderful."

"I said no." Olivia's blue eyes crinkled. "I didn't want to wake you or Carlotta."

"Please, it would be lovely." Emery nodded once.

Olivia stood and pursed her lips. "Morgan, what would you like?"

"*Lu sua scintilla*?" he said.

"Ah." She pulled in a deep breath. "A favorite of Ronald's. Forgive me, Emery, it's in Italian."

Olivia straightened her back and posed like she was on a grand stage. Opening her mouth, the pure clipped musical notes and words spilled forth with emotion and delight. Emery was in awe of the clarity of her voice and wished she knew what the strange words meant. Watching Dr. Hastings and Morgan, their faces held such pleasure and admiration. Gifted with a high soprano voice, Miss Bradstreet commanded it to rise and fall in perfect tempo.

For a fleeting moment, Emery was the teen back in Hangtown inside the Snider mansion; she and Gianna were in their black uniforms and crisp white aprons serving the guests at Arnold and Finny's wedding party. Miss Cassidy sang that evening. She also had a voice that could move mountains. Her songs had been American and easy to follow.

The men clapped heartily, and Emery came back to the moment. Balancing the baby, she clapped also. Before anyone could ask, Olivia broke into a bouncing tune about tulips in Holland. Forging a smile at the light entertainment, it fell away as Morgan approached. Slipping Gus from her, he tucked the baby into the crook of his arm and took her by the hand. Before she could understand, he pulled her away from the wall.

"What are you doing?" she hissed.

He pulled her arm up and forced her to do a turn.

"Dancing," he smiled.

"Stop it." She jerked her hand away and reached for Gus. Morgan stepped back and lowered his eyes on her.

"We don't dance, Morgan." She protested while Olivia sang the chorus.

"Maybe we should. Gus likes it." Morgan rocked him in his arms.

Emery felt sharp words starting to form and locked her jaw. "I've decided to go home. To Eureka Creek."

Morgan froze, then turned to watch Olivia hold out the last pure note. Placing Gus back in Emery's arms, he clapped. "Brava, brava," he cheered along with his father.

"That's enough for tonight," Olivia curtsied then held her hands over her heart. "We don't want the deer and woodland creatures coming to complain." She laughed lightly.

"Would you two excuse Emery and me for just a moment?" Morgan asked. "She has brought something to my attention that I would like to speak to her about."

He took Emery by the elbow and walked her and Gus past Olivia and Maxwell. "Your singing was pure heaven." Morgan nodded to Olivia as they went out the front door. His long stride seemed hasty as he walked her out towards the greenhouse. The moonlit night laid shadows along the dried grass.

"What did you say?" He turned so quickly that she almost bumped into him.

Gus wiggled in her arm. "You heard me." Emery looked toward the barn. "I need a ride tomorrow. I've decided to return home."

"Home?" He spread his hand open in front of her, then pointed left. "Back to Eureka Creek?"

"Yes." She huffed. "I was hoping you would take me?"

"How many months, Emery, did I offer to take you and you would have none of it?" She opened her mouth, but he didn't wait for her answer. "I can only imagine that having my father and Olivia—ah, Miss Bradstreet—is informing your decision now?"

"Yes and no." The baby gave a few squeaks, and she bounced him up and down until he settled. "We shouldn't be out here." She shook her head. "They will wonder what we are doing."

Morgan grimaced and ran his fingers through his hair. "So, this will be goodbye?"

She couldn't meet his eyes.

"Tell me, Emery." His hand gripped the back of her arm. "If they had never come, would you be leaving me?"

Emery hated the way her body began to tremble. "It doesn't matter, Morgan," she whispered. "Because they are here and they belong to you—to who you are and to your future."

Morgan dropped his hand from her arm. "Only God holds my future."

They stood in the shadowy silence. "That is true." She admitted his words were always exact and true. "And if tomorrow I don't have a chance to say it—" Her chin began to quiver, and she repressed the emotion. "Thank you, Morgan." Emery tried to hide the tightness in her throat by kissing baby Gus on the head. "I know you felt there were so few you could save in the war." Her breath hitched. "But please never forget . . . you saved us. You may not think two people are much, but we are two who can turn and look you in the face and mean what we say." Her eyes locked on his. "You've forever given us a chance." Thinking of how deep her gratitude really was, she pulled up on her toes to kiss his cheek, but his fingers threaded across her neck and into her hair until he brought his lips down on hers.

An instant tingling coursed through her, lessening the twisted knots in her belly. His lips were warm and tender, and she'd no desire to pull back. Her free hand rose up, touching his lean back as her eyes drifted closed with the sweet lingering moment. Lost in the tenderness, she felt his cheek rest on hers and ragged words next to her ear.

"You said you loved me."

Until Gus squeaked, she'd forgotten about the baby stuck between them. Her heels lowered to the ground. "I do." She tried to find her missing senses, already missing his kiss, his touch. "That's why I need to go." Conscience returning to its rightful place, she turned with a swish of her skirt and hurried back to the cabin.

Morgan watched her until she slipped inside. He'd lost sleep thinking about how to explain their relationship to his father and Olivia. Every time he rehearsed the truth, it left him more daunted. He'd also lost too much sleep thinking about what it would be like to kiss her, to feel her tender touch against his skin when it wasn't red with poison oak.

Morgan closed his eyes and let out a low groan. It had been better than he'd imagined. As soon as she moved toward him, it was as if he had no choice. The flickering shadows were setting the encounter with moody approval. She was soft and curious, relishing the tender moment as much as he did.

How did the woman snarl at him when he took her hand to dance and then give him the sweetest lips for his own taking? His belly was still giddy. How did he come out here in anger and shock, then become a thirsty man who could only be satisfied by her? His body and mind still swirled.

Should he enjoy the momentary blessing, or curse the future without her?

Forty

The next morning, Emery untied her small bundle on the bed. She'd already checked it over twice after breakfast, and it hadn't changed from the last time she examined it. Two baby gowns, two blankets, and five diapers. Her nightgown, nursing poncho, and extra underthings. Using the extra baby flannel from Gus's baths, she rewrapped the bundle and retied the string. Her sweet little boy with the wisps of dark hair slept soundly in the middle of her bed. After the sour looks from Carlotta this morning, she hoped to sneak away with him without any painful goodbyes.

"Emery." Morgan rested his scarred hand on the door jamb and looked in.

She startled at his voice; he looked so incredibly stoic, yet handsome. "Yes." She almost forgot to answer. His clean-shaven face and suspenders pulled around his broad shoulders made her look to the ground.

"While he's asleep, can we talk?"

Emery nodded and felt her mouth go dry. If he planned on getting her alone for another show of affection, she would crumble into a pile. Stepping outside, the wagon was hitched and waiting.

Feeling like her insides were eggs whipped with a fork, she followed him to the barn.

"I think you should take the goats. I got them for you." They simultaneously butted against his simple pen as if begging for a new home.

"No, I don't want them." *They would be a constant reminder of this place.* She pulled the collar away from her neck.

He opened his mouth for a rebuttal and then closed it. "What about the plants?"

"Those are for you and the medicine you will make." Trying with all her will to stay steady, she took a small step back closer to the barn door.

Morgan closed his eyes and rubbed the lines between them.

He looked distraught, and a terrible urge flew up her spine. If she could be back in his arms and take all her good intentions back. Maybe . . .

"There you are." Olivia swished her thick skirts into the barn area. "Morgan, please tell her she must visit soon?"

He scratched his head and rolled his tongue inside his cheek. "Yes, of course," he said unconvincingly.

"I'm ready whenever you are." Face to the ground, he stalked past them.

Olivia and Emery stood in the awkward silence.

"He really does admire your cooking," she said faintly, swatting a fly from in front of her face.

Emery could think of no reasonable conversation to have. Olivia stood in all her beauty, purity, refinement, and grace—everything Emery was not.

"I must be on my way." Emery walked past her.

Morgan secured Gus's cradle to the back of the wagon. Emery looked everywhere, the sight making her stomach twist. She was interrupted by Dr. Hastings as he walked out the front door, smiling.

"It was a pleasure to meet you, Emery." Dr. Hastings nodded. "Morgan mentioned your father is a miner also. I suppose that's the way of it in this country."

"Yes, sir." A strange gust of morning wind swirled around them. "Excuse me, Dr. Hastings, I need to get my son." Fretful, she rushed into the cabin door.

Turning into her room, she found Carlotta holding Gus and singing to him in Spanish. Gus's wide brown eyes watched Carlotta intently. In just a few seconds, all the agony she had held back, came forward and pinched in her throat.

Carlotta's scratchy song and lyrics ended when she frowned at Emery.

"I know what you're going to say." Emery sniffed. "Please don't. Let me say this first." Emery closed the gap and grabbed her thick dark wrinkled cheeks, and kissed them. "Thank you." Her eyes narrowed. "You have been patient with me and my disruptions and even stayed with me into the night until he was born."

Carlotta's chin began to quake, and she kissed Gus's head. "You have been like a granddaughter to me. That is no lie." Carlotta pinched Emery's chin. "You go." Carlotta handed the baby over to Emery. "And take this." Carlotta pulled a length of bright Mexican fabric with two ends tied around a stick off the bed. "Stick to your back." Carlotta lifted Emery's braid and pulled the fabric over her shoulder and under her other arm. "*Rebozo.*" She pulled Gus up and tucked him in the folds.

Emery nodded. She'd seen the Basque women work and carry their babies in the woven wraps. "*Gracias.*" Sorrow laced her voice as she squeezed Carlotta. "*Adios.*" Emery grabbed her wrapped things off the bed, wiped her face on her sleeve, and turned to leave.

Olivia waited on the porch, and Morgan reached for her things and placed them under the wagon bench. "I'm saddened our acquaintance has been so short." Olivia frowned. "What a wonderful baby sling." She peeked open the fabric to see Gus inside. "I think he likes it. I saw your grandmother making it this morning." Her voice was so cheery, while Emery felt insurmountable fear and depression through every limb.

She faked a smile. "It was nice meeting you, Olivia." Unwilling eyes finally glanced to where

Morgan waited. "I hope you . . . you find . . . ah . . . whatever your heart desires." She blinked quickly and stepped away. Taking Morgan's offered hand, she climbed up onto the bench. Tucking Gus close against her chest, she looked forward as Morgan jumped up, and the wagon rolled out.

With only the dry dust swirling off the wheels, Morgan tried to watch the road and fight the thousands of questions in his mind. The first hour they rode in silence, each lost in thoughts and things left unsaid. For some strange reason, he hadn't seen this coming. He must have been so distracted with his father and Olivia that he'd not noticed Emery's distress.

Morgan knew it was Olivia who had pushed her from his home. Certainly not intentionally, but the woman had a presence that could command a full dance hall to attention. Maybe he was secretly relieved that he'd never had to tell Emery's story, the unpleasant truth of what happened to her. What would his father and Olivia's reaction be? He would look like some sappy do-gooder with a needy stray pup and a hundred reasons why he wanted to keep her. Sinking back against the bench seat, he knew that he'd fumbled any resolutions, prayed, and then shortly after lost hope. Now, too soon, she would be gone and their connection, their little moments that made him happier than he'd ever been, would all be over.

Baby Gus began to cry. He led the horse to the side, stopping under the shade of a group of trees.

"Thank you." Emery finally looked at him. "I will feed him, and we can . . . can . . . carry on."

Morgan studied her and wanted to say something, but Gus let out a long cry. Setting the brake and jumping down, he walked a few feet from the horse and took a long look over the land. Long rolls of dead, yellow summer grass ran in every direction, green groves of oak trees scattered here and there. Morgan sighed and leaned his arm against the tree nearest him. Dropping his head onto his hand, he closed his eyes. "Lord help me, give me the words. What is there to say?" Morgan glanced over his shoulder to the wagon. Emery's head was down, gazing into the baby sling Carlotta had given her. *She loves her son.* The thought brought a moment of peace. Emery had come from forsaking the baby to adoring him. That was something to be thankful for. She looked up and met his gaze before he walked around the tree. After a few minutes of walking and fretting, he came back around to the wagon. Emery had Gus over her shoulder.

"Can I tell you something?" Looking up at her,

his voice was low and strained. "You said last night that I made a difference."

She nodded slowly.

"You are by far the bravest person I've ever met. And you know I saw men die for their country."

Emery's eyes narrowed with disbelief as he set his arm across the wagon front. "It's bravery far beyond holding a gun, and maybe only women possess it." He shrugged. "I know at first you didn't want to live, but you fought past that. You had such a love for your sister that you would have done anything to make sure she was safe. The courage to fight back is stronger than a hundred oxen pulling a load."

Emery took a deep breath and looked long over the landscape.

"And now, though you have no assurance of open arms, you will risk walking up to your family's door. You will introduce them to Gus and they will need to know where he came from. Your father may hate you and possibly condemn you. You cannot be sure. Your mother may embrace you or shun you. How do you know?" Morgan waited and she lightly shook her head.

"What if they have open arms, but the other miners, the women, the community will have nothing to do with you? Your willingness to go forward and find out," he huffed, "Emery, that is a faith, a trust that I don't know if I've ever seen."

She sighed and tucked Gus back into her front pack. "Thank you for those words, Morgan. I'm truly scared to death. And these things you say of me? My only assurance is that I'm not alone. God is with me."

He stepped up, and the wagon seat rocked as he crossed over to his place. "Would you like me to stay, to explain the stupidity of the Derry brothers?"

The wagon bumped, jerked and pulled out onto the road. "I don't think so." She shook her head.

Morgan felt his chest squeeze. The harsh truth, he supposed, was that she wanted to leave his help and interference behind and find her own way home. "I'm going to miss Gus," he murmured.

"He will carry your middle name with as much pride as a little boy is allowed." Her smile faded fast, and she looked away.

Morgan blew out a long sigh. He'd prayed for the right words. He wanted them to convince her to stay with him. He needed words to explain what happened to him when they kissed. Something conclusive about a road or path they would travel together. Yet all he could tell her was the profound courage he saw in her. It seemed lacking compared to the tight constriction in his chest. With closed eyes, he pulled in a breath before he tapped the reins. The horse picked up the pace as the wagon got closer to Eureka Creek.

Maybe God knew the misaligned words was all she could hear.

Forty-One

Morgan noticed Emery clasping her hands and wiggling in her seat as they approached the road to the miners' camp. Her nerves must be on the far end of her skin. Not only would she see her family, but she would also have to relive the pain of all that had happened to her. His own stomach twisted for the next few moments, wishing there was something to ease her—"

"Morgan, stop!"

He gently pulled the wagon to a stop. "Is that the mining shack you went to last time?" Emery leaned close and pointed to the third shack from the top dirt road.

"Yes, I believe it is."

"Can you see? Do you see that girl there? The one with wood in her arms?" She stood up from the bench. "I think that is Gianna!" Her voice squeaked between joy and a sob. Before he could set the brake, she had pulled the baby and the sling over her head. "Please, for a moment." Her voice broke with emotion, and she handed baby Gus into his arms.

"Gianna!" she cried out as she jumped to the ground.

Morgan wanted to thank the heavens. The brown-haired teen turned and her face burst out in a shocking smile. "Emery!" She dropped the wood and started to run down the road.

Morgan felt his heart pound as he watched the two sisters run full force into each other's arms. Reunited at last, they hugged and weaved, searching each other's wet faces and then back to hugging. A young boy came around the shack and grabbed ahold of their skirts. Emery looked down and picked him up. Holding him close, his legs dangled down around hers. After one long kiss on his cheek, she placed him on the ground and embraced Gianna again.

"I think this is good." He smiled at baby Gus looking up at him. "Your mama is happy to see her sister. Happy to be home." Morgan glanced down at her small, wrapped belongings. Pulling them from underneath and setting them on the bench, his free hand rested on the flannel that he'd bought in Auburn. He held one hand protectively around Gus and the other over all her worldly possessions. A fierce wave of pain swept over his body. He should have done more for her, promised more. The piercing truth of them being out of his sight, his arms empty, choked his breath. "I love you, son." He tenderly kissed baby Gus.

Swiping the dampness from his face, he carefully stepped down from the wagon with Gus. The two sisters approached, linked arm in arm—Emery thinner and a few inches taller,

Gianna rounder in face, but with the same thick, wavy brown hair tied back in a bun.

"Morgan, this is my sister Gianna." Emery's expression shined every ounce of delight mixed with dirt-streaked tears.

"Pleasure to finally meet you." He nodded. "I've heard wonderful things about you." Morgan's face froze. *Should he have said that?*

"And this little baby is my son, Augustus." Emery pulled back the fabric to see his face.

Gianna's eyes jolted open, glancing back and forth between them.

The little boy crowded into the middle. "Let me see the baby!"

Morgan lowered his arms.

"And this little *muchacho* is my brother, Ferdinand." Emery ruffled the boy's hair.

"Your husband is very handsome," Gianna whispered loud enough for Morgan to hear.

"Morgan is a dear . . . friend." Emery reached out for the baby.

As soon as he let the warm baby loose, Morgan turned to untie the cradle. He would leave quickly and not spoil one moment of her happiness.

"You look strong." He set the cradle in front of Ferdinand. "And this too." Reaching back onto the bench, he set her things inside the cradle.

"I can carry it," Gianna said, looking puzzled. "Emery, are you home to stay?"

"I am." She grinned. "Just when you had a spot

to sleep to yourself." Emery hugged her. "Here I come." Her voice cracked.

Gianna's eyes flashed at Morgan. "Can I offer you some water? My mother is just inside our home, and I'm sure she would like—"

"Oh, no." He stepped back from the group. "I will say my goodbyes here and head back to Auburn." For the life of him, he could not look Emery in the eye. A cold surge ran up his back as he climbed back on the wagon. Morgan raked his fingers through his hair and unlocked the brake. Before he could pull the reins back, her hand touched his knee.

"Thank you doesn't seem enough." Her voice trembled. "But thank you, Morgan." Her eyes swam with tears, and she pinched her lips, stepping back.

"Take care, Emery." He pulled the wagon to the left and around the back onto the road. He gripped the reins the first hour out of irritation and frustration, but wondered if the worst wasn't the last hour traveling the road of self-pity and regrets.

That evening, Emery held her brother Ferdinand on her lap at the table, just like she'd done a hundred times in her other life. Her father never looked up from stirring his potato stew. His face turned red, then white, then back to red again. The news of what Arnold Snider had done to her had produced no words from his mouth, just a cold searing in his eyes.

Her mother held her and wept, but neither of them had looked upon baby Gus for even a second. Gianna was the only one who spoke after Emery had confessed everything. Finny had delivered a girl in San Francisco, she told them, and Arnold had hired a nanny and paid for Gianna to return to Hangtown.

Like cowards the Sniders left Gianna with the sorrowful news to carry home on her own. They said they were in a hurry to sail down to the southern end of California and start their life there. Gianna was the first to tell her parents the news that Emery had gone missing from the boat. The shock that she might have drowned brought the entire family into deep despair. Then the letter had come to her parents—Emery was alive and well, but Gianna was no longer safe in the Sniders' employment. Gianna held Emery as they both cried; she'd been home and secure for weeks. Gianna whispered for only Emery to hear—Arnold had never touched her.

Late after everyone had gone to sleep, Emery placed Gus into his cradle and crawled in next to Gianna. Gianna spread the blanket over them both and reached for Emery's hand.

"I'm just so sorry for everything you went through," Gianna whispered. "I will help you with the baby, just like we did with the boys."

She squeezed Emery's hand. "Mommi and Poppi will need time. Give them time, yes?"

Emery nodded and felt Gianna rest into her shoulder just like they did when they were girls. It was strange, somewhere deep inside—she knew these smells, sounds, and rhythms of her home. Her little brothers had grown by inches, their English practically fluent, but their banter and silly questions were so familiar. When Ferdinand asked how she got off the ship, Gianna had piped up that it wasn't important and to finish eating. Something about Gianna's tone took her back. It was like *she* needed protecting now, and Gianna had taken her place as the older sister. Emery wondered if anything would ever feel right again.

They were both teens when they'd started working for the Sniders. Unfortunately, Emery's youth was taken, stolen from her. In this past year, Gianna had missed so much, and Emery was thankful for that.

She pulled the blanket closer to Gianna's shoulder as she slept. The despair of knowing her sister was abused, too, would have made this homecoming beyond bitter. Emery tried to close her eyes and get comfortable. She was thankful. Her father would need more time, her mother was right. The man carried guilt as deep as the ocean.

She wondered how Morgan fared. Had Carlotta, Dr. Hastings, Olivia, and he sat around the table at supper? Did they ask questions that Morgan didn't want to answer? Probably not. Olivia undoubtedly thought this granddaughter of Carlotta was here and gone with little importance. Emery could feel the heavy pain inside her chest, picturing Morgan and Olivia talking about a future, their new life in California. Would Morgan try to gain interest in the animals and garden with Olivia? The lady couldn't help but be smitten with him. As long as he asked her to help, she would do anything, Emery supposed.

Emery tried to keep her eyes closed, but they kept opening again. Even with Gianna asleep next to her, this was another strange place to her. It didn't feel like home. Certainly, she wasn't the same young woman who had left so many months ago. It had been difficult to tell her parents the truth of what had happened, but she'd never expected to feel like a visitor, a stranger in her own home. Just like her father, she groaned inwardly, she needed time.

Baby Gus let out a snort. Her life was as a mother now, of course. She wouldn't feel the same. This body that had carried Gus, the body that held his milk, everything felt different. Gianna breathed lightly into her shoulder.

Can a person put their past behind them? Emery tried again to rest and calm her thoughts, but Morgan was in her mind's eye. The soft brown of his eyes, the way his kiss melted everything within her. The way his hands were gentle when he touched her back or waist. Oh, she loved his smile, his soft laugh, like sweet medicine; she sighed, drifting to thoughts of being held by him.

Her eyes flew open. Maybe she was not as broken as she thought. She imagined being loved and taken away by his affection. Why was she so sure she would spend all her days appalled by a man's touch? Feeling the fluttering of her heart, she listened with a new resolve. Morgan wasn't just any man. He was thoughtful and self-assured, appreciating her without asking anything in return. The light tingling around her skin started in, and she willed herself to sleep. *But Olivia was perfect in body and in heart,* and they had a long friendship and Ronald in common.

Forgetting the past would involve forgetting the love she now felt in her heart. So much good entwined with so much bad.

Oh Lord, how do you listen to one so confusing as me? I will choose to keep all your goodness close. Amen.

Morgan would always be her first love.

And likely her last.

Forty-Two

The fresh air of Jacob's tidy working ranch caused Morgan to enjoy his change of surroundings. The family's loss was great on these very steps he stepped down, but walking inside the barn, it seemed life would carry on. Morgan appreciated the distraction of a week spent helping his father purchase a horse and wagon for his upcoming trip to Grass Valley. The irony was, the horse and tack came from Jacob's small herd—Jacob, who had lost a daughter when Morgan could do nothing. They were glad to see him and graciously thanked him again for his help.

Maxwell Hastings handed Jacob the money.

"Thank you, sir." Jacob nodded and put the money in his pocket. "She'll be a good mount for you." He glanced over to Morgan. "It's been a good thing havin' your son." He turned to his father. "He's been a great help to the folk down around the camps."

Maxwell agreed. "He's a good doctor."

"It was a great comfort to the missus and me. Losing our sweet Biscuit . . ." Jacob swung his head to the barn floor; fighting the emotion, he kicked some hay. "Sorry." Jacob tried to clear his throat. "Place just ain't the same without her."

Morgan stepped closer and squeezed his shoulder. "I'm sorry too. I wish there was more I could have done."

"No, no." Jacob swiped his sleeve across his wet face. "What you did with a needle and all that." He choked again. "We was lucky to have you."

Morgan nodded and helped his father bridle his new horse. The three walked the horse out to the wagon.

"I heard a family got some sickness over by the Elk Bridge." Jacob glanced at Morgan as he backed the horse into place and strapped it to the wagon.

Morgan wished for something different. Maybe he just wanted to have his seclusion back. "I will check on them later this week," he hesitantly agreed.

"Thanks, Doc." Jacob smiled a crooked grin. "Word's got out about ya." He came around the rig, and the men shook hands. "Holler, if I can do anything else." Jacob waved before he went back to the barn.

Morgan began to move towards his horse.

"Son," Maxwell stopped him, holding his elbow before he could jump up onto his wagon. "God has given you a gift."

Morgan shrugged and stepped away. "Anyone who has the will can learn what I learned."

"No." Maxwell narrowed his eyes. "Can you

listen for one minute to an old man who taught doctors to be doctors?"

"Of course." Morgan blinked back his discomfort and took in a deep breath.

"When a man who lost his only daughter feels thankful for your help," Maxwell said, "you have something special. His grief is raw and yet he shook your hand."

Morgan nodded, looking at his dusty boots.

"You can't teach that. And you can't get it from a book." Maxwell reached again and squeezed his son's elbow. "You carry hope."

Morgan shook his head and looked out over the ranchland. "And there is the problem." The regretful silence filled the space between them. "Many times, Lord knows, it *is* hopeless." His voice held the familiar discouragement he carried in his own heart.

Maxwell shook his head. "And then there is a new hope. The man hopes you'll check on the sick family. He still has hope you could help them. Do you see that?"

"Yes," Morgan answered, rubbing the crease between his eyes. "I hear what you are saying."

"Something wrong, son?" Maxwell pressed. "It's none of my business, but something changed after Carlotta's granddaughter left."

"I'm sorry." Morgan jammed his fingers into the hair at his collar and squeezed it until it hurt. He wished they could be on their way. "I'd . . .

I'd grown a special attachment to her and to the baby." He pulled his shoulders back. "Are you ready to try your new rustic coach?"

"Wait a minute," Maxwell said, and Morgan turned to face him. "I think it prudent to come out with this now." Maxwell's voice sank with concern. "Do you see yourself having more than friendship with Olivia?"

Morgan closed his eyes and pulled his hand down his chin. "No, I don't." The words felt harsh, but he'd changed. If he disappointed his father, his plans for the Hastings lineage, so be it. She was Ronald's love, not his. Unfortunately, Morgan knew what he wanted. Why would he hope Olivia to be someone she would never be? There was only one brown-eyed woman who filled his thoughts day and night. "I have a respect for Miss Bradstreet, but nothing more."

Maxwell chewed on the corner of his lip and stroked the velvet nose of the chestnut mare. "And you don't see your affections growing . . . in the near future."

"I'm sorry." Morgan frowned and shook his head. "It would be unfair to her to make her think that would change."

Maxwell tapped his chin and looked in a circle. "I didn't want her to come. I tried to tell her it would be too difficult. I'd heard after a few months she'd stepped back into society, as it should be. Her loss of Ronald was great, but I'd wanted her to move on and marry, have a life with a home and children." He puffed out a strained grunt. "Then, out of the blue, the young woman shows up on my doorstep." The horse dipped his head for a clump of weeds and munched it. "I suppose Olivia hasn't told you the whole story."

Morgan shuffled his feet. "No." He looked away. "I'm afraid I haven't been in the mood to stroll and converse with her."

"And I only have sons, and work with male colleagues and students." He lifted his eyebrows. "As if that was the reason I know nothing of the fairer sex." He huffed a chuckle. "Olivia is a wonderful young lady." Maxwell sighed. "Your mother was a wonderful woman."

He nodded. "Yes, she was." Morgan appreciated his honesty; the frank talk with his father was worth the wrath that didn't come. Maxwell seemed far off in turmoil.

"Will you take Olivia to Grass Valley to the new mine?"

"What choice do I have?" Maxwell glanced about. "I've become a guardian, an uncle of some sort."

Morgan held his mouth open, looking for the right words. "I have no help to offer. I seem to know nothing of the fairer sex myself." Funny, he'd often daydreamed about a life with Gus, if Emery wanted to give him up. He would've been a good father to a little boy. Or maybe his fumbling motive was from his own desire to make a home with her and keep them both close.

"We'll make our plans to move on right away." His father climbed up on his new wagon. "I won't assume her wishes. I just think it would be helpful for her to find her own place in this new land."

Morgan nodded and walked back to his horse. Olivia, in all her pomp and flair, had come quite far. From Illinois to California, she'd known he could be married by now. Or what if he'd decided to return to Texas or Chicago? He tapped his horse forward and led his wagon down the dirt lane. And what would she think about this personal secret that had yet to be told? It was hard to look into those pure blue eyes and see anything amiss. His father knew what was driving her and her pretty façade to leave everything she'd ever known. Maxwell Hastings was a smart, reasonable man; he knew that limited options awaited a refined young woman from back East—at a mine full of soiled working men, no less. The Hastings line had an old family connection with the wealthy Bradstreets. His father would help Olivia with her next step in life.

Morgan could hear his father's new rig plod along behind his. And what about him? What was his next step? Everything had been fine until the Derry brothers had ridden onto his land, depositing a shackled woman on his front porch. Shouldn't he look forward to having the cabin back to himself? Now that his father was to settle only an hour or so away, could he seriously entertain the thought of following his friends to Oregon? Shouldn't he be thankful that Emery had done the hardest thing and gone back to her family? How many months had she seen her circumstances as hopeless? Maybe he did give people hope.

Morgan gave the horse another tap. Yet, then why did hope seem impossible to find for himself?

Forty-Three

It was cholera. Morgan had seen it rampant among the troops. The Texas battle camps had been filthy with putrid waste and death. These poor mining folk had lost two daughters on the wagon ride from the east. His anger spiked. They must've been told how to prevent it.

"You cannot use the same water to drink from." Morgan tried to settle his voice. The thin-boned, distraught mother at Elk Creek had tears of exhaustion running down her cheeks. "I'm sorry for your loss." He washed his hands in the hot water they provided. "You must boil the water before you drink it. You cannot ever be sure what has contaminated it upstream."

With vacant eyes, she nodded her head and Morgan wondered if she understood him. He turned to the oldest child who remained without symptoms. "Only drink the water after it has boiled. When it has cooled, it is safe." A toddler with nothing but a sagging diaper watched him while holding on to a chair. The bowed legs of scurvy seemed his only malady. Morgan pulled out the apples and lemons he'd gathered before he'd come. "Make sure the little one has a bite of apple every day. Mix the lemon in the cooled water for drinking. Keep giving it to your brother," Morgan nodded to the sick child in the corner. "Sips of water. He may recover." Morgan tried to lighten his voice. What had his father said about giving hope?

The mother lifted a sad smile. "Thank you." She'd a thick accent from some unknown European country.

"And tell the other miners they can't drink the water." Morgan dismissed his own words. The boy likely worked from sunup to sundown. Who would tell these people who came and went every day?

"Maybe we could dig a well?" the boy asked, wide-eyed.

"Yes." Morgan smiled at his knowledge. "A well would be wonderful."

Morgan let his washed hands drip onto the floor. There was nothing clean in the small shack to dry them on. "I will return next week."

The woman pulled a small coin purse from her apron pocket.

"No." Morgan shook his head. "No money."

Letting himself out, Morgan saw the other eyes of the thin and ragged miners watching him as he pulled out in his wagon. He knew they and their children often lived on the brink of starvation. Never enough gold, never enough money to pay for the supplies and feed their families. Morgan didn't want their money.

Payment meant he was working as a doctor,

and he had sworn off the profession that led to his own melancholy and desperation. Tapping his horse across the creaking planks of Elk Creek Bridge, Morgan rolled the tension in his shoulders. When word got out he wouldn't take their money, wouldn't just more people seek him out to doctor their families?

Trying to absorb the ruts and dips in the dirt road, Morgan groaned. It had been two days since his father and Olivia had moved on to the gold mine at Grass Valley. Any moment he should be able to return to his own peaceful life, his stride. Maybe it was the confusion in Olivia's eyes when he kissed her hand goodbye, which brought his unrest. She'd tried to start a conversation, offered to sing in the evening, but he'd been a coward, never engaging or asking her about her reasons to move this far from home. He didn't want to know, didn't want to care. Morgan huffed. Wasn't he the one who had to know, had to help everyone? Emery hadn't withheld the reprimand—his chivalry was a weakness. Maybe one unsettled woman was enough for his lifetime.

Morgan pulled his rig in front of his barn and hopped down. Unhitching the horse, he watered it and tossed it some hay. The plants they'd started weeks ago in the barn had grown tall. He took a cup and watered each one. Seeing the motherwort and echinacea in front of him, he fingered the feverfew and peppermint. Fruit was what the gold mining children needed. He stepped back, scratching his head. Apples, oranges, and lemons were too scarce for all the immigrants flooding into the area. The merchants tried to ask a day's wages just for one lemon. Each home should have a bowl of fruit to keep the children healthy. Stepping from the barn, Morgan looked long over the garden that Emery had brought back to life; he realized he could double its size for the planting of the herbs.

Morgan walked the length of his land that was least covered with shrubs and trees. With a fair amount of chopping and clearing, an orchard could be next. A foreign spark of energy filled his being. He'd had so little motivation, and even though he'd said it to his father, he didn't want to admit to himself that his travail was centered on Emery and Gus going home. Yet this felt right. He would grow trees and give the fruit away. Even though it would take years, soon it would bring essential medicinal health to the new Californians.

The following week, Morgan's tanned bare chest glistened with sweat and dirt. Pulling one last long scrub tree by the branches, he dropped it in the monstrous burn pile. He'd cleared at least an acre himself and stood back to see the remarkable progress. He'd been to Auburn to order the trees from San Francisco and read everything he could find about planting fruit trees. One of Emery's favorite goats bumped his shin as he looked out along the vast, disrupted terrain.

"Could'a used some help." Morgan drew his wrist across his wet brow.

The goat watched him for a second and went back to chewing the dry grass.

"All you and your friends could have asked to help." Morgan grabbed the hoe and began to break up the ground. "All you do is eat all day." Puffing out a breath, he shook his head. "Take your time, no rush now, but chew up the rest of this by Friday." Morgan forcefully whacked the hoe into another clump.

Truth be known, the hard work was good, distracting. Staying clear of the poison oak, he washed in the creek and fell into bed each night, aching and exhausted. Just like mining, working the land had so little mental demand. The simple life was where he belonged, where a man could walk humbly with God.

The thought stopped his pounding of the ground, and he gripped the handle of the hoe. He was keenly aware that there had been no humble thoughts and no walking with God. It was a nice platitude, but it wasn't his truth to spout. Not recently, anyway.

Out of the corner of his eye, Morgan watched Carlotta whip a stick against the rug she'd tossed over the clothesline. She wouldn't live and tend to him forever. That was a humbling thought. What if he was alone all his days? Just the log walls and simple furniture, no baby son of his own to come home to. Would he curse God for the woman and family he wanted but never would have? The question felt too familiar as it settled in his thirsty mouth like sour milk. With an irritated snap, the hoe struck the ground again, and Morgan tried to resume what he was doing.

No. He stilled and felt righteous ire run up his backbone. God had given him life when Ronald, and so many others his age, were cut short on the battlefield. God had given him provisions and this peaceable land. A light breeze cooled his sweaty skin. Yes, he'd been suffering. Certainly, God knew the hurt of the human heart, but it was time to let his expectations, his dreams go. Time to let the sound of Emery's voice or the baby's squeaks fade from his head.

He needed to stop hungering for her touch, stop rehearsing his desires, as they swept in and out of his heart. Morgan kicked at a ball of unearthed roots. Thankful now to have his father nearby, their plans to meet next month in Auburn was something to look forward to. He would choose this day and decide to rejoice in it. God had given him so much, and yet he'd been angry that it wasn't everything on his list. He dropped the hoe down hard again. How selfish.

"Please forgive me, Lord," he whispered. "Your

mercy, grace, and the future You have for me, is what I thank You for." Staring at the dry earth and the clearing he'd created in front of him, his thoughts swirled.

Strange how hard men work to unearth the gold from the rock, river or streams. Daily we search, digging the soil for specks or nuggets. We strive and strain, toil, and sweat for what we want, what we think we need, Morgan thought. He shook his head to clear it.

He'd felt like God had spent the year pounding out the hard spots in him. His fight not to doctor had been pushed and remolded into something as simple as a garden and some fruit. Maybe God's hand had been at work this whole time to unearth the true gold that was to be in his life. Would he be a lonely, bitter man always feeling like a victim of unreciprocated love? Can a person be a victim when God is the director of all things?

Or would he look to the heavens and find the gold, the good in all things? The opportunity to help Emery and Gus—just to be there for them when they needed him. Morgan scratched the back of his head. It was time to quit chewing on all his regrets. Walking the hoe back to the barn and setting it in the corner, the goats followed him, begging for his attention. *Quit reliving the loss and pain,* Morgan told himself, and just accept the piece of dirty rock he was, full of hidden gold that needed a season of chipping and rinsing. Was it possible that God was showing him acceptance, grace, favor, and truth even now? Walking out across his yard, he stopped, feeling lighter, his gaze rose upward. "Thank you," he whispered, turning.

A refreshing dip in the creek was in order.

Forty-Four

Morgan checked the crease in the paper again. The dried echinacea leaves and petals were still there, and he rolled his eyes, feeling unfocused. The paper had been on the bench in the barn, just as he'd left it for the last four days. The problem was it did no good just lying on the paper. It was only useful in the hands of those who needed it.

Emery had been the one to plant and nurture the garden, and the only reasonable purpose of the echinacea was to get it into her hands to help the people around her. Four days was enough to pray and procrastinate. The weeks were passing and summer had already faded into fall. Maybe she wouldn't even be there.

Morgan focused on folding the edges, creating a pouch for the herbs. He took a pencil and noted on the paper the amount for a cup of tea and the various things it was suitable for. He'd already told Carlotta he'd be gone most of the day, just not where. The idea of seeing Emery again played havoc on his new sense of inner harmony. Carlotta would likely say nothing, but one word about Emery or her meddling opinion on what he should do might convince him he was not as stable as he'd thought.

Pulling the horse out, he raked his fingers

through his hair. Overthinking was getting him nowhere. All these herbs were grown to assist the hurting. After buying more fruit, he would ride into the Eureka Creek camp and do what he did best. Help people.

An hour after buying the fruit and riding towards Eureka Creek, Morgan pulled the wagon to the side and jumped down. Taking his canteen, he swallowed a large gulp and let the water run down his chin onto his shirt. Hoping that would settle his gut, the drink did the opposite. He scratched the back of his head and walked around in a circle. Why had he thought this was a good idea? Morgan leaned against the wagon and tried to steady his heartbeat. The herbs. Remember, *you are just dropping off the medicine. Morgan and his medicine,* she might say. Maybe Emery would smile and be happy to see him? But then he would say goodbye, turn away and drive back to Auburn. He would be glad to have seen her, but worse for the wear, no doubt.

Strangely, his scarred hand itched as he grabbed the seat. Morgan jumped back up on the wagon bench and rubbed the scars on the side of his face before he tapped the horse forward. Interesting, he'd thought his burn scars were hideous to anyone who saw him. It was one of the reasons he'd gone on to California instead of returning home. Yet, Emery never looked appalled and or shocked. Olivia, who had known him before, had never looked away, never asked one question. Morgan huffed, shaking his head. The Derry twins had saved his life and disrupted his intentions of being a sulking hermit hiding his burns in peace. Something in him wondered if he owed them double gratitude for bringing Emery to him.

Morgan pulled the reins back and rode into the mining camp slowly. Some children screamed and splashed around a bucket of water. A dripping wet little girl with blonde hair stopped playing to wave to him. At least the children looked well.

He smiled back and searched toward the area he'd seen Gianna come from. Pulling the wagon to a stop, Morgan lost all focus on the surroundings and locked his eyes on two young women. Even far away with their backs to him, he knew the one with the long brown braid wearing the clothes he'd bought was Emery.

Setting the brake, he jumped down and fumbled with the box of fruit. Before he could reach the nose of the horse, Morgan saw her turn. Her lips parted, and she seemed to straighten taller. Without taking her eyes from his, she said something to her sister and handed the baby over to her sister's arms. Her mouth grew round and eyes wider, and after a few long strides toward him, her face broke out into the largest, warmest smile he'd ever seen. Without thinking, he set the box to the ground and stepped forward, watching her now running down the path toward him. He didn't remember his arms opening, just the fact that Emery flew into them, and he held her off the ground until he thought his heart would explode from his chest. Her face buried in his neck, his arms wrapped her body as if he would never let her go. Only out of propriety, he finally released her feet back to the ground. She leaned back, gripped his arms, and searched his face like a blind woman getting her sight.

"Morgan," Emery whispered, beautiful and winded. Blinking wide-eyed, a sudden pale, stricken fear covered her face, and she stepped back. "How are you?" She sucked in a needed breath. "How is Olivia?" Stiffly, she shuddered and dropped her arms. "Your father?"

"They are well. They've moved on to Grass Valley." Morgan couldn't help smile and stroke her cheek, where the breeze caused a strand of hair to flitted around her mouth.

"Will you be joining them?" Her soft brown eyes narrowed.

"No." He tried to be patient, but every limb just wanted her back in his arms. "They will be living there. I'm not sure what Olivia will do." His hand draped down her arm and took her hand. He ached for her warm greeting again. "Were you happy to see me?" He bit his lip, watching her very conflicted expression.

"Yes." Emery nodded slowly. "But I thought you and Olivia would have a . . . an understanding by now. The families, the obligation to . . ." She stopped. "Did you know that's what she wanted?"

"I did." Morgan's eyes held hers as he intertwined their fingers. "But I don't love Olivia." His thumb caressed her palm, holding back the depths of his affections.

"You don't?" Emery glanced down at their fingers, pressing her lips together.

"No, I don't." As her eyes looked up to his, Morgan pulled on her hand and wrapped his arms around her again. "I'm in love with you." The truth couldn't be contained any longer as his mouth lingered near her ear. Feeling her hands cling to his back, he pulled her in tighter. The pleasure of her embrace, like his emotion, riddled through every part of him.

She turned up to face him. "And I love you, Morgan. More than anything." Emery ran her hand tenderly down his cheek.

Every pent-up fiber in his being wanted to yell something in celebration, but this was all he needed, to hold her, smell her, see her brown eyes now filling with misty tears. "Will you marry me, Emery? Would you and Gus want to return to Auburn?" A crooked smile arose from the corner of his mouth. "I'm an uncommitted doctor who does a fair bit of mining, and now I've decided to grow fruit trees."

Her face beamed with light, and she released a chuckle. "And what about that oath you held when I first met you, 'to help people'?"

He leaned back while still holding her. "I forgot I'd said that. I was just trying to convince you to come inside."

Emery stilled, catching a tear before it ran down her face. "You were always an answer from God." Her chin quivered. "I still cry at night to think I would have ended my life and Gus's too." Another tear rolled loose. "Where would I be if you hadn't come for me at So Chen's? I would have given him away and hid away myself—never to join my family or believe that I could have a real family." She held her fingers over her lips, slowing her rambling. "So many times, I should've been left in my misery, but you were always there, helping, prodding me to overcome. I knew you were an amazing, strong, smart, caring person. I just figured Olivia was better suited. Better for your future. So I came home."

Lifting a small smile, Morgan blinked, breaking their powerful gaze. "I'm not sure if you ever answered my question?" His brows narrowed.

"Oh, yes." Emery laughed. "I would be honored to marry you and support your unorthodox doctoring and mining and help you grow . . . trees!" Her eyes glittered with another laugh. Reaching up to gently brush his chin, she whispered. "I'm ready. Ready to take your words into my heart and let go of how undeserving I am." Slowly, she pulled her hand down over his heart. "I'm ready to believe God can take my past and give me a beautiful future. I'm ready to be your wife, to be your companion, lover, and . . ." Emery stopped.

Morgan's expression flushed red, and he looked side to side, thankful no one was listening. "So, you are saying someday . . ." He tried to breathe normally. "Gus could be a big brother?" Morgan inched closer, putting his hand around the back of her neck, allowing his fingers to rise into her hair. *Could this be happening? Could Emery want him the way he wanted her?*

"Likely, he'll be a big brother many times." Her eyebrows flicked higher for a split second.

Taken back, Morgan felt the land beneath his feet shift, wondering if this was more than he'd allow himself to dream. Yet, here she was, looking long and sultry into his eyes. "Emery, if I kiss you now, will your father come out from the creek . . ." His gaze jumped over her head. "And point his shotgun at me?"

"I'm not sure, but I'm willing to risk it." Her coy smile was ruining any of his common sense.

He drew his other hand around her neck, cupping her face. "What am I going to do with you?" Morgan whispered, drawing her nearer.

"I could think of a few things." Emery squinted and rose up on her toes.

Oh, this remarkable beauty. He wanted to kiss her so badly just as he had done before, but he had to quit smiling. His joy overflowed to see this love, this courage, this miracle of light flowing from her. As he lowered his hungry grin and lips to capture hers, he believed their hope would carry them all their days.

"Find what makes your heart sing and never let it go."
   Cassidy to Emery in *Truitt's Truth*

Author's Note

Every story I write has a theme: Redemption. In Luke 4:18, Jesus came to heal brokenness, bring deliverance, sight to the blind, and freedom for captivity. I've known and seen these things work in my own life. Though redemption looks completely different in all of us, I write these characters with confidence in what God offers them. The next huge thing is Acceptance. Grace and acceptance for those warts, messes, mistakes, sin, wounds, and scars. Morgan carried his scars on the outside and the inside. Emery would likely never forget what happened to her. But the life of Christ in us is how we accept *(not tolerate with grinding teeth)* the flaws and failures of all those around us. Let's be honest, the people we care for the most often hurt and disappoint us the most. The antidote feels counterintuitive. Punishment and withdrawal is the easy road. Walking through the repentance and understanding and acceptance of the wounded one is much, much (one more—*much*) harder. I would say: It is the deeper life of the Christ follower.

    This is more than a simple "note to self." But I pray you would first take a baby step to give acceptance to yourself. Show Him that scar of self-loathing or_____. Maybe in return He'll show you the scars on His hands, back and feet. He understands. Let Him heal you from the inside out. From there, you should be able to give it away. Isn't it really what we all want? Just to be accepted as we are?

Freely give it to yourself and others as you walk the road to redemption.

Walking with you,
Julia

While roaming around lovely Auburn, California, I was caught trying to steal a bit of gold from this larger-than-life miner.

Thank you, Bernhard Museum. A local museum in a hotel built in 1851. Placer County Museum. Local artifacts in a historic courthouse and The Gold Rush Museum.

Now on to the next mining town—

Books are produced in the United States using U.S.-based materials

Books are printed using a revolutionary new process called THINKtech™ that lowers energy usage by 70% and increases overall quality

Books are durable and flexible because of Smyth-sewing

Paper is sourced using environmentally responsible foresting methods and the paper is acid-free

Center Point Large Print
600 Brooks Road / PO Box 1
Thorndike, ME 04986-0001 USA

(207) 568-3717

US & Canada:
1 800 929-9108
www.centerpointlargeprint.com